# STORIES ABOUT A GEORGIA MOONSHINER

## Larry English

authorHOUSE®

*AuthorHouse™*
*1663 Liberty Drive*
*Bloomington, IN 47403*
*www.authorhouse.com*
*Phone: 1-800-839-8640*

*Published by AuthorHouse 1/16/2012*

*ISBN: 978-1-4634-2946-1 (sc)*
*ISBN: 978-1-4634-2947-8 (e)*

*Library of Congress Control Number: 2011911563*

# SHORT STORIES BY LARRY ENGLISH

I do not need to hear how mean and sorry that I was during my young life, I already know that. But Judge not, and ye shall not be judged. Condemn not, and ye shall not be condemned. Forgive, and ye shall be forgiven, that is what I like to hear. Luke 6:37

These stories are created and narrated
by Larry English

This is a work of fiction inspired by true stories, about one teenagers life during the 1940s, and 50s, in the north Georgia Mountains. There are 10 other stories, other than the whiskey stories, in this book and they are fiction also.

---

## THE ENGLISH FAMILY

In the community where I grew up, making whiskey was a way of life. There were no jobs in our County back then. Grown men with families earned.75 cents per hour, if they could find work. If you could not find a job then, you may have to help make some whiskey. The normal pay for that was $50.00 per day, working in someone else's still. A day may be 8 hours, or it may be 24 hours, but it is still a day, and $50.00.

In 1946 I was 13 years old. This is when I ask for a job working for the English family, and I got it.

The English family lived within sight of our home, they made a lot of whiskey and I knew where two of their stills were, and they knew that I knew, so that is who I ask for a job. Everyone in that family knew me, but Grub is the person that I went to and ask, because I knew him better than the others. I knew all of the family but it just felt like I could talk to him better about this, because it was a kind of a guarded subject to talk about, especially with someone that was outside of the whiskey business circle, and I was.

Grub told me that if I could tote a 100 pound bag of sugar from the barn to the place (still) that I had the job. The two of us went to the barn and we both shouldered a 100 pound bag of sugar.

It was dusty dark by now. Together we walked the trail around the corn field, and crossed over the creek on the bridge, then as we started up the mountain, Grub stopped and laid his bag of sugar down. Grub told me then, that he thought that I would not make it that far, and if I wanted to work, that I had the job.

Sugar come in by the load and was kept in the barn, usually 80 bags at a time. My job was to carry sugar to the still. My pay was $ 1.00 per bag. I only carried about 10 bags on my shoulder, then I used a mule and a packsaddle. I think Grub let me carry that 10 bags to see if I really wanted that job.

With the packsaddle on a mule I could take 3 bags of sugar at a time, and I still got the same money per bag. If they were running the still, at the same time that I was hauling sugar, I brought 2-10 gallon barrels of whiskey back to the barn, and I got $ 1.00 each for them also. Each still was only run every 4th day, so I did not get to bring out the barrels all of the time.

Grub's father was the boss of everything

there, and I only talked to him one time while working. He told me that I would never be caught if I would take good care of the mule. Give that mule plenty to eat and all the water it wants and that mule will tell you when anything or anyone is close by. Nothing or no one can come close to you, without you knowing it, if you watch that mule. Those ears both turn 360 degrees, if the ears turn in different directions you are safe, but when both ears point in the same direction, at the same time, get ready to run, because something or someone is there.

In this business any one that gets caught is on their own, you pay your own fine or you build your own time in jail. This is why you make so much money.

Grub hauled most of the whiskey himself. One time he ask me if I would be interested in driving a truck into South Carolina loaded, and they would pay me.50 cents per case to drive. I said that I would and the next night, I drove a truck loaded with 200 cases of whiskey to South Carolina. Grub had taken me to the place and shown me where to park the loaded truck. Five minutes after I got to the unloading place, Grub was there, in his car, and told me to get in. We drove down the road to the nearest restaurant and had a cup of coffee, waiting for the buyers to unload the whiskey from our truck onto their truck. The truck that I drove was an old farm vehicle, it was muddy from the back roads that I had been on, and it did not have a tag on it. Their truck was new, it had a cattle bed on it, and there were two mules in back with the whiskey. The mules covered the suspicion of the truck being out on the country roads at night. The revenuers looked at every vehicle that came down the road, when they were in your area. Usually a runner would be 10 minutes in front of the loaded vehicle. The law would go after that runner and the runner would not stop, but would cause the law car to be miles away from the vehicle that was loaded. This happened a lot of times.

Grub handed me a one hundred dollar bill and

told me to take the truck back home and park it in the barn.

[Do you have any idea how much $100.00 seem to be then to a teenager, in the 1940's, when clerks made $15.00 to $25.00 per week?]

The English family had two haul cars. Both were 1940 ford coupes. One had a Cadillac engine and the other one had a big Mercury engine and both were supped up to race. Grub ask me if I wanted to buy the ford with the mercury engine for $ 1,200.00 and I could work it out. I did, and I paid the $ 1,200.00 in 12 weeks. The car I bought was too hot to haul on. It had out run all of the law around there and all of the nearby areas, and the law wanted that car for themselves, they really wanted that car.

This English family was amazing. They had two large farms and both were run at 100%. There were two son in law's and two sons and Mr. English, and they all worked from daylight till dark and they had another man that lived with them part time to work in the stills. I had a lot more work than I wanted. I worked with the English family for about 18 months, and although I was new in this business, they made me feel like I was important, like I was one of the family. They were all good folks.

One time three of us was working in a still and it was about 3 am, Lloyd, Dip and myself and we only had about two more hours to be finished. I stepped out from under the shed, that covered the still, to urinate, and I saw a light up the mountain above us, the light was coming towards us. I told Dip and Lloyd and they saw the light also. We all three ran, Lloyd went one way and Dip and I went another way. Dip and I ran for over two miles and came out of the woods near Fish Bait Inn, a small grocery store. Then we walked up the road to the house. Later in the day we went to the still and nothing was damaged. We still do not know what the light was, but we all saw it. Dip's Mother said it may have been a ghost. We worked there, in that still, for about a year and then just quit.

## THE END OF THE STORY

# MY FIRST STILL

I was in the 7<sup>th</sup> grade now, and Ted was in the 7<sup>th</sup> grade also, he was 4 years older than I was, but he was still in the 7<sup>th</sup> grade. Ted's family all made whiskey and always had, they never did anything else but farm a little bit. All thru that year of school, I worked with Ted's family and they became like family to me.

When we ran the still it was always at night, and About 3 or 4-0 clock in the morning, Ted's mother would come to the still and bring us cornbread and milk to eat, this was not just regular cornbread, it was full of sweet corn kernels and very good.

If Ted had of gone to school and studied he could have done anything that he wanted to do, he would have been one hell of an engineer. After we started running the still with steam, Ted and I figured out a way to make the still run faster. Simply by putting a pre heater on the water that would refill the boiler, after each still full was run. After we did this, our production almost doubled.

Ted had a down side also. We were putting a new still in, and each one of us had a list of supplies that was our part to furnish for the new still, and our responsibility to pay for. Two of Ted's items were 30 bushels of corn meal and $60.00 for lumber. Each of us had $60.00 worth of lumber to pay for. I gave Ted the money for my part, and he was going to buy the lumber and take it to his house. Instead, Ted stole the lumber from a saw mill, and when the owner of the mill missed that lumber, he called the sheriff. It had rained and the dirt roads were mud roads now. The sheriff tracked the mud grip tires right to Ted's house, and Ted was there cutting the lumber into 4 foot lengths, for boxes. [a box is 4 foot square and 40 inches deep and holds

400 gallon, it is used to make beer in.] Ted was caught. Also he used his brothers truck to haul the lumber, and the sheriff made a case against him too. Ted had to pay $ 300.00 for the lumber, and no case was made against any one.

About a week later, after Ted got caught stealing, Ted and I were in the back bed room of their house. Ted's dad come in with a leather strap about six feet long and started whipping both of us, he did not care who he hit the most, he was just swinging that strap. I made my way to the door and ran, Ted could not get out so he took a beating. Ted's dad said that "there never has been a dam thief in my family, and there won't be one now." After he found out that I had nothing to do with that, he came to me and apologized, with tears in his eyes.

Then, when it came time to cook the meal, we were going to start work at 3 am, so I slept at their house that night. At 1:30 the alarm went off, I ask Ted why we got up so early and he said we had to go after the meal. The meal was his responsibility. Ted was driving the truck and he stopped about a half mile from the grist mill. We walked the rest of the way to the mill. The mill had shutters instead of windows, and Ted got one of the shutters open and went in. He threw the meal out of the window, and I did help him carry it to the car. We cooked the meal that night, and made a sweet mash, we worked that still for over a year, which is unbelievable to run one still, that long, without it being caught and cut down. We just had good luck. Ted and I had some serious discussions about the lumber and the meal that was stolen, and as far as I know that is the last thing that Ted ever stole. Ted and I were good friends and we worked together off and on for another 10 years after this happened.

This was a very exciting life. We made the whiskey there in walking distance of Ted's family's home. Then we loaded it onto Ted's brother's 1936 ford, and it was hauled to South Carolina, sometimes Ted and I went along just for the ride. Ted and I got $16.00 per case for the whiskey and Ted's brother made about $10.00 per case for hauling it.

## END OF STORY

# BIG SUITCASE

When I was in the 10<sup>th</sup> grade in school I was offered a chance to go to Detroit and work for the summer season. A friend, told me that we could board with his sister for $10.00 a week and there were plenty of jobs there for us, so we planned to go. Vern had a friend that was going to Detroit the following Sunday so we got a ride with him for $ 10.00 each to Detroit, Michigan. This was one week after school was out for the summer, in 1948.

Vern told me that we could get $ 60.00 for a case of whiskey in Detroit, and if I would get the whiskey, he would get a big suitcase. So on Saturday night we took our suitcases, 3 of them, and loaded them into the trunk of the car. One suitcase had 6 gallons of 100 proof moonshine. We left on Sunday morning and made good time until we got up to the state of Ohio. Then the rear end of the car started roaring and sounded like it was going to come out, so we stopped at a garage to find out what was wrong with it. Vern said that we better tell his friend, that we were riding with, about the whiskey, because we may be broke down on the road. Vern told him just after we left the garage. He immediately pulled over to the side of the road and put both of us out of the car with three suitcases. There we were, on the side of the road up in Ohio, with 6 gallons of moonshine.

Vern called his sister and she and her husband came after us. We told them what we had, and what happened, and they both said that we could not put that whiskey in their car either. We drove away and left 6 gallons of whiskey in a big suitcase, setting there on the side of the road in Ohio.

This was a bad start for our trip to work for the summer, but it got worse. I had good luck and got a real good job in a General Motors plant, tying the electrical wires together, that goes under the dash in trucks and buses. A clean, easy job that I probably would have stayed with, if things didn't happen the way they did.

There was a food wagon in the plant that come around and sold drinks and sandwiches. On the sly, the operator sold whisky in small bottles, probably 2 or 3 ounces for $2.00. I heard him tell someone that he was out and could not get any more whiskey. I got a chance to talk to him when no one was around. I told him that I could supply all he wanted. He told me that he would buy it if it was good, and we agreed on a price. I called Ted down in Georgia and told him about it, and three days later Ted was up there with 36 gallons of whiskey.

Ted was driving a car that he and I built from parts from a junk yard. It was a 1939 ford with an Oldsmobile engine. It had air lifts to keep the car level, when it had a load on it, this was a car built to haul whiskey, and we had no papers of any kind on this car, so that it could not be traced to us, if it was caught.

Ted and I contacted the buyer of the whiskey by phone. He met us at a service station and looked at the whiskey and tasted of it, then he smacked his lips and said "man that is the best shit that I have ever tasted". Actually, I was ashamed to show that whiskey to the man, it was the worse whiskey that I had ever seen, but Ted said that it was all that he could find, and he had bought it on credit. The man that made it had a reputation for making bad whiskey. The buyer bought only 3 cases, Ted had brought 6 cases, so there we were with 18 gallons of illegal whiskey in Detroit, and no place to put it.

Ted had rented a room to stay in while he was up there. We got some grocery bags to carry the whiskey into Ted's room, and we put it all under Ted's bed.

We decided to go to the buyers house and try to sell the rest of the whiskey to him.

## stories about a Georgia moonshiner

We had the address but was having a hard time finding the right place. We were in a neighborhood that was totally black, we were the only white boys anywhere around there, and that was in 1948. We did not care about that, but the people that lived there did not seem to like us.

We found the number on the house. There was one porch, and two front doors on this porch, but only one number on the house. I was driving the car and I parked on the corner, caddy cornered, while Ted went up and knocked on the door to see if we were in the right place. Before anyone came to the door, a police car pulled up to the front of our car and two black policeman asked me, what we were doing in this neighborhood. I told them that the transmission on our car was going out and that these people had a junk yard, we wanted to buy a transmission. I was ask for the title and insurance on our car, and we did not have either one. One policeman handcuffed me, and locked me in the back seat of the police car, while the other policeman went up on the porch and got Ted. When the other policeman ask Ted what we were doing here, he said we were lost and I was just asking directions. Now Ted and I were both handcuffed, and setting in the back of the police car. We had been searched and everything we had was taken from us, and our belt was taken and our pockets were pulled inside out. We watched as a wrecker pulled our car away.

We were arrested for auto theft, then taken to Pontiac and put into a cell with several other people and they all stunk. I think they were all drunks that had been picked up off of the street. The second day of being in jail a policeman came and got Ted and I, and carried us to another jail on the other side of town. There we were questioned, about the car theft ring that they thought we were a part of. We stayed there one more day, then on the morning of the fourth day, I ask to make a phone call.

I called my Mother in Georgia and before I

could speak to her, an officer grabbed the phone from my hand. He told her that I was being held on suspicion of auto theft, then he gave the phone back to me. I explained the situation to my Mother and asked her to call the sheriff, for help. The sheriff knew the car and he knew that it was not stolen, he called the GBI in Atlanta, they called the police department in Pontiac and then Ted and I were released from jail. Now everything was okay and back to normal, right?

No way. The car was in the police pound, and we could not get it out. I had lost that good job that I liked so much, and there was 18 gallons of moonshine under Ted's bed, that we had to do something with. Not only that, but we were 750 miles from home and broke.

I did still have a check coming from the plant where I worked, and it should be about $70.00, but we had things to do right here before I could go after it.

There was a city park one block away from

Ted's room, we carried the whiskey in paper bags to the park, and left one bag on each park bench until it was all gone. Then we went into Ted's room and put his clothes in paper bags, and then we went to the bus stop, carrying the clothes in our arms. We had to slip out of Ted's room, because his rent was due, and he could not pay. I got the check and it was $68.00. The bar that I cashed the check in charged me $2.00 for cashing it. We got on another city bus and rode to the greyhound bus station, where we bought 2 one way tickets home. There was less than $4.00 left over, and as I was dividing that money with Ted, I dropped a dollar bill on the sidewalk, and a black lady picked it up and swiftly walked on down the street. Ted ran after her and took the dollar from her. I had told Ted to spend his part anyway he wanted to, but I was going to ration mine out, because it is a 24 hour ride on the bus to get home. We eat candy bars and drank water on the trip. This was not a successful trip. We still had to pay $96.00 for the whiskey, that Ted had bought on credit.

Two months later Vern got our car out of hock for us, and drove it home to Georgia, we had sent him the money to get the car out, and to pay for the gas for the trip home.

## END OF STORY

# "THAT'S HOW IT WAS THEN"

If you think that this book is mostly about the whiskey business in North Georgia in the 1940's and 1950's, you are right. This is all during that time, and I am telling about what I did now, and before I am finished I will tell some things that other people did. I would not tell it, but I know it happened, because I was there.

In the 8th grade I was 6 ft. tall and weighed 170 pounds. I had a birth certificate that I had changed, that said I was 19 years old and, with it, I could get a job any place I went to outside of this area. I went to Michigan two or three times and always found a job. I even went to the atomic plant in Oak Ridge Tennessee and the fake birth certificate worked there just as well.

Back then there were no computers, no radar guns to check your speed, police cars in our part of the country did not have two way radios. The cars that the law had then were not as good as the cars we had. It was no trouble to out run most of the law. But sometime the Federal or State law would come to our county and they would catch you if you were not very careful. On nights that the moon was bright it was not uncommon to see the law driving the country roads with no lights on, in certain parts of the county every car would be stopped and searched for whiskey, because in this area a lot of people made and hauled whiskey. Sometimes the law would park near the homes of the known whiskey makers, knowing that sooner or later there would be some activity there, if not tonight, then later. When activity was spotted the law would watch and wait until the most vehicles could be caught, or the most people could be caught and then they made their move. It was the same when a still was found, they did not get in a hurry to cut it down, they watched and waited and then when the most damage could be done they moved in. Many times, by waiting that way, not only the maker was caught, but the hauler that come to buy the whiskey was caught also. This involved 2 or 3 cars or trucks and usually 4 or 5 people.

As an example, the last still that I knew about made 420 gallons of whiskey every day. The supplies that was used every day was 4,000 pounds of sugar, 300 pounds of barley malt, 70 cases of ½ gallon jars. There was 26-400 gallon boxes for mash. One car and one truck and three people were involved every night. We worked in daytime, but at night is when the supply truck came, and it and the third man was there only for about 90 minutes.

Think about it. The reason it is against the law, to make whiskey, is because of the taxes. You can buy all of the whiskey you want at the local whiskey store and that is okay, but it's against the law to make your own.

The families that I grew up around were fine

people. Some of them did not have much education but remember, we are talking about 1946, and the family men and women would have been raised in the late 1800's or early 1900's. Every one that I knew then was land owners, they paid taxes, they went to Sunday school and church and were very serious about God and Jesus Christ. They, mostly, did not have regular jobs, because there were no jobs to have. They did everything they were supposed to do, and for money they made some whiskey. We did not believe it was a sin to do this, it was a man made law that could be changed at anytime.

When they went to town to buy anything the merchants were very glad to take their money. During those days whiskey money circulated all thorough that area, and I never did hear of anyone refusing it because it was whiskey money.

All of that sugar and malt and yeast and jars came through the merchants in town. Cars and trucks, were bought with cash, gas and oil and tires were bought regularly and service station owners, loved to have a person in the whiskey business as a customer.

I said all of that to say this. A few people around this county looked down their nose at the makers of whiskey, because of what they did for a living, But, many of them were involved in the same business, mostly merchants.

## END OF STORY

# MY DAD'S HOG PEN

In 1947, I met Christine Hodges, we dated for 5 years. and then we were married in 1952. Every stupid thing that I ever did, she was there, and telling me how wrong that I was. She wanted me to get a job and quit what I was doing and I always would not. The numbers were wrong, I could see that there was no possible way for us to live on what I could make on a job.

My dad had a 1936 Oldsmobile and I was driving it one night. I had gone to Mountain City, which was only 3 miles north, to get Christine and we went to the movie there in town. After the movie was over I told Christine that I had to go and get a load of sugar and I ask her to go with me and she agreed. We went to Tiger, Ga., which was only 3 miles South, and bought 800 pounds of sugar from a Mr. Ramey. I loaded that old Oldsmobile and we started towards my home. The motor mount was broken and the motor sometime would raise up on one side. I did know that this happened sometimes, especially when the car was loaded, so most of the time I carried a 2x4 about 6 feet long in the back seat. I put the 2x4 under one side of the motor and pried it up a little bit, and Christine set on the 2x4 while I put a pin back in place and then we could go again. This happened to us twice that night. We finally got home and I carried the sugar and hid it in our hog pen, we had no hogs at that time. The sugar was covered and it would stay dry. Then Christine and I went back to town.

One week later my dad and my uncle Tallmadge brought two hogs to put in the pen. They put the hogs in the pen, and put the sugar out of the pen. My dad was very mad at me again. He already knew that I had been making whiskey, but at that time, I was working for someone else, now I have my own still and he was furious. He told me then, that if I was going to do that, not to ever ask him for anything, and if I get caught not to call him to get me out of jail, and that I was on my own from now on, and since that day, I have been on my own. I was 14 or 15 at that time.

My dad was not a business man. He owned a ½ interest in a welding shop and had owned other business interest but he did not get interested in anything. It looked like he did not care if he made money or not, in other words he just had no ambition. But he did show a lot of interest in hunting and fishing, and that is what he and I did together.

## END OF STORY

## OUR HUNTING CAMP

Back there in the 1940's, my dad and my uncles and some of their friends started a hunting club. A group of 12 friends bound together and purchased 3 acres of land down towards the South Carolina line. about 12 miles East of town on Goldmine creek.

3 acres is not a large amount of land for a hunting camp. But it was 3 acres in the middle of nothing but woods. It was the most private, secluded place there was anywhere in the area. There was an old logging road that had been there a few years before that, but it was not much of a road.

One of the members had a 1931 Ford model A strip down, that was used to haul our supplies in to the camp, and our deer back out. Usually we spent more of our time pushing that old Ford than we did riding, but looking back, I remember that that was fun also.

On work days all of the members would show up and work on the camp. They built a camp house that 12 people could sleep and eat in. There was a spring house where the milk and butter was kept, and a toilet about 200 feet down below the cabin. There were no windows in the cabin but there were two doors, one in each end. The floor was wide boards and there were cracks between every board. The roof was tin and there was no insulation. The rafters was just popular poles, there was nothing fancy here in this cabin. Slabs from a saw mill were used for the walls.

A small creek ran down beside the cabin and there were trout in that creek. It was just a beautiful place to be. When we first started hunting and camping there it was just the way that God made it. But, as usual, the more that man was there and the more that man used the place the more that it became contaminated.

That cabin was used for a few years, there was many good times had there, it was a good thing. But that slab cabin wore out, it started leaking when it rained and Tallmadge, {every one considered him to be the leader}, after asking all of the members about doing this and voting on it first, said that we should build a new cabin.

In a joint effort everyone pitched in and a new log house was built. I wanted to be there to do my part, but at that time I could not be there. I paid for a man named Paige to notch the logs for the cabin, it was $ 60.00 and Tallmadge said that could be my part.

In this new cabin it was good, it was warmer and everything was improved, even the road was better, we could now ride all of the way in with no pushing. But, the old cabin was more fun. I remember one night that it was very cold and Tallmadge did not want to have to get up and go outside to pee during the night, so he got a quart jar and put it under his bed to pee in. Tallmadge went to sleep, so his brother

Coot got the jar and peed in it and slipped it back under the bed. Coot did not fill the jar, so his other brother Obis got the jar and peed in it and filled it full. Before daylight Tallmadge had to go, he reached under the bed and got his quart jar. He discovered that it was full and he spilled some on his fingers and in the floor. He was as angry as I have ever seen him. He took the jar out and emptied it, he had to go out and pee anyway and wash his hands. My bunk was about 3 bunks away from Tallmadge's bunk, but I could see all that was taking place. It was all in fun. Otis and Coot laughed about that for a long while. Before breakfast was over the next morning Tallmadge was over his angry spell, and laughed with the others.

It was against the law to hunt deer with dogs then. But We had several dogs there in the camp and every morning at the break of day Tallmadge would have the dogs down on the creek and turn them loose. You had better be on your deer stand before that because deer would be moving. The first day of the season we killed bucks or does, does for camp meat and bucks to haul home. After that first day we could only kill bucks, this was our camp rule.

We made our own rules, if you broke the rules we had our own court system, and we held our own court. If you shot at a deer and missed, you would be tried in court. If you were found guilty [and you would be] your shirt tail would be cut off, and used for a dish rag there in the camp.

Another rule, every day one person had to stay in camp and cook and wash all of the dishes and get wood for the fire and just keep the camp clean, and you could not hunt on that day. On my dad's day he was there in camp doing the chores. One of the dogs was running a deer. The deer was coming towards the camp. My dad grabbed his Sears and Roebuck J.C. Higgins bolt-action shotgun, and killed the deer, right there in the camp. The group tried dad in camp court and he come clear. He said that he shot in self defense, the deer came into the camp after him. He is the only person that ever come clear in that court.

The original 12 men that started the club spent a total of $12.00 each. That paid for the land, the camp house and everything that they had to pay for. I never heard anyone arguing or disagreeing about anything, it was just a group of friends being together.

The funniest thing that I saw happen there happened to Coot. He was dating this lady named Dorothy and they had a date that Saturday night. We all got up early and went hunting that morning and got back to camp about noon. Coot wanted a nap before he went into town so he laid down on his bed and dozed off to sleep. One thing we did not have in camp was a mirror. Tallmadge and Obis got soot from the stove and blacked Coot's face. Coot had to go right by Dorothy's house on his way to town, so he stopped to pick up Dorothy. He knocked on the door and when she came to the door, there stood Coot with a black face.

When there was work to be done on the camp, I always felt disappointed if I could not be there to help. Not just for the working part, but I missed not being there with Tallmadge, Coot and Obis and my dad, because I knew that they would be gone someday, and they are.

Dan Godfrey was the game warden then, and way back then, he was already an old timer. Dan was one of the first wardens in that area, and he rode a mule every place that he went, even to town. Dan would come to our camp and stay 2 or 3 days at a time. He never mentioned the dogs that we had there to hunt with. Dan would ride up on his mule and set and talk for a while, then he would tie his mule up and ask if he could get a drink of water or something. Everybody there knew what he wanted was a drink of whiskey, and he got all that he wanted. Dan would stay two or three days at a time with us, and when he was ready to leave, he would just get on his mule, and ride on up the road. We always knew that Mr. Godfrey would be there enforcing the game laws, so we would always have hay for his mule.

When the season ended one year, my dad and I, and two more of the members decided that we would put a still down behind the camp because no one was ever there unless it was hunting season. We did put a still down there and we all lost our shirts. We had put a big steamer down there and it got caught on the 2$^{nd}$ round. We all lost about $600.00 each. I should have quit then, but I didn't. [A round is one cycle. You put sugar and malt on the part left over from the last round, and in 3 days it is ready to distill again, that is a cycle, or a round.]

I was down at the old camp just a few years ago and I just set down and started reminiscing and it was sad, because they are all gone now, but 61 years ago we had the best of the best.

No amount of money would replace the fun, the good times and the memories of the deer camp on Goldmine creek.

## END OF THE STORY

## ROB AND GENE

There was a branch that come down the mountain and thorough our yard. But a few years before our home was built there on that branch, it was just a stream of water coming off of a steep mountain, and had no importance, my family living there on the branch made the difference.

Eugene lived up the road a mile or so from our house, and he had made whiskey here, on this branch for several years. Then when our home was built, Eugene stopped working here. Eugene was about 10 years older than I was, but one day he came to our house and told me that he needed some help. He said that he had 30 cases of whiskey sold every week to a man that owns taxi cabs in town, and he wanted to put the still back up on the mountain above our house, and he wanted me to help him. We discussed this, and I decided to do it.

There was a water shoal, a steep formation of rock, about 200 feet long, up above our house. At the top of the shoal there was a flat spot that was only 10 feet wide and 20 feet long, just enough room for a small still, then the mountain turned straight up for a quarter of a mile. It was very hard to climb up this mountain, so there was no hikers or hunters in this area.

From our yard, you could walk in the branch and step from rock to rock up to the water shoal, so there would be no trail for anyone to follow. This is why Eugene wanted to work up on this branch. From the foot of the water shoal, we dug steps out in the ground so that we could walk up this steep mountain without slipping, and falling.

It took Eugene and I a month to put the still up and get it running, but then we ran that still for about 6 months, and the man buying the whiskey was there every week with the cash.

No telling how long we could have gotten by there, if Eugene had not got scared. We had worked all night and finished running the still just about daylight. We had the sugar there, in the shed, and was ready to put it back on to start another round but we was taking a break first. We both laid down on the bags of sugar for a short nap. Just as I went to sleep, I heard a car door shut, it woke me up and scared me, I thought we were caught. I shook Eugene to wake him up, then when I went to investigate, I saw that it was Rob. Rob was Christine's Brother. Rob wanted me to go with him someplace, He knew that I made whiskey but until now he did not know where. He had caught a ride to my house, not knowing what Eugene and I were doing.

The three of us discussed this situation, we decided that Rob would help us finish our work, then Eugene and I would go with Rob.

The three of us all picked up a bag of sugar each, and started up the branch towards the still. Eugene and I got there with our load and laid it down. After resting for a minute or two I looked down the trail and I could not see Rob anywhere. I started down the trail to look for Rob, when I got to the steep place I found the sugar laying there and Rob was gone. I walked all the way to the highway and did not find him.

After Eugene and I finished our work I cleaned up and went to Christine's house, Rob was there. I ask him what happened to him over on the trail and he said that anybody that works like that has got to be crazy, you must be some kind of a dam fool. I could not argue with that.

This happened a long time before Christine and I were married.

After this happened Eugene would not work there in that place anymore. He told me that he would never work in a place [still] that anyone had found, no matter who it was.

It was at this time when I found out why Eugene was so afraid. Three years before this happened, he was driving a load of whiskey down near Atlanta and he got caught. They tried him in a court and he had no attorney, he was sentenced to two years in the chain gang, and he escaped.

## END OF STORY

## TED AND BILL

In 1947 and 1948 the law, state and federal, was clamping down on moonshiners. They rotated the areas that they worked, and at that time it was our area. We had to be extremely secretive about what we were doing, I did not run around with whoever I was working with. I always cleaned up and wore clean clothes when I went anyplace. Still beer on your clothes or shoes is a dead giveaway. I always had to lie about where I was at a certain time or place. The big sin in making whiskey is the lies you think that you must tell.

Revelation 21:8 plainly says that all liars will see their part in the lake of fire. But you can be forgiven, and I sure am glad.

Almost all of the people that I was involved

with then, are dead now. And I must say that most of them stopped the whiskey business when factories started coming into the county. They were good people, they were just forced into an illegal business to survive.

Two of my best friends that I worked with for a few years turned mean. They drank a lot and they both wanted to fight. I stayed away from them, for a while, because of this. Ted was one and Bill was the other. Ted was killed in an argument, and I had to tell bill that I could not associate with him any longer, because of the way he was. He was mean. Bill left town about this time, but I heard talk about him from time to time thorough the years and it was good news. Bill changed his life, he accepted the Lord as his savior and he witnessed every time he could. He has witnessed to me several times.

Back then we lied a lot, we thought we had to, but I did not think of it as a sin and I did not think of the whiskey business as a sin. Anyway, I have had 50 years to ask for forgiveness for that, and I have.

After I retired from the job that I had for 31 years, Christine and I moved back to North Georgia. We were building a house in the County when a strange car drove up one day. I went out to see who it was, and it was Bill. He ask me if I remembered the last thing that I said to him, and I did, I told him what it was, about not wanting him around, because he was the meanest person that I knew, always wanting to fight. I know that Bill changed a lot and I tried to change also. Bill and I are still good friends to this day.

## END OF STORY

# **VOTING**

The first time that I voted was a joke. A real serious, and illegal way to vote. If it had not been for the sheriff at that time, I don't know what would have happened. To start with I was only 15 years old, Ted and I had worked all night in a still, and just about daybreak, we saw a stranger coming up the trail to the still. Ted and I both ran, when we got to the top of the ridge we stopped and looked back. The stranger come right on in to the place [still] and yelled for us to come back, we recognized the voice as being Rosie, He was a good guy and had done a lot of favors for the people in the whiskey business. Now he wanted Ted and I to do him a favor. He said that he would help us to finish our work, if we would then go and help him. We did not ask what it was, we just told him yes.

In an hour we finished the last still full and then we had 11-10 gallon barrels full of whiskey to carry to the house. We cleaned up and got into Rosie's truck. On the way to town we ask Rosie what we were going to do. We are going to vote, was his answer. I told Rosie that I was not old enough to vote, and he said that did not make any difference.

We went to Derrick's service station there in the center of Clayton, and in the bathroom we were given absentee ballots and we voted right then and right there. That was easy.

The next day The Sheriff come to my house. He called my dad outside and they talked for a long time. Then my dad called me out and ask me, in front of the Sheriff, if I had voted in this election. I knew that we were caught and to lie would just make things worse, so I said yes, I voted yesterday. They ask me where, and I told them. They both laughed and the Sheriff told me that I may be in trouble.

The next day Rosie come to our house and

called my dad out, they sat on the porch for a while and then they called me out. Rosie told me that we had been caught voting illegally, but nothing was going to be done about it, just do not worry.

Rosie owned a construction company and he did work for the County. This election was for the County Ordinary. Now it is called County Commissioners, then it was called County Ordinary. Needlessly to say, Rosie kept on doing the county work.

The sheriff was our friend, he was everyone's friend, unless you tried to lie to him or do him harm. The local people around there appreciated him because this was whiskey country, and he was not too interested in catching someone just for making whiskey, but he would catch you, if he had to.

## END OF STORY

# MY EATONTON TRIP

In 1949 I was 16 years old and a senior in high school. I was in the last class to graduate from the 11<sup>th</sup> grade in Georgia, and Christine was in the first class to graduate from the 12<sup>th</sup> grade in Georgia.

Christine's Sister Margret and her husband Bill was 2 of the most important people in our lives. They helped us when we needed help. They were our friends, and we could depend on them. Bill had been involved with whiskey now and then, and he knew a lot of people that was in the business.

I could trust Bill 100%, so when he first told me that he had some whiskey sold down in Eatonton, Georgia, and he wanted me to haul it, I was not worried.

I did have a 1940 Ford, but Bill and I traded it on a 1940 Chevrolet 1-1/2 ton truck. It was in the process of having a trap built between the frame that would hold 20 cases of whiskey. The cattle bed and the top part of the frame was removed, then 3 x 6's were screwed to the frame and then the other part of the bed was replaced. A floor was put into the bottom flange of the frame, a spare tire box was built on the very back, so that you could not see the floor of the trap when we went over a steep hill. The trap would hold exactly 20 cases and it just looked like you was going down the road empty.

Finally the truck was completed and ready to go. Then Bill told me that it was two Georgia State patrolman that had bought the whiskey, At that time I was still not worried.

On Friday night we hauled the whiskey to Bill's house, on Bill's car. Then we loaded it into the trap between the frame on the truck. It worked perfect.

On Saturday morning very early I headed South on hwy 441. I had one hot spot that always scared me, and that day was no exception. In Toccoa I I had to make a right turn and there was a red light at that intersection and the Ga. State Patrol office was there on the corner. My not having drivers license did not help any. I was 16 now and could get license but I just forgot about it. License will be no good if you are loaded anyway, because you have to jump out and run or else be caught. It would be nice to have them if you get stopped on the way back home. No one even looked at that truck on that Saturday morning.

Bill had given me a detailed map of how to get to the buyers house, showing me every turn to make. I was making good time but when I got to the city limit sign, I really got scared. I, then, realized that it was Georgia State Police that I was selling 126 gallons of moonshine to. I was scared and wanted to turn around and go home, but no way could

I haul that stuff back up the road. I forced myself to go on.

A large 2 story house set in the middle of about 10 acres. I turned into the driveway and pulled to the rear of the house, between the house and a three car garage. I could not be seen from the main highway that was about 300 feet away.

I knocked several times on the back door and no answer. I walked around to the front door and it was the same. Then I went to the garage and tried to look in thorough the windows in the garage doors, but they were too high. I found a metal 5 gallon bucket and stood on that, then I could see in. There was a Georgia State Patrol car in the garage. When I saw that, it scared me so bad that I could not keep from running. I ran around the house, down through the front yard and across the main road, then thorough a corn field and into the woods, then I looked back and no one was after me, so I set down on a stump to rest.

After 10 or 15 minutes I settled down some and realized that I knew all of this before I left home, It just scared me when I saw that car.

I calmly walked back to the truck and set down. About 10 minutes later a car pulled in and Two Georgia State Policemen got out. They were calm, not in a hurry and they were friendly to me. Then they looked the truck over and ask me where the whiskey was, it was hid that well. I pulled the 3 boards from the center of the floor that had been dummy nailed. They both looked at the whiskey and tasted of it. Then they paid me, and ask if they could get another load next week and I assured them that they could. But I lied, no way would I ever do that again.

When I got back home I told Bill that if he ever sold another load to any kind of law, he would Have to drive it himself, he just said okay.

## END OF STORY

# TRADING CARS

Sometime during the 1940's, Christine and I had a 1937 Chevrolet. It was a pretty good old car, it had a good heater and all windows were good and it would start with the starter. That is how we determined if a car was any good or not. This was just a car to ride around in, it was no good to haul whiskey on. The only problem was that it would jump out of 2$^{nd}$ gear sometime.

One day Christine and I was just riding around in town. The train was stopped at the depot, and traffic was backed up all the way up town. Christine and I were in the line of traffic waiting. Vern pulled up beside of us and ask if we wanted to trade cars, I said yes, and we traded there, then. There was no money difference, no paper work, no discussion. Vern and Betty got into our 37 Chevrolet and we got into their 1938 Ford. The Ford had a cracked windshield, but I thought the rest of it was okay. I found out later that the Ford was not much good at all. I traded it off in just a week or so.

Forty years later Christine's class had a class reunion, Vern and Betty were both in that class also. After the reunion party was over with, a group of us was setting around just talking. I ask Vern if he remembered us trading cars in the middle of the road that day while we were waiting on the train to clear the road. He was still mad about that, after forty years. He said, "Hell yes, I remember, and you did not have to do me that way." He told me about the transmission jumping out of 2<sup>nd</sup> gear, I never said anything about it to him, but that Ford was no good either.

Back then Mr. Simmons was clerk of court. We could take a motor number written on any kind of paper and tell him what color the car was, and get a tag and a title. This was a few days before computers, and things were easy and simple.

## END OF STORY.

# DOWN BY THE RIVER

In 1950 Whiskey got so hard to sell that the makers was cutting the price down to $ 13.00 per case. That is $ 2.55 per gallon. It cost $ 1.50 per gallon to make it. Sugar was $ 8.00 per 100 pounds and would make 10 gallons of 100 proof whiskey, or close to 12 gallons of 90 proof. But then you had to have malt, jars and maybe yeast. It was a hard life, a lot of people quit the whiskey business. If you got by for 6 months or so, and then got cut down you lose all that you thought you had.

Ted and I figured it out. We had to take advantage of these low prices and buy the whiskey, instead of making it, then haul it to the State line and sell it to the customers that we already knew. We spent one day in South Carolina and sold more than we could ever haul. The buyers would meet us on the South Carolina side and then switch the load to their car. A schedule was made that suited both buyer and seller.

A spot to transfer from our car to theirs was picked out. Just across the bridge on highway 76 there was an old road that went out into the woods a short ways, then stopped at the river. We were going to use this place for a while then find another spot to transfer loads.

We switched 4 or 5 loads there and everything was perfect. We bought for $ 13.00 a case and sold for $ 24.00 a case.

We found a house for rent that was only four miles from there, we were going to rent the house starting in two weeks, as soon as the people moved out. Then we would use that house to switch the loads.

My car was in the shop getting a new motor put in, Ted had a 1941 Ford and his brother borrowed it and tore the transmission out of it, and for only 2 or 3 days, we both were out of a vehicle. But, during that time our best customer wanted 24 cases one night. Ted borrowed his brother in law's 1936 Chevrolet pickup, a raggedy old truck but it ran good.

We loaded the 24 cases on the pickup and was down by the river on time. The haulers were there waiting on us. They had a Buick car fixed to haul, and to run. On the road the law could not catch them.

Ted was on the back of our truck bed, I was up in the front of the truck bed handing the cases to Ted. Ted handed the cases to the man on the ground, and he handed them to the man in the car. We were almost finished when everyone started yelling. In the truck bed it was dark but the dome light was on in the car, at a glance I could see that there were too many people here. One officer was in the truck with Ted and I, he had his arm around Ted's neck, and had me by the collar of my leather jacket. My jacket was not zipped up and I slid out of it, I jumped to the roof of the truck and then onto the hood, and then onto the ground, then up through the woods. The last I saw of Ted, he and that revenue was down in the floor of the truck wrestling around so I knew that he was caught. Both of the haulers were caught and the car and truck was caught and I do not know what they did with the whiskey and the money.

This happened about 10:00 that night. I ran through the woods in total darkness for a little ways. Then I stopped and laid down so the law could not hear me running, I was afraid to start walking out too soon, because they may still be near here, waiting and listening for me, so I waited until almost daylight to get up and start walking.

After daylight I walked to the highway. The first vehicle to come by was a cattle truck and they picked me up and took me all the way home. Me and Ted had to pay for the pickup, $ 500.00, the whiskey $576.00, Ted had to pay a $2,500.00 fine, To the State of South Carolina.

The following week the sheriff of our county saw Ted in town, and said to him, laughing, "boy those South Carolina officers are bad, aren't they? We need to keep our money on this side of the line. Ted just said "yea".

## END OF STORY

# MAKING BRANDY

After that disastrous deal down there by the river, I decided to work on a job for a while and let things cool off. I got a job with Gabriel steel company in Pontiac Michigan. It was a terrible job, but I made almost $ 3.00 an hour. I only wanted to work for two months just to be away from the whiskey business.

I worked only 6 weeks and I quit and went home to Georgia.

The whiskey business is a different kind of life. You may make money and you may not, but if you do, it is a lot of money. Also there is an excitement with it. A gamble that makes your blood circulate faster, gets your adrenalin rushing thorough your body. If the law is after you, you can run twice as fast as you can normally, you can see further and you can think faster. In the back of your mind you are always thinking about doing time in one of the prisons, or paying a huge fine. The deal on the river was the second time that Ted and I was working together, and the law come in on us and Ted was caught, and I got away, both times.

When I got back home I saw Ted's dad in town and he told me that Ted would be gone for a while, probably 1 year. Then he ask me if I would help him with his brandy this year. He made the best brandy around this part of the country and everyone knew this. Ted usually helped him but now Ted is gone. I agreed to help him, he has always been good to me. He told me that he would give me half of everything we made. He also said that it is time to start today. Peaches are ready right now. We got to their house and started working. In the barn there was 16-55 gallon barrels, we rolled them all to the back porch and washed them out real good, then covered them with white cloths. Then we eat supper and went to bed. At 4 AM we got up and left for South Georgia in his 36 Chevrolet truck. He drove 35 and 40 miles an hour all the way.

He knew the farmer that he bought peaches from, he goes there every year. We picked peaches up off of the ground, some had spots on them some were over ripe but perfect to make brandy with. We loaded every peach we could get on that truck and paid the farmer $5.00.

When we got back to the house supper was ready. We had had nothing to eat all day, but we ate supper and rested about an hour. Then he said "let's do some peaches". We started taking out the seed and the bad spots and putting 5 gallons in each barrel. Then sprinkling 1 gallon of rye meal over that, the same thing over and over until the barrels were one foot from the top. Then 5 gallons of water. 3 ounces of yeast and one gallon of corn malt that we had made our self was added and then stirred a lot. It was 10 AM when we finished and we went to bed and slept all day.

That night we shelled 5 bushel of corn, and put it into burlap bags. Each bag half full, and laid it on the front porch. We heated water on the stove and dampened the corn with Luke warm water, we turned the bags of corn over every 4 or 5 hours and in 3 days it had sweet smelling sprouts on it. We spread the sprouted corn out on the roof of the wood shed until it was dry enough to rattle, then we took it to the grist mill and had it ground fine. This was corn malt.

The next day we got the still, and all connections that went with it out of the barn loft, and went to the furnace to set the still up, by the end of the day it was ready. [The cap goes into the top of the still, the arm of the cap goes into the dry barrel, then the thump barrel then the heater and then the condenser. It is all connected to each other by pipes that are 3 inches in diameters.] All of this is called the "outfit".

## stories about a Georgia moonshiner

I was told that we would have nothing to do for 2 or 3 days while the peaches were working [fermenting] so I went home.

When I got back we added 30 pounds of sugar to each barrel, then 2 or 3 gallons of water and then we stirred it a lot, then we covered all of the barrels with the cloths and left them alone for 3 more days.

We hooked the mules to the wagon and went to a neighbors' house and got more 55 gallon barrels. We could haul only 8 so we made two trips. These barrels were already clean but we rinsed them out any way and they were ready to use.

We cut wood for the furnace and hauled it to the still on the wagon. The still was in the upper end of the pasture and about 50 feet in the woods under thick pine trees. We were on top of a ridge but we had water piped in from higher on the mountain. This still had been here for several years but it was only used in the fall when peaches and apples were ripe. He did not make whiskey, he only made brandy.

We were now ready to distill the peach pluming. We loaded the clean barrels onto the wagon and pulled them alongside the porch. Then we dipped the pluming from the full barrels on the porch to the empty ones on the wagon and the mules pulled the wagon to the still.

Each one of these barrels of pluming makes one still full and it takes 45 minutes to distil each still full, and each still full makes 4 gallons. It took us all day and all night to run the 16 barrels of pluming. We had 64 gallons of the best peach brandy that anyone could have.

Whiskey sells for $3.00 a gallon and brandy sells for $20.00 a gallon. $120.00 per case of 6 gallons. That is why he only works in the fall of the year. A man come from Ashville N. C. and bought the 11 cases that we had made, it was gone within 3 hours from the time that we got it to the house.

Just as soon as we got everything cleaned up we went after another load of peaches and did the same thing.

Then we did one load of apples. We made the apple pluming on the porch also, but it snowed before it was ready to distil and we could not haul it to the still because of making tracks in the snow, for someone to see. We were a week late distilling the apples and it lost some strength but we still made 48 gallons. The same man bought every bit of it.

I was paid every dime of the money that I had coming. I ask him why he paid me half of his yearly income and he told me that he didn't. He said that we made twice as much brandy as I usually do, and you did all of the work. I made the same amount of money that I always make. This was one nice family. They were as good to me as my own family was. I miss not being around them.

## END OF STORY

# MY MOTHER IN LAW

My mother-in-law always stood up for me, we got along very good. She did not like what I did for a living and she would tell me so, but we always were friendly. One or two times she had a reason to be mad at me, but we always worked it out.

One time I had an old Ford panel wagon that I used as a truck. I hauled fire wood and anything else that I needed to haul in it. I had cut the body off of it and made just a strip down, it was a handy vehicle. I had gone to the feed store to buy cow feed for Mrs. Hodges, Christine's Mother. I backed the truck up to the place where she kept the cow feed and unloaded it. Then I walked up to the house and just left the truck setting there. That old Ford had cotton seats in it.

The soft seats that you set on was made of cotton. That cow ate the seats in my truck, then she walked to the stream that was nearby and drank a belly full of water. That cotton swelled up inside of that cow and she died.

Mrs. Hodges was very nice about it all. She said that I should not have left that truck inside the pasture, and for me to go buy her another cow. I did buy her a cow that day. $ 60.00 I paid for a cow from a neighbor, she knew of the cow and approved, so everything was okay.

The only other time that she may have got mad at me was when Dickey, her son, wanted to sell his car. He tried to sell it to me, it was a 1940 Plymouth. I told him that I would buy it when I sold some whiskey that I had. He said that he knew someone that he could sell the whiskey to and he would take 3 cases for the car. I used the car to go after the whiskey and we made the deal. Instead of selling the whiskey, Dickey kept it. He hid it up on the mountain above their house and he and his friends drank that 18 gallons of whiskey. Mrs. Hodges had a reason to be mad at me at that time, because I sure was wrong.

But the worst thing that ever happened between us was not my fault. Christine wanted to go to Franklin N.C., which was only 20 miles, to buy groceries. I had 36 gallons of whiskey that I was going to deliver to a man that lived on the way to Franklin. Christine and I decided to do both things at the same time.

I took the back seat out of the 37 Chevrolet and put the whiskey where the seat had been. I covered the whiskey with a bed spread and you could not tell that it was there. Christine and I had 2 little girls so the four of us started to Franklin. As we backed out of our driveway we heard someone yelling at us. It was Christine's Mother. She ask where we were going and we told her to go on into the house that we would be back shortly. She said wait, I'll just go with you. Christine got into the back seat with one baby and Mrs. Hodges got into the front seat with the other baby.

As we crossed the North Carolina State line everything was good, but one mile from there we met the N.C. State Patrol. They did not look us over, but I thought they did. My imagination started working overtime, I rushed as much as I could and still be safe. As I turned into the driveway we saw the man setting on the porch that was buying the whiskey, he could tell we were scared so he ran out to our car. Christine and I both yelled for Mrs. Hodges to get out of the car. She jumped out like the car was on fire. I unloaded that whiskey in about 10 seconds. The other man run around the house with it and hid it someplace. He had our money counted out and when he handed it to me we left in a hurry. I have never seen anyone madder than Mrs. Hodges was. We were up and down the aisles in the grocery store and she would not speak to us.

That is the only time that we did anything

like that, ever. And I can promise you this, it will never happen again. Our babies that was on that load of whiskey with me and Christine are now 50 years old, and when they read this, it will be the first time that they have heard about it.

## END OF STORY

# CHICKEN HOUSE

Margret and Bill, Christine's sister and brother-in-law and the two of us, were all very broke. It was the worst winter we had seen in several years, and it was about 6 weeks until Christmas. As we set in the house by the fire discussing how bad everything was, Bill said that we could put a still in the chicken house, we certainly can't put one in the woods now, with snow on the ground. And we had all tried to find a job, but there were no jobs.

Once we decided just what we were going to do, we got all hyped up and made some plans. Tomorrow morning we would start buying the supplies we needed. I had built several stills and I knew what we needed and how much it would cost. When the stores opened that morning we were the first customers. We bought what we needed all on credit. When we got back to Bill's house we run the chickens out of the chicken house and cleaned it out. Then we lined the inside with tar paper and the next job was to run an extension cord from the kitchen to the chicken house, then we had lights and we could work at night. It was only 50 feet from the back door of the house to the chicken house.

We worked about 20 hours a day, we built 8-4 foot boxes that was 4 feet square and 40 inches deep. We built our own boiler to generate steam to run the still and that still was complete in 4 days. A small stream ran down thorough the edge of the chicken lot. We went up the branch and put a pipe in the branch to run water into the still house. We took 4-15 gallon grease drums and welded them end to end to use for a smoke stack. We had to wait until dark to put the stack up, and it had to be down by daylight. All of the hard work was done. The money was spent. Everything was ready to get started.

## stories about a Georgia moonshiner

Christine's Mother lived about 200 feet from the still, and she hated whiskey, but she was gone to her daughter's house in Florida for the winter. Everything was working out real good.

Bill and I bought the rest of our supplies on credit. Corn meal, sugar, malt, and jars. We bought it all and put it all in the chicken house at one time to cut down on the traffic.

On the very day that we were going to cook a mash, Mrs. Hodges came home. We really had a problem now.

Bill and I talked it over, nothing we could do but go ahead and run at least enough to pay for what we had bought on credit.

After dark we put the smoke stack up. We mixed the cornmeal and water and filled the still and the heater box. We fired up the boiler and the steam started flowing thru the outfit, this would clean everything out good, and we would be ready for the next time that it was run, for then there would be some whiskey made to sell.

When it started to steam, the thump barrel made a thumping noise, because we put water in it, I walked out to the road to see if I could hear it, and I could. I walked down the road about 200 feet and I could still hear it. I rushed back to tell Bill and see what he wanted to do, because it was his chicken house.

I met Mrs. Hodges in the road. She said "what in the world is that noise?" I told her to come and tell Bill about it. She and Bill and I talked. She did not agree with anything that we said. But she did say, that if the law comes here I will tell them that it is yours. Bill said, "If the law comes, they will already know who it belongs to, because it is my chicken house and the light cord is hooked up to my house." We went on and run this still for three rounds. We paid for all of the stuff that we bought on credit and had some money for Christmas.

One man bought all that we made. Courbet,

from up in Tennessee, said that he would take everything that we made. But it was impossible to get by here very long. When the law comes there is no way to get out of it, you are just caught.

We ran good whiskey and kept everything clean, we were making drinking whiskey. This was a goldmine if Mrs. Hodges had not come back home when she did. What made her the maddest was, We burnt the handle out of her shovel, and used her wash tub, and she would not take them back. We had to buy her a new shovel and a new tub.

## END OF STORY

# TOO CLOSE

Oss was a cousin of mine. He was as good to work with as any one that I have ever known. Oss had a place that he wanted to put a still and he ask me to help him. It was very close to his house, and I thought that it was just too close to several houses, but he insisted.

Across the road from Oss's house, there was a very old man that lived there alone. He could not see very well and he could not hear at all. The old man was in his 90's.

Oss had it all planned out. We would haul everything to Oss's house and then carry it across the road and go the trail to the old man's toilet, that was down below his house. Then we would put a wide board across the branch that was there, to walk across, and not make a trail to be seen, if any one happened to be down there. We trimmed a trail up the steep ridge for a ways, then went on a level around to the stream that was in the hollow. This was a good plan. We could see several houses but our trail was in laurel thickets, and they could not see us. We carried all of the stuff we needed there on our backs. It took about 3 weeks to do this. But when we finished we had a nice still. Oss was right in everything that he planned.

We could see car lights from the road. We could hear people outside their houses, if they talked loud. Dogs would bark at us if we made a noise, the dogs could hear us but the people could not. We could not hammer, we had to use a brace and bit and screws to build everything. There was a shed over the still built out of poles and all of that was tied together with strips of bark.

When We left the still house and was going to be gone for a day or so, Oscar walked out backwards with a stick in his hands and flip leaves into the trail, so it would not be seen from an air plane. He carried a spool of green sewing thread with him and would tie it across the trail from one bush to the other. If that thread was broken he would not go back to the still. Oss was very strict in the still house, it must be clean or he would be mad, he said that he may want to drink some of that himself. He was the best.

One day we were coming out the trail from the still, and both of us had a 10 gallon barrel of whiskey. We stopped to rest and we were straight across from one of the houses. This house did not have a window on the side we could see from our trail, but it had a door, and we had never seen it open before. There was no porch or steps just a door on the second floor. As we set there resting, the door opened and a girl peed out the door, from a standing position. That was enough proof that those people did not know that we was there.

Another time I was there at the house waiting for Oss to go to work. Some of their family came to visit and we had to wait until they left, so we could go. They eat a meal and then we were all outside talking. Oss had a bad case of gas, and the conversation got around to would a fart burn. Oss said yes it would and I will prove it. We all went into the bed room and Oss got on the bed on his knees and elbows, and told his son to get a kitchen match, and when I tell you to, you strike it and hold it close. In a minute Oscar said to strike it and he let a double flutter buster. A blue flame run out about 6 inches and it blistered Oss's butt, but not bad; he proved his point.

On the other side of the ridge there lived a man named Sammy. He made a small amount of whiskey and was known for making very good whiskey, and he drank most of it himself. His trail to his still was about 100 feet from our trail and he never did know that our still was there. Sammy's son hauled almost all of our whiskey and he knew where both stills were, yet he was honest with Oss and I. He never talked about Sammy's still to us and never did tell his father anything about our still.

Time flies by. That was 60 years ago and I still have pleasant memories of Oss and his family. Oss has been dead for several years now, but some of the stories about the time we were working together, I will always remember.

When I retired from my job, My wife and I moved back to Georgia. We started going to Church there at Liberty Baptist Church in Tiger. On our first Sunday there, The lady setting in front of Christine and me turned around and ask me if I did not remember her. I told her no, I don't believe that I do. She said "don't you remember when I would take the rifle up on the mountain and pretended to be squirrel hunting while you and daddy was working in the still"? I was watching for the law while you worked. After she said that, I did remember that happening. That was Oss's daughter. All of his children lived close by home.

**END OF STORY**

## BIG STEAMER

In 1956, Christine and I were in Detroit, Michigan. She had a job in a grocery store and I was working at a Chrysler plant in Detroit. We both had fair jobs but I never did like any job in Michigan. The money was about 4 times as much as we could make on any job that we could get in Georgia. I worked as many hours as I could for about 4 months, then I got laid off.

As soon as I heard about the layoff, I went to the phone and called Christine, and told her that we were going back home. Then I called Harvey and ask if he would be interested in furnishing a big place. [still] [To furnish means that he furnishes all material and I furnish all labor, for $3.00 per case.] He said to call back the next day.

When I called back, Harvey said yes that he was interested. He also said to come into Rabun County at night, do not let anyone see you, and come straight to my house. We did that. Christine took me to Harvey's house and dropped me off, and she went to her mother's house. Harvey had everything ready to start working. I knew someone that I wanted to help me if I could get them, and I went that first night to ask and see if he wanted to work. Not only did he want to help, but he was ready to go right then, this was Oscar, that I had worked with a few times before.

Harvey took me and Oscar to the location that he had picked out. We got there 2 hours before daylight and we took tools to work with, drinks and food and sleeping bags. In 2 days Harvey would be back with everything to set the still up. In 2 days we were ready for the supplies. We had trimmed out trails from the road to the still, and built a corral for the mule that Harvey was going to bring. We had built a sled that would haul 600 pounds, and fixed a place for Oscar and I to sleep.

Harvey brought the lumber already sawed up for 25-400 gallon boxes, 3-55 gallon barrels, complete still and outfit and 50 bushel of corn meal, and 25 bags of coke for the furnace. This would be the biggest steamer that I had ever run, or that I had ever seen. The shed over it was 50 feet square. It took us two weeks to get it up and running. But when it started producing, it produced a bunch. We loaded out 420 gallons every day 7 days a week.

Oscar and I went up on the mountain, above the still, and built a platform out of poles that was the size of a mattress and 5 feet off of the ground. It had a slanted roof over it to keep out the rain and snow. A camouflaged tarp was used for a cover. We had a mattress on the poles and we had water proof sleeping bags to sleep in. The only time we were cold was when we first got up. We had to build a fire in the furnace at 4 A.M. and when the temperature was down near 20 degrees it was cold at getting up time. I tried to sleep with my clothes on a few times, but I would sweat while I was in the sleeping bag, and then I would stink. I had to stop that because it never did warm up enough, there in the woods, to take a bath.

One night I heard a strange noise, I thought an animal of some kind was trying to get into our bed with us because when I heard the noise, our bed would shake. I unzipped my bag and raised up on one elbow to see what it was. Oscar had a small hole in his sleeping bag, right at his breathing hole. The bag zipped up all but a small hole to breath thorough. When he moved any at all, the down in the bag would puff out. Oscar had a throat and mouth full of down and he was choking. After spitting and puking feathers for a few minutes he was okay.

When the truck came with supplies they stopped right in the middle of the road. No one ever touched the ground. A wide board was put from the truck to the top of the bank of the road, and it was all carried across that board. The whiskey was loaded that way also.

A large tree had fallen there above where we unloaded. We put everything behind that downed tree until the next morning, then we hauled it to the still on the sled. The mule made so many trips that we did not have to use a bridle, but we had to turn the sled around and then load it and the mule would go to the same place every time and stop. It was a perfect set up, but we knew that it would not last very long, it never does.

Me and Oscar discussed how we would run when the law come in on us. We knew it would happen, it always does. There was a very large patch of running briars just above the still house, so we agreed that no way could we run up thorough there, and would you believe that when it happened, that is the way we ran.

One day about noon, two men came running down our water line. We piped our water almost 1000 feet because we were in a dry hollow. We did hear these people coming because they were making a lot of noise and me and Oscar ran from them, not knowing who they were. We stayed gone all day, we had no car to leave, and we knew that Harvey would be there that night. We walked through the woods and watched for the truck to warn him to turn around. Harvey already knew about it, those people had a still about a mile from us and the federal law ran them off and cut their still down and chased them almost to our still. They told Harvey that they saw our water line and followed it, they knew what it was and they wanted to warn us. It was two months later when the law got us. Late one afternoon a small airplane come right over us flying real low, they made a wide circle and come over us the second time and dipped their wings two or three times. We did not know if this was a law plane or not. If it was they were flying over North Carolina. We were in Ga. But right on the line.

We told Harvey about it that night and he said to take two or three days off. So we went home for the first time in three months.

When something like that happens and you have beer in the boxes ready to run, that is called scared beer. You are supposed to have people there to watch for you when you work, in those circumstances.

Oscar and I both figured that the plane was not law, if it was they would have cut it that day, but they did not.

We decided to keep on working but to be extremely careful. We worked one at a time in the still, and the other one would be up on the hill watching. We rotated doing the tempering, the only time we were both in the still is when we were filling the heater box, that was 10 minutes.

We worked this way for a month, then one day Oscar was in the still house and I was on my way out the trail to watch for him. As I walked out the trail, I met Bob Kaye, Federal agent, and I stopped and looked at him, he did not call my name. I turned and ran back out the trail and about half way to the still someone jumped up behind me. I could hear them, but I did not look back.

The sled was setting there alongside a ditch that the water had washed out. I knew that the ditch was there so I put one foot in the sled and jumped across the ditch. Fay Blalock, I found out later, is who was behind me. He jumped over the sled and went down into the ditch. Oscar saw me running and then he took off running. Oscar looked back when he heard the noise because he thought it was me that fell, and he saw Fay blalock. Oscar went thorough that briar patch like it was not even there and I went through the hole that he made. We were both scratched up and had a lot of briars in us but we both got away. We ran to the top of the ridge and I was give out. I could not breath and my throat felt like it was on fire, I just laid down on the ground and Oscar got me by the color and said "come on boy or they will catch us". Oscar was 52 years old and I was about 22.

The first thing they did was turn the mule

loose. Then they cut up the gears and then had to carry all of that sugar out on their back. It took them two days to tear up that still, we worked there for four months.

Harvey had borrowed that mule so we had to find it. You would think that a mule would be easy to track but it took us 3 days to find it and get it back to its owner.

I went back to that spot 5 years after that and could find no trace of any glass. When we left, there was at least 70 cases of whiskey in ½ gallon jars.

Do you think the law sold that 70 cases of whiskey?

## END OF STORY

# CLAYTON POLICE FORCE

In 1957 the Mayor of Clayton hired me as a policeman. For several years I had been in the whiskey business, and I had been buying all of the supplies to build stills from the Mayor, because he owned a hardware store there in town. I suppose that my reputation was as good as anyone else's around there, or he would not have hired me.

Whiskey was the number one job in our County. It was the best paying job in the County, and it was the only work that was available in my neighborhood. It paid $50.00 per day and everything else around there paid $.75 cents an hour. That $50.00 was for a day, it may be 10 hours or it may be 20 hours, but it was still $50.00.

This police job paid $56.50 per week. For the

time that we was on the job, that amounted to about $.35 cents an hour. You had to be crazy to take that kind of job. But I did. And the only reason I did, was that I expected it to open doors for me in the whiskey world.

While I was on the police force there in town I kept on making some whiskey, not much, but some. I hauled a little bit also, I had to so that I could survive. Everybody I knew was doing whatever they could to make a living. A lot of folks was getting commodities, some were on welfare. My Mother worked for $15.00 a week and my dad was a welder and sometime he did not make anything. My family had it as good as anyone, it just did not satisfy me. I never was that smart, but numbers do not lie, and I could see that my family's future did not look very promising.

Some of our county business people was against unions. There was no such thing as a retirement plan, there was nothing at all for workers. Young people had to leave this county if they wanted any kind of a future.

The City Police force consisted of one man, Elbert Page. Then I was hired, there were two people on the police force. The police car was a 1952 Plymouth, and it was a joke. The police station was an iron post on the corner by the water fountain with a telephone on it. This town was as far behind times as you could get. There was no red light here then. I was on duty from 6 P.M. until 6 A.M. There was hardly anyone in town after 7 o'clock at night, except on Wednesday and then after the movie was over the town was deserted again. On Saturdays everybody was in town and Saturday nights would be busy until about midnight. I was working for nothing, but I saw everything that happened in that small town.

I could see the Sheriff department and the jail house from up town, when the federal or State law come to this county, I knew it. So most of the haulers that lived there in the County stopped to talk to me, I am sure that I kept some of them from being caught, and I knew when I could do some of my own work. I was aware of how serious it would be, if I got caught with a load of whiskey and me a policeman. I hauled a few small loads on the police car, when I had to just move it from spot to another spot. That was just too dangerous and I stopped doing that.

I knew that pretty soon I was going to have to leave this County. No one could do what I was doing very long without getting caught.

One day a friend of mine brought a person to talk to me and introduced him as "L" and that is the only name that I ever knew him by. Denton told me that L was okay and I could trust him 100%. So I did. L wanted a lot of whiskey. He wanted me to find it and buy it, and have it ready for him to come after. He said that he would not come for less than 200 cases, but there was no limit how much He would take.

Sometimes there was plenty of whiskey, and sometimes it was hard to find. What I needed now was regular suppliers.

A man named Henry said that he would let me have 100 cases a week. A man named Lester said he would let me have 80 or 90 cases a week, then there was a few that come up with 20 or 30 cases pretty regular. One man let me have 40 cases every week and he had a place near town that I could accumulate all of this whiskey for L.

L brought a large grocery bag full of money to me and Christine. It was not in bundles and counted; it was just dumped into the bag. L said that he did not know how much was in the bag, but I never did believe that. He told Christine and I to buy our groceries with the money out of that bag, and pay for the whiskey. We paid for the whiskey and that is all. We never spent a cent for anything else.

One time we bought 230 cases from Henry. As soon as L was gone with that load, I went home, and Christine and I counted out the money in 100 dollar piles in the floor. When Henry come in, the money was in the floor. We insisted that he count the money but he would not. He raked it up and stuffed it into his pockets. It was over $5,000.00 and there was a lot more in that bag. After this deal was over we found out that Henry could not count. He took the money home and his wife counted it.

One of the people that we bought from was a regular, two times a week he had whiskey for us. He had a full load one time and said we could load it at his place. We went to his barn and got the 200 cases. I drove my car and L rode with me to their house. When the whiskey was loaded L rode back to town with them in the truck. I checked the roads with my car and they would follow me 10 minutes behind me.

L sent the truck on back to Charlotte, and after everybody was gone, L come to my house and told me that my supplier had tried to cut me out of the deal. That was a surprise to me. I kept buying from him, but I knew to watch out for that guy, no way could I trust him. If I stopped buying his whiskey now, he may have reported me to the federal law.

The first load that L hauled out of the County was 200 cases. The Sheriff, had told me before that if the Police car ever gave a problem to come get his car, and then he showed me where the keys were kept. I got the Sheriff car and lead L to the South Carolina state line. Then I returned the sheriff car to the jail house. L thought that I could do anything that I wanted to here, but I could not, and I never told him that I could, but he seemed to think so.

The Sheriff of the County would work with you, but you better not try to take advantage of him. He was as tough as a nail. I told him that I used his car and he said that that was okay, to get it when I needed it, but that was the only time that I did that.

I was not the only person that needed money. most of the people like policeman, revenuers, lawyers, judges, merchants, most of these made a little bit of money from the whiskey trade.

Revenuers got more than their share. They

were nice enough to talk to if you was not in the whiskey business. But they was a dirty underhanded bunch of bastards that would do anything. I thought for a long time that they were doing the job the best they could. Then I found out that they were out for money. Some of what they caught was sold for cash. Cars, trucks, full loads of whiskey, and pay offs. if you were caught in the woods. $300.00 was cheaper than a fine that the Judge would put on you in court, and everybody was glad to pay that, the best part is that there was no record. But look how much that was to the revenuer that caught you and collected the $300.00. Did you ever wonder what happened to the money that was paid in fines when you were caught for whiskey? It did not go to the County or State to build roads, it went into the pockets of officials.

The most honest people in this whole thing was the maker of whiskey and the hauler of whiskey. The people trying to catch them was trying to profit from their labor, and they did. Most folks just did know about that. I was there when a sheriff and a deputy accepted money for sugar and the pickup truck that was hauling it. I was there when a car load of whiskey was let go for the sum of $500.00. This was good of the sheriff to do this. I was a law officer at that time also, but I was not receiving any money on these deals, but I helped arrange it, on behalf of the haulers. The only time that I received any money like that was a mistake. A car come through town and I could tell that it was loaded, but I thought it was a friend of mine. I pulled the car over and as I walked up to the car, they rolled the window down a little bit and stuck something out the window and I took it. Then they took off very fast. I looked at what I had, and it was $30.00, I still do not know who it was. I saw the person that I thought it was and ask them, they said no it was not them. I kept the money handy so that I could give it back, if I found out who it was but I never did. I spent the money. It was a lot different for a local person than it was an out of Towner, it was harder on an out of state person.

L and his deal was over with. I do not know what L was. But I feel like he was much more than a whiskey hauler. He seemed to be better educated, he was a polite man and he did everything that he said he would do. On his last trip he stopped at our house and ask if we were even, did he owe us any money. We told him that we were even. The bag had money in it, and we kept it in the freezer because the freezer had a lock on it. Christine got the bag and handed it to L and he left, and we have never heard from him again. Denton was right, L could be trusted 100%. L was the best thing that happened while I was a policeman. The City did not want to pay very much to a policeman. What they did not know, is that I would have taken that job for nothing.

About a month after this deal was finished, I went to Lester's and got 20 cases of whiskey and did not pay for it. I put it on my 1939 Ford and hauled it to Elberton, Ga. It was 3 AM when I got back and I went straight to Lester's house to pay for the load that I had hauled and to get another load. I had his money counted out and it was rolled up with a rubber band around it. I knocked on the door and no one answered, the lights were on in the living room. I stuck my head inside and yelled for Lester, no answer. I could hear both of them snoring, so I went into the bed room and shook Lester, he raised up on one arm and I told him that here is your money, and I need 20 more cases right now. He took the roll of money and stuck it under his pillow, and told me to go ahead and get 20 more from the back porch, I did. I drove straight back to Elberton and delivered that load. It was 4:00 in the afternoon when I got back, because I slept some in the car. I handed Lester the money for the second load and he said NO, you owe me for 40 cases. I explained that I had already paid for the first load. He did not remember that because he was asleep. I ask his wife to look under the pillow and Lester and I went with her to look. She found the money and Lester just Laughed about it. Lester had money laying around his house everyplace. I thought he was a millionaire.

## stories about a Georgia moonshiner

Not long after this happened My family and I moved to Florida, to get away from this business. After a year or so I found out that Lester had died and was broke. This was hard for me to believe. Lester would let me have anything I wanted at anytime, but you better never lie to him about business.

## END OF STORY

# 1936 HOMEMADE
# CHEVROLET TRUCK

Ted's dad's barn was in front of their house. Over beside the barnyard away from the house there was a couple of old cars and one of them was a 1936 Chevrolet. It was rusty, very dirty, The chickens had been roosting in it for a year or so and weeds and vines had taken it over.

The tires were slick and flat but Ted said that the car was running when it was parked there, about a year ago. We decided to try and clean it up and use it if we could. We got the mule from the pasture and put the gears on it, and hooked the mule to the old Chevrolet. We pulled it out to the chopping block on the other side of the barn. It took all day to clean it up. We went to town and bought used tires for $2.50 each. We got 5 gallons of used motor oil from a service station and went home to work on our new car.

The reason the car was parked there is because it was too hot to use. It had been a whiskey car and the law all knew it. They stopped it every time they saw it on the road, so it was parked behind the barn and just forgotten about. The car had 16 inch wheels and mud grip tires on it and was high off of the ground. It was good for the mud roads that we had in our area. Sometimes the roads were so bad that we could not get to town, but this old Chevrolet would plow right on thorough the ruts in the road.

When the car was cleaned as good as we could get it, which was not too clean, because we had to carry water from the spring in a bucket, Ted decided to make a truck out of it.

We took a pencil and marked it off where we were going to cut it off. Then we took two pole axes and cut the top and back fenders off of it. We left the front fenders and the roof on the front part. We did not cut off the head lights or the tail lights. We found some old used lumber and built a bed and side boards and a wall behind the front seat. The wall had a cut out window in it. Then we went to town to the western auto store and bought a battery for $9.00 and 10 cans of black spray paint. We changed the oil with that used oil and put the battery in and that car started right up. The car had been gray before, so the black paint covered good. We painted the whole thing black and most of it got 2 coats.

After we finished painting the car, we set on the porch for about 2 hours, and admired our handy work. Then we loaded 16 cases of whiskey on our new truck and covered it up with stove wood. We hauled it to Anderson South Carolina and never had one bit of trouble. That is why we needed a vehicle, not to out run the law, but to slip thru with a load. The law probably thought any one would be crazy to haul whiskey on a trap like that.

It seemed like we would have plenty of money one day, and the next day we would be broke. We have had cars and trucks that cost a lot more than this 1936 homemade Chevrolet pickup truck, but none of them did any better than this one did. It was there at the right time, and Ted and I were both at the bottom of our business adventures.

## END OF STORY

# SUGAR DEAL

The year of this story I am not sure of, but I had moved my family to Florida and would come back home every time I could. When I first started on the job, in Florida, I would get laid off occasionally, and would then come back to work in my old profession, with my old business partners. Sugar was becoming hard to buy. The revenuers had found another tool to use against us. The sugar bags were numbered and they could tell what merchant sold the sugar and it could be traced.

My job in Florida was in a brewery, and In the lunch room at work there was one of the truck drivers that hauled beer away from the brewery and to a distributor up in Georgia. He ate lunch with us 2 or 3 times a week. One day I ask him if he knew of a place to buy sugar by the truck load. This truck driver knew all of the right answers. He told me where he could buy it, and I knew that he was right. He told me how much it was, and I knew he was right on that also. He told me that a truck company could buy 300 bags at a time, but it had to be cash. He also told me that he owned the truck and trailer and he just contracted loads for a Distributing Company in Vidalia, Georgia. A full load of 300 bags was $2,400.00. plus $1,000.00 delivery. It would be $1,400.00 down and $2,000.00 upon delivery, and that included the haul bill. I went to see Ted and he wanted the deal. He and some of his friends got the money ready. We called H.D. and the load was ordered. Ted wired the money to H.D. for the down payment. Delivery was supposed to be on Sunday night at a barn just South of town. We were there on Sunday night, but H.D. was not. We waited until Tuesday morning and then H.D. called. He was setting in a weigh station in South Georgia near Savannah. Savannah is where he was supposed to get the load, there at the docks. He said that they had him for being over loaded. They, whoever they were, wanted $1,280.00 in fines and then he could leave. Ted wired the $1,280.00 to H.D. The truck still did not show up. We waited another 4 days and then Ted and I decided to go and look for H.D.

We was not too worried about this yet, because we knew that H.D. worked out of Vidalia, Georgia. We knew where to find him. We was going to leave tomorrow morning to hunt him. I was picking Ted up in Town in the morning, when I got there Juke was there with him and Ted told me that Juke was going along just to have something to do, I said okay.

The three of us went to the Distribution Company in Vidalia. We went into the office and ask for the boss. This man come out and said he was the owner, and what did we want? He was not especially a nice person. We ask if H.D. was there and that boss got real mad, he was yelling at us and he called 3 other men from the loading docks, then we explained what we wanted, and just what the deal was. We told them that H.D. had told me that the tractor and trailer he was driving belong to him, and he contracted loads to this Distribution Co. They let me know in a few unfriendly words that the truck and trailer belonged to them and H.D. owned no part of them.

After it was all straightened out, We were invited into the office and they explained a few things to us. H.D. drove for them. He had been gone for a week and no one knew where he was. He had bought tires, and several other items, on the company credit card and the tractor was left on the side of the road, they had gone after it. The police are looking for H.D. now. H.D.'s wife is over there in the hospital right now with a new born baby and were hoping that he will come here when he comes after his wife. As we started to leave we were given some more information. H.D. has a sister in Savannah and we have her address. If you find him, call us and we will send you some help, if you need it.

The three of us went to the hospital as fast as we could get there, and we had a plan. Ted and Juke would watch the doors on the floor that the wife is on and I would go to the room that she was in. Ted and Juke had never seen H.D. but I could give them descriptions so that there was no way he could be missed. Both of his ears looked like something had chewed them up, they were jagged.

We ask at the nurses' station what room she was in, assuming that they were married, and they were. Ted and Juke was where they were supposed to be. I went to the room and the bed was messed up, but no one was there. We waited for an hour, then we ask about her. We were told that the baby and the lady was gone and could not be found. They skipped out and left the hospital bill, the baby was only 2 days old. The lady and the baby was here this morning and no one saw them leave.

We called the owner of the trucking company and gave him a full report. Then we left there and drove straight to Savannah. We did not know, that that is where they would go to, but we had nothing else to go on.

The address that was given to us was way out in the country, 15 miles of dirt roads. When we found the number on the mailbox we could not even see the house. We walked up a long sand road and then there was a fence and a double gate. We went thru the gate and several hogs was running lose in the yard. Chickens were roosting in trees right by the porch.

After we saw the house we made a plan. I was going to the front door. Ted was going to the back door and Juke was going to watch 2 windows that was on the same side of the house. We knew that H.D. would run if he was there, and saw us coming. As we started Ted come out with a pistol that I did not know that he had. I got the pistol away from Ted because I knew that Ted would shoot H.D. if he got the chance to. When I knocked on the door an old lady answered the door. As I spoke to her, Ted kicked the back door open and ran through the house, He jerked the phone out of the wall and told the old man to set on the couch and be quite. I explained what was going on, and why we were hunting H.D. Surprisingly, they understood. They said that H.D. come to see them and bought things on their credit there at the local store, and they had to pay for them.

We found out that H.D. was not welcome in their house, and that he had not been there in a year. We fixed the back door and gave them $20.00 to have the phone repaired. We left there with a half way good feeling with these people. Then we headed back home. We drove for about 100 miles then we stopped to buy gas. It was raining and I pumped the gas and went inside to pay. I was probably in there for 5 minutes. I ran back out and got into the car and left. It was still raining. In a little while we stopped to get something to eat and then I saw it. Ted and Juke had stolen a water pump with a gasoline motor on it back there at the station. It was my car and I was driving, if we had been caught it would have been me that went to jail, not them, and I did not even know about it. H.D. did what he did and we have never seen or heard from him since then. I do not know if Ted lost all of the money or if he had partners in that deal. I just know that I did not lose any, because I did not have any. I probably drove 1000 miles and spent 100 dollars, but all the way around, this was a bad deal for everyone.

## END OF STORY

# GASOHOL

After I had been in Florida for a while I heard about an experimental program that the U.S. Government was doing to make gasohol. High proof alcohol to use to mix with gasoline, or to use in the place of gasoline.

I knew how to make alcohol, but I did not know what the proof was. My brother-in-law Ralph, and I decided to put up an experimental still. We acquired a permit from the bureau of alcohol, tobacco and firearms and started working on the still. It was the first legal still that I had ever built.

We used syrup in place of sugar. We used hog feed in place of corn meal and yeast in place of corn malt or barley malt. This was a lot of work and it was all done on weekends.

This still was set up in a boathouse there in Ralph's yard. We moved the boats out and used the concrete floor to support this still. We cut a hole in the roof for a smokestack and put a steamer in there that would have made 500 gallons per day of 100 proof or 250 gallons of 200 proof. We worked all day and sometimes all night until it was ready. Then we notified the bureau in Atlanta that we were ready to run this still. We had permission to go ahead and run it but to keep all of the alcohol on the property, they would be here to inspect everything, especially the proof of the alcohol.

The first time we ran this still it produced 191 proof alcohol, 200 proof is all alcohol and no water in it. That is what we wanted. We were told by the inspectors from the bureau that they saw a lot of stills that were prettier than ours and a lot that cost much more than ours, but that ours run the highest proof of any still that they had checked, and the alcohol was the clearest.

We had a still sold to people in Africa, they did

not want gasohol, they wanted whiskey. We made a deal with them to build the complete still here, and ship it to Africa and Ralph and I would both go there to set it up and teach someone how to operate it. We were to have it ready to run on a Saturday morning for them to see. We had it all ready for them and no one came. A few days later we were notified that two people were on the way to Lake Okeechobee to inspect the still, they were in a car wreck and both of them were killed. There were only two prospects we had to sell a still, now there is only one.

The other prospect was a group of business people from Jonesville, Louisiana, they went into the gasohol business and was getting it from Brazil, but they wanted to make their own and they really liked our still. Gasoline dropped some in price and there were gas wars all around. The Louisiana people backed out on the deal.

The companies that produce gasohol now are just taking money from the government.

There is not enough alcohol in corn to pay for producing alcohol, much less make a profit. The stupid people in the government have been duped.

The best part of this gasohol still for me, was the location. On the bank of Lake Okeechobee. While we were not working, we could fish. And we could catch all of the fish that we wanted. We had all of the fish we could eat and sold hundreds of pounds of fish every week.

Ralph and I both had air boats and we both had fishing boats. Christine and I each had permits for 60 traps. We trapped specks, that is crappie to some people. We always sold the fish no matter how many we caught. The most that I ever caught on one trip, about 5 hours, was 1,400 pounds, and we had two wash tubs full that were not weighed and sold. The boat was level full, when I would hit a wave some of the fish would slide off of the boat into the water, that was a good day.

We made more money fishing than we did working.

We never did intend to make whiskey on this still in Okeechobee, we wanted to sell stills to other people and teach them how to run them. There was one person there in Lakeport, Fla. That wanted us to make whiskey in the boat house and he said he would buy all that we made, but we did not. We would make more money fishing.

**END OF STORY**

# THE SAWMILL

This story has nothing to do with whiskey, but it was about my family, and what my dad was doing to try to make a living in 1941. I was 8 years old. Dad had a saw mill in Apple Valley, off of War woman road. He bought timber from the forest service for logging and dog wood from the same area that he was cutting logs. The dog wood was sold in Clayton, Ga. And that was turned into broom handles and hammer handles, this work was done at the stave mill just across from the golf course and swimming pool one mile south of town. The logs were pulled to his own saw mill there in Apple Valley, now named Sarah Creek, and sawed into 12 foot long boards, and hauled to Atlanta to sell.

As an eight year old, the most exciting

thing in my life, was to go to work with dad whenever I could. It was always a thrill to go down there and watch the team of oxen pull the logs to the saw mill, he had a team of horses also, but I just enjoyed seeing that team of oxen strain to pull the logs.

The big saw was turned by an old Chevrolet truck, strip down. The rear of the truck was jacked up off of the ground and a wide belt went from the tire to the pulley that turned the saw.

Up on the hill above the mill, there was a one room cabin. It had a cook stove that also provided the heat that was needed. On a bench outside the door was a bucket of water for all of their purposes. The 7 man crew lived there from early Monday morning until late Friday night. Then it was pay day and a Saturday and Sunday off to be home with the family.

A lot of weekends dad and I would stay there at the camp to feed the animals and watch over his possessions. We fished in the creek and always caught fish to eat, there was plenty of deer and turkey there in Apple Valley, and although we never did kill any, there was always some there. The crew managed to have plenty of meat to eat. My dad was an expert with a Dutch oven. Hot biscuits, chicken and gravy and pork & beans was the regular meal, that's what he liked.

One of the crew's name was Conrad Holcomb. He smoked but never did buy any tobacco or leaves. Back then everybody rolled their own smokes. My dad smoked Prince Albert and that come in a metal can. Because Conrad had a habit of bumming all of the time, dad fixed some special tobacco for him. In a prince Albert can there was enough tobacco for about 2 smokes. Dad found some dry horse manure and crushed it up and mixed it and the tobacco in the can. When Conrad ask to borrow some makings dad just gave it to him and told him to keep it, that he had some more. Conrad smoked it, after 5 or 6 smokes Conrad said "dam" N.J. how long have you had this tobacco? It taste like it's getting old.

I often went with him to haul lumber to Atlanta. One time we were going to haul a load of lumber on a Saturday morning. When we got up it was not daylight and it was raining, but he thought it would stop raining so we went any way. Where we turned off of the paved road we had to go through a pasture and there was a barbed wire fence to be opened and closed back after we got inside. As I was closing the gate, made of wire, lightning struck a tree on the mountain above us and it knocked me down. I felt nothing, it did not hurt, but for a few minutes I was out. We later drove by the tree and saw it, it was busted into small pieces. I remember how good it felt and how warm it was when dad got me back into the truck out of the rain, and I remember thinking how powerful that lightening strike was. Not because it knocked me down, but because of what it did to that tree.

A few times I have gone back to Sarah's creek

and just sit there and think about how it used to be, about how it used to look. I can almost see dad all bent over the Dutch oven making his famous dumplings and I can almost smell bacon cooking, I can almost hear the saw ripping thorough the logs, and I know that it is not possible, but it is still a memory of mine. Out of the eight or ten people that was there, at that moment in time, I am the only one still alive.

## END OF STORY.

# ACID WOOD

Another deal that my dad was almost involved in was cutting acid wood. I always heard that gun powder was made from acid wood. Acid wood was chestnut trees that was dead. In the mountains there were as many chestnut trees as there were oak or pine or anything else, but a disease killed them all out. For several years the dead chestnut trees stood there on the mountain side, and when the sun shined on them, they stood out bright and shiny. Then a market was found for the wood, and the woodsman started cutting them down to sell.

My dad and two of my uncles was preparing to cut acid wood. This is when dad put the sawmill on Sarah creek to cut logs for lumber, instead of acid wood.

My uncles hired two more people to help them in the woods. Two of them would run a still and two of them would cut the acid wood. I was there and saw the still but at that time I did not know anything about a still, I was too young. A few years later I realized that acid wood was just an excuse to be there in the woods, whiskey was where the money was. This acid wood was hauled to town and sold. The whiskey was sold on the road. One mile from where the still was, the whiskey would be hauled out on the back of the logging truck. The person buying the whisky would transfer it to his car and would be gone with it in less than five minutes. Money was never handled at this time, That was done the next day. Two years they did this and no one ever caught on. The guys lived in the woods in a small canvas house, not tents, but a house built with canvas and they went home one time each month. The money from the acid wood was my uncles, after expenses were paid. The money from the still was divided 4 ways. All four of the men involved in this deal made a lot of money. They cut all of the acid wood on that mountain, then they cut all of the dogwood, and then they had to quit the still, but they did okay.

## END OF STORY

# MY LAST DEAL WITH TED

About 1956, after I was out of the Marines, Money was really hard to get. Ted and I put a still in a chicken house down in the next County. The farmer had quit the chicken business and was going to move to Florida. He was in the process of moving, at that time. Chickens were still in one end of the chicken house, when we started the still.

Ted and I, had a hauler that wanted 60 cases of whiskey every day. We moved a still and outfit that was already built, and set it up in 2 days. We had 20-four foot boxes. We worked 80 sacks of sugar there, the boxes were full of still beer and with the steamer that we had, we could run the 60 cases, [360 gallons] in 9 hours. One man was to haul all that we made, and he wanted a load every day.

Then, I was offered the job as a city policeman. Ted said go ahead and take that job. We can hire someone to do your work and you will still make money. That sounded good to me so I did that.

This worked perfect. In one more week I would be making money from the still, while I was working as a policeman in town. Then, the farmer came back home and saw the big still and how much it was producing, and he wanted half.

In just two more days of operating the still I would have been out in the clear and making a profit. Ted and I negotiated a deal with the farmer for him to get 1/3, and to do his part of the work. That worked out okay. As soon as I paid off all of the supplies that I had bought on credit, I quit.

Ted and I agreed, I was going to quit now, and he was going to work there until we could get another still built and in operation, then he would quit. This was the only way that we could keep the hauler. This hauler had a lot of connections.

Three weeks later I was setting there in town in the police car at night. Ted walked up and set down in the car with me and told me that it was all over. He had caught the farmer stealing whiskey and selling it. 10 cases at a time, that is 60 gallons. Ted said he was going to destroy the still and shoot the farmer. I knew Ted, and I knew that he would do just that. I persuaded him to back off, do not shoot anyone.

That still is run every day. You call the law and tell them where the still is, and let them cut the still down. You do not go back to that still anymore. Ted took my advice. He made the call, and then stayed around home where people could see him, he could prove that he was at home.

The still was cut down by the federal law. No one was caught there in the still. A case was made against the farmer because the still was on his land. He swore in court that he did not know the still was there. The farmer came clear. The farmer and Ted was on speaking terms after all of that happened, but the farmer never did find out that Ted reported the still.

## END OF STORY.

This completes 24 short stories about SOME OF THE THINGS THAT happened in the life of this Georgia moonshiner. My family lived a hard life, because of moonshine. It is not an honorable life, there is not one thing mentioned here that I can be proud of. However, I never felt like it was a sin against God.

I handled many thousands of dollars. None of it stayed with me, it did me no good. I knew that I had to get out of Georgia and away from the whiskey business. When I moved my family to Florida, I had to move on credit, in an old unreliable car, that was not paid for. I was so glad that the whiskey life, was over with.

## THE END OF THE WHISKEY STORIES.

The whiskey stories are over with. Some people will think that those stories could not have happened, but there are enough of the old timers still around to  verify that it could and did happen just the way that you read it.

The way of life that I lived back then in the 1940's and 1950's is history. We did the best that we could. The people that I lived around were mostly poor, but they were honest and hard working, and would do you a favor at any time.

## THE END

# PRIVATE BUSINESS

It is winter time now, the snow is piled high outside on these prison grounds, I can see it through the window of my 10 foot by 10 foot room, that I have occupied here for the past six years. I was sentenced to ten years, but I may have a chance to get out in one and a half more years, if everything goes well.

When I come to this federal prison here in Minnesota, I had almost two million dollars hid in various places, known only by my wife and me. The money has been spent on attorneys and pay offs, here in the prison, for favors that make it possible to survive. Now that the money is gone, I may have a chance to be pardoned.

The trail that led me here to this hellhole

started out good; I kept thinking that in two or three more years I could retire and live any way, and any place that I wanted too. Some of the people that I was involved with made out worse than I did. They died a violent death.

In 1950 two of my neighbors and I were involved in a large-scale whiskey trade. We were making almost one thousand gallons per week, and buying that much more, and it was all sold in Detroit, Michigan. We were all making plenty of money. It cost us three dollars a gallon to make it, and we were getting $15.00 a gallon for it, we were getting rich. We did know that it was a group of men that belong to an organization called the mafia, that we were dealing with, but we did not care.

Then in February of 1950, I was drafted into the army, after six months training I was on my way to Korea. Korea is a desolate, nasty, cold, hard place. The farmers use human waste to fertilize their rice patties. The most expensive thing over there is a cow; the least expensive thing is a human being. To leave America and a huge income and go to a place like that, was unbearable for me. I was not a patriotic person, I was forced to go and to say the least I was bitter. All I could think of was getting back home alive, and every day it looked like I had a very slim chance of doing that. I was wounded two times, but neither of them was bad enough to get me home, one did not even get me a day off. I originally was supposed to stay over there for one year, but at the end of the year my time was extended, and I was there fifteen months.

About the end of the first year; when I thought I was going home, I wrote a letter to a friend of mine that was big in the whiskey business and ask him to be partners in a big operation with me. I had it in my mind to renew the business deal in Detroit.

I received Randy's letter and was shocked to learn that one of my previous partners had been killed in an automobile accident. Randy was not in on the deal, that we were doing when I got drafted, but he knew about it and wanted to be in on it. Anyway, Randy told me that he was ready for us to start a business as soon as I got back home, for now he had bought a taxicab company and was operating it.

When I left Korea I only had two months left to do in the army, and I had almost that much leave time coming, so they just discharged me early and I went home. Randy had my plans all made for me. I moved into his house with him and his wife. My room was away from the other part of the house, you could only enter it from the front porch, and it was very private. The walk in closet in my room had a hidden door in it that slid open, and entered into the closet in a spare bedroom in the other part of the house. There was a small room between the two closets that was only about two feet wide and twelve feet long; Randy had used it to hide whiskey in, back when he bootlegged twenty years ago. I lived there with them for two months before I knew the room was there. Dixie, Randy's wife told me about it, and said just do not mention to Randy that you know about it. Dixie was thirty years old, Randy was forty-five, and I was twenty-five.

The first week that I was there, Randy handed me two hundred and fifty dollars, and said go down and enter the sheriff race on the democrat ticket. "We are going to put you in, as the next sheriff of this county". Sheriff Johnson will not be running but no one knows it yet, he will be driving a cab for me, he will drop out of the sheriff race at the last minute and you will be elected. We have a lot of plans for you, Johnson already has connections, and we plan to cash in on them. All you have to do is work with us.

Sheriff Johnson gave me a list of everyone in the area that made whiskey, and every one that hauled whiskey. One at a time I contacted all of them and told them what we wanted from their production. It was not excessive. Everyone was glad to pay, because it was easier than worrying about being caught.

New people getting into the business would be caught, but first we would break them by taking cars and trucks and equipment and supplies. Supplies we took from them went to our friends for a small amount of money. This county was being organized; we protected our friends and closed down all others.

Buyers from out of state, or from out of this county, could come to the pool hall and arrange to buy any amount of whiskey and to have a guarantee to be escorted to the state line, with no problems from the local law. Just one person could arrange this kind of deal, and it always took two or three weeks for this to happen, because Randy took our attorney to their hometown and investigated them completely. We could not afford to have undercover agents break into our organization. Two of the neighboring county sheriffs worked with us and was paid by us, as was the judge, two of the county commissioners and everyone on the police force. One man handled all of this money for all pay offs, and his name was Patch.

The bars were different, some of them were all legal and they did not pay, but they were watched, if they stepped out of line for anything they were caught. Once in a while, we had to catch somebody and make a big show of it, and be sure it was in all the papers. There were five black bars in town. They all had bands, and dancing, and anything else that you wanted, and they made more money than all the rest put to-gather. One thing was not allowed any place in the county, and that was dope of any kind. If you were ever caught with any kind of dope, you were history. Everyone in or near this county knew this, so we did not have the problem.

I have found a farm that I want to buy, and I have the cash to buy it with. $6000.00 for 60 acres of beautiful land. I told Randy and Dixie about the farm, and that when the house renovation was complete that I would be moving into my own house. They were o.k. With it, but said that I could stay there as long as I wanted too. Later in the day, Dixie said she wanted to talk to me, after

Randy went back to work. Late in the day just before dark there was a severe thunderstorm and a lot of lighting. I was lying there on the bed when Dixie come in thorough the closet, she knocked on the closet door and ask if she could come in, and I said yes, so she sat down on the bed. It was plain to see that she was ready; she had on a thin cotton dress and no under clothes at all. Dixie had laid down on the bed and her dress was up to where I could see everything she had. I wanted her but not there and not then, I told her that it was going to happen, but not now. I told her to go back thru the closet and be in her side of the house. I followed her thru the closet and the hidden room, and in their living room, on their couch, neither of us could wait any longer. After that, we talked a long time and made some rules to go by, because I knew that Randy was mean, and he was powerful in more ways than one, and we could not take a chance on him finding out what we had done.

I had stopped driving the cab but I still hung

around the garage where the cabs were kept, all of the news in the county and the surrounding area come thru the garage. The scanners picked up the police calls from the high way patrol and all sheriff depts. Within forty miles of us, if it happened we heard about it.

Dixie had told me that Randy has a girl friend over on Beacon Street that he goes to see, everybody in town knows it, and they know that I stay here for the money. We have been married for twenty-one years and Randy has things tied up so that no one can get it, not even me.

I had to get out of that house and have time to think, things had happened that I did not plan on. Randy was a friend of mine, and a business partner, I did not feel right by seeing his wife this way; I think I better move out while I can.

At two thirty the next morning I was sound asleep when Randy shook me by the arm, and told me to get up and get dressed, naturally I expected the worse. We went out and got into the car and drove to the cab garage. Inside they had a stranger that I had never seen before, and they were holding him at gunpoint. Patch was doing all of the talking. This stranger was stopped over on Highway 25 for driving on the wrong side of the road, when they looked in the car he had over sixty pounds of dope, and he was under the influence of alcohol. I was not sheriff yet, and I could not arrest this man, and none of us could afford to call the sheriff and start up a new scandal, it was only one month until I went into office. Randy told us to handle the problem, and before he left he took the two bags of dope with him, Patch put the man in the car, and gave me the pistol and we drove until almost daybreak. At the end of a bridge out in the country, Patch took the pistol from me, and let the man out. I did not look, but I heard two shots, then Patch got in and drove away. We never got home until almost noon. We never heard any news about anyone being found dead.

As soon as I went into my room Randy come to visit me and he come thru the closet and Dixie was with him. We talked a long time and Randy ask if I had used the secret passageway, and I said yes, because I did not know what she had told him. He said that is o.k., Come anytime you want too. But do not come when I am here. If I am home you are still welcome but use the front door and knock. If you come to see Dixie, you can come thru the closet, when I am not here. Don't be shocked, just know that I do not care about her, and I won't be home very much.

Now I am very worried, I am afraid to sleep, I have no security at all. I have to find a way to close the closet door, or I have to move.

I bought material and installed another door next to the door on their side and it had an alarm on it. It could not be opened from their side of the house, now I was o.k., I told Dixie that when she wanted to come over to let me know and the door would be open for her, and she was over there almost every day.

Two weeks after the doper was taken away, Randy come into the pool hall and gave Patch and me $15,000 each, he did not say what it was for, but we knew. Two hours later he gave me more money and told me to leave town until the first of the year. Randy told me to take Dixie if I wanted to, and I did.

I was back home two days before I went into office. People come from everywhere wanting favors and handing me money. I did not accept any money from anyone, I just told them no. Later I gave their names to patch and he contacted each one of them. Everyone in our group gets paid. Everything is cash. None of us were allowed to have a bank account. We were not allowed to spend a lot of money. Randy made the rules and patch saw that they were carried out. Bank accounts were for home expense only.

My deal on the land and the house was made before I went into office. Both were paid for with cash, and there were no questions about any of it. In my utility room there was a trap door in the floor under the wood box, where wood was kept for the stove. It was dug out and poured in concrete. A safe with a door on top was put in the hole and concrete poured around it. It could not be seen even if the wood box was moved. I did all of the work myself, no one else in the world knew about it. I had to have a place to keep money. My money comes every day. Randy and patch gets money every day also. All the others got money one time a month. Every still in the county that we knew of, was paying $1.00 per case for all that they made, and we could find out how much they made very easy. If a hauler come from out of town and bought whiskey, he went to the pool hall and made arrangements with patch, they paid $50.00 per load for protection, no matter how many cases they had per load. We caught an average of two loads per week that tried to slip thru without paying. We sold their car and sold the whiskey, but we let them jump out and run, and let them get away. If the car was old, we would leave a few cases on it, and dump the whiskey out where people could see us, then auction the car off to the highest bidder. The bars and bootleggers all paid a flat fee, usually $100.00 per week.

Elections in this county were a joke. We put who we wanted in office. We did not care about politics; we just wanted our private business to be done quietly with no interference. Any of the people that did business with us we protected them, and helped them to make money. Our group controlled the courthouse and the city hall. No one was forced into our group; they ask to be in it. Things were going good now. There was no interference from the state or federal law so it was a good time to go to Detroit and look up some of the boys that I worked with, before I got drafted. I had one phone number that I could call, and leave a message and Roger would call me back usually within an hour, but that has been three years ago, I guess all I can do is just try it and see what happens.

I got a recorder on the other end, but I left a

message anyway. I just said this is Georgia Boy call this number, and I left the number of the pay phone in front of the pool hall. Ten minutes later the phone rang and it was Rogers wife. She said Roger is in jail but he will be out in about two months. We can go see him anytime, if you need to see him. I told her that I would be there the next weekend. I had been to their house before, and it was easy to find. Roger's wife and four kids and I all went to visit Roger; he was a trustee in the Michigan State Prison. We talked and our deal was made. Roger was only the driver of the truck that hauled our whiskey to Detroit before, but he knew everyone in the organization. He could set up a deal that would work. Roger told me that he was going to set me up with a man that would get us started now. I told him "no way" we will wait until you get out, then you handle this end and I will be on the other end, he said that was okay.

When we got back to their house I let the four kids get out of the car, and I talked to Roger's wife. I ask if they needed money until he got out of prison and she said no, Roger is on a salary, and I receive the same amount every week, just as if Roger was working.

I got back home on Wednesday afternoon and the shit had hit the fan. Everyone was mad, and scared. One man that lives near one of our biggest operators, had called the federal law and told them that Mr. Nichols was making whiskey, the feds called me and said they would be here tomorrow morning to search for Mr. Nichols still, and would like for me, as sheriff of the county to assist them. I told them that I would be glad to help and that there may be more to look for, because the wellborn family has been known to haul whiskey. Mr. Wellborn is the man that called the federal law, and he had just bought a new Oldsmobile.

In the middle of the night we sent someone to plant 36 gallons of whiskey into the new car. Next morning I told the feds that Mr. Wellborn had a reputation of hauling whiskey, but I have heard nothing about Mr. Nichols being mixed up in that business. We searched the wellborn car, and found the whiskey and confiscated their new car, and when Mr. Wellborn went to court the judge fined him $3,500.00. We never did have any more trouble from the Wellborn family. They moved away.

The equipment barn for the county has a hall way large enough for a tractor trailer to drive thorough, so at a certain time on a certain date an empty trailer would be parked in there. All of the makers in the group would bring their prearranged number of cases of whiskey, and load them onto the trailer then go to the pool hall and Patch would pay them in cash. The trailer would have 1500 cases of whiskey, and behind the whiskey, we loaded four pallets of floor tile. The load bill said there were 30 pallets of tile. The doors had locks and secure ties on them from the South Carolina wholesale tile depot in Charleston, S.C. The drivers were teamster drivers from Detroit, Michigan.

Absolutely the worst thing you can have in this business, is a woman that will get mad enough to call the law, and report what you are doing. We have the possible making of that right now. Randy has already got rid of Dixie; she is with me for the time being. I do not want her, I want to move into my own house and do things my way, but we cannot afford any trouble.

I went to talk to Randy about this. He said to let him handle the problem and for me to stay out of it. Randy told me to move on out to my house and to leave everything but my clothes, so I did just what he said. I moved that day and Randy moved one of the men from Detroit into the room that same day. He was a young man and had plenty of money, and did not want anyone to know who he was or where he was from. He hooked up with Dixie on the second day there. On the third day he gave Dixie money to buy a new car, with the agreement that he use it when he wanted too. He worked for the gang in Detroit, and we knew him only as Herschel.

After one month I was all right; living in my

own house and Dixie was gone from my life. Our business was going great and there were no problems, but anyone with a brain would know that this could not last forever. My plan was to have money saved to go anyplace that I wanted too, and I put thousands of dollars into the safe every week.

On the second load for Detroit, Patch had an argument with one of the drivers, and cut him real bad, he bled to death before help could get there. Patch and Randy loaded him into a truck and hauled him to the next town and dumped his body behind a bar. He was found the next day and the newspapers said that he had been killed in a bar fight. This town where they dumped him was a hundred miles from where we live.

As sheriff of the county, I knew enough to realize that sooner or later Patch would get mad at me or Randy and try to get rid of us the same way. We better make changes soon, or ease out and disappear while we can, patch must be eliminated.

I went to Randy and told him we had to have a talk without Patch knowing about it. He told me a place in Knoxville to meet him on the next Saturday morning and I was there. It was sixty miles away and I left early Saturday morning, Randy left the day before. No one knew we were gone from home. I told Randy my thoughts and he admitted, that he also had that thought in his mind. Randy said he would take care of the problem.

When Randy got home he went straight to Dixie's house, the new person living in my old room was there with her, so Randy told both of them, that they had to cool their relationship some that people were talking. Not that he cared, but it is bad for business. Randy sent Patch and Dixie and Herschel on a cruise, and Randy gave all three of them the money for the vacation. Before they left Randy secretly told Herschel what he wanted. Patch and Dixie will not be back. Get rid of them any way you want too, either on the way there or on the way back. Just be sure they do not return. Also, you go back to Detroit, and I will be up there to meet with you in three weeks. He gave Herschel $25,000.00 for the job, plus the trip money.

In my mind I am thinking that Randy and Hershel are no better than patch. Now I do not know what to think. Four people have been killed, and still I do not know who to be afraid of.

Back home I am taking care of all the collections. The money from the whiskey makers total about $20,000.00 per week. When a load goes to Detroit there is about $ 43,000.00 profit on the load, the bars bring in about $ 12,000.00 each week. It keeps me busy just counting money. I take my part out and put it into the safe. I keep all big bills. 100's and 50's go with me, I take nothing less than 20's, and their part is in small bills. Each month I go and pay everyone in our group, this month they got $3,000.00 each, and there are 16 people on the payroll. Randy hired people to drive the cabs, and run the pool halls, but they know nothing at all about other private business.

Everyone is gone except Randy and me. Herschel is not supposed to be back down here, and I don't know about Roger, I don't know if he will work here or in Detroit. Randy's money is in a bushel basket in my old room there in his house, the basket is half full and most of it is 20's.

Randy returned on Sunday night, and first thing he wanted was his money, we went after it and he was pleased with the amount. He told me that it was just the two of us running the business now, that the others were gone. We decided what job each of us would do, and that we would not be seen together very much. This will keep talk down.

Trouble started our way, but I think we may have avoided the worst part of it. One of the makers in the south part of the county had their still in a large chicken house. One of the haulers that hauled the whiskey away got drunk and told some people where the still was, when the law came to cut the still down, the one that got caught, is the one that did the talking, all the others got away. It happened to be a black man from Virginia and while he was in jail, the federal officers offered him a deal. Tell us who the local man is that owns the still, and we will let you go free. The Virginian told them that he would tell. Later, when he went to court, he was ask to identify the owner, just point him out, and the real owner was told to stand up. The Virginian looked at the man and said "no sir that isn't him; the owner was red headed and freckled faced", so he got off. And the Virginian went free also. The still was destroyed, but no one got caught. The property had been leased from out of state owners, that knew nothing about the still, so no charges were made.

Randy has over six thousand, 50-dollar bills and no place to keep them. He asked me what I did with my money, and I just told him that it was out of state, and in a safe place. We both get money every week.

Having this kind of cash has become a

problem; we both know that there are a lot of people that would kill us for the money if they knew where it was. My safe is full and I have taken out all of the small bills, there is nothing but 100's in the safe now and I get more all the time. If I put a safe anyplace in the house it will be found sooner or later, and I just can't take that chance. As sheriff I get $1,250.00 per month and that all goes into the bank and that is all that I can put into the bank. I have to be real careful with what I do.

On Friday, the 12th day of December, Randy stopped production in Michigan and come home for a break, He had been making 700 gallons of whiskey each day, while he was up there. He paid every worker and gave them a nice bonus.

The middle of January, Randy left to return to Michigan to resume production of the still. All of the workers showed up for work, it would be a week before any whiskey would be ready, so there would not be any money, everyone got paid by how many cases were ready to sell. While everyone was gone on the break somehow the sheriff department found out about the still. Two deputies come there on our second day back, they did not try to arrest any of us, they just wanted a pay off. They never got any money, but Randy made a deal with them to protect us from other law officials, and to patrol the roads in our area, and watch for us. They were paid $300.00 a week each. We had a scanner in the house and could pick up police calls; they knew how to send us a message if they needed too. The five workers in the still were from Newport, we were not worried about them, but any of the others could send us to prison for a very long time. Because of the conflict Randy stopped working in Michigan.

Now Randy and I are both home. The operation here takes care of itself; all we do is collect money. I dug another hole and put another huge safe in it. That one was in the chicken house under six inches of chicken manure. It is a steel safe with one foot of concrete poured around it and it is full of money, over one million dollars. No one worked on it but me, Lois knows where it is, and she is the only one. When my term as sheriff is over I intend to farm and travel the country, and it will take a lot of money.

Randy is in a lot of trouble with his money, he has no place to keep it, and he asks me to help him. In his house in the hidden room between the closets, is the only place that I can think of. The two of us sealed the door with a solid wall in the closet that was in my bedroom. In the other bedroom we built a hidden door that opened into the secret room. That room is only two feet wide and twelve feet long, but we went to Knoxville and bought two large fireproof safes, now Randy has plenty of room for money, and he and I are the only ones that know about it.

It was late on that Saturday night when I got home from work. It was a cold rainy night in November, and as I walked from the car to the house, I found tip, my dog, lying there dead on the walkway. He had been killed with a blow to the head. I rushed inside to tell Lois, but she was not there. The house was destroyed on the inside. Walls were torn out. Floors were cut up, cabinets were torn off the wall, and someone was looking for money. Lois was not in the house. I called the City Police and I called Randy for help. Randy was their first and he had called someone that had tracker dogs, they were all there within 30 minutes. The traffic in and out of our road had wiped out any stranger tracks, that may have been there. Lois's body was found behind the barn, she had been beat to death with a 2x4, and the 2x4 was lying there beside her. We were very careful not to touch it because we could see blood and hair on it.

The Tennessee Bureau of Investigation was there before daybreak. We had kept everyone away from the house and barn but still no fingerprints, or other leads were found. Someone had been very careful.

One safe was in the utility room off of the

back porch, the utility room door did not even have a lock on it, but the safe was buried under the wood box, and in the ground with concrete around it. They did not bother the utility room. The other safe was in the chicken house fixed the same way, and it was under chicken manure. It was not found either.

Still no one knows about the money or the safes. If Lois had told them where the money was, it would have been gone, and she may still be alive.

Randy called Roger in Detroit and gave him the news; Roger was in Newport the next day and wanted to help find the people that did this. Because Roger had been there most of the time when the truck was loaded with whiskey to go to Detroit, he knew the people that brought the whiskey to be loaded. There was no stopping him, he found every one of the whiskey people and questioned them. He insisted on knowing where they were, on that Saturday night and you better be able to prove it. Roger had two other men with him. They were big gangster type people that you just did not want to lie to.

After a week of visiting all of the farms of the whiskey makers, Roger come to me and said that he was not sure about it, but one family was very nervous and did not want to answer some of the questions, then I went with Roger to the Ramey farm. Rip and Poke, the Ramey twin sons, managed to get into their car and get away. Roger told Mr. Ramey to find the boys and bring them in. They had 24 hours to report to the Sheriff in Newport, and if they are not there by then, we will hunt them down. At this time we notified the Tennessee Bureau of Investigation about Rip and Poke Ramey, and an all point bulletin was put out in the entire area. At the break of day the next morning Mr. and Mrs. Ramey brought the Ramey twins in and turned them over to the T.B.I.

Now the problems could start. The twins could tell about the whiskey deal, that involved almost every family in the county. The twins had completely destroyed the inside of our house looking for money, and did not find any; this was the only plus for us. The twins know about the group but could they prove it? Roger and Mr. and Mrs. Ramey were allowed to go in and talk to the two boys. They were told that one of the best attorneys in the State would be there to represent them. It could be arranged for a deal to be made that would make it a lot easier on them, but they could not mention anything about the whiskey deal with the group and the sheriff. They agreed, but they did so out of fear.

Since the two boys had been in jail, they did not meet face to face with me but one time, and then it was very brief, and we were not alone, but they could see the hate in my eyes. They both were aware of the killings that had taken place, and of the disappearance of people in our group that had stepped out of line, but no one knows how or why or who is responsible. At this time the safest place for them is in jail, because they knew that if they were out on the street they would be in great danger.

Both boys requested that either their Mother or Father be present, when they are visited by attorneys or anyone else. The county judge denied this request because the jailers had to take food to them three or four times every day. It was also requested that Roger, never be allowed to visit them in jail, because he was not an attorney and did not know anything about the circumstances of the case, they thought. Roger's attorney in Detroit wants to have the brothers transferred to another county to be tried. He said if anything happened to them, that it would leave all of us here in Newport in the clear.

The coroner here determined that Lois had been raped, and then bludgeoned to death with blows to the head. This is when the public wanted to get Rip and Poke out of jail and hang them. Our county judge and the T.B.I. agreed to move them to another county, for the trail because everyone in this county wanted them dead, they could never get a fair trial here.

45 miles to the west, was Mountain City, Tennessee. A small town, and they had an old jail, but it was secure. This is where the brothers were moved to for the trail. Word got out that the prisoners were being moved and about 60 or 70 angry people gathered there at the jail to protest. To avoid trouble there, we dressed both boys in Tennessee State Trooper uniforms and they walked right out of the jail with two other troopers, and our city police, and left for the jail in Mountain City. No other problems occurred that night.

Victor Callaway is our attorney for the group. As far as I know, there is nothing that he cannot take care of. Dirty, crooked, thieving, underhanded, and dangerous. This is just part of the words that describe him. But if he is on your payroll you can depend on him.

Rip and Poke had been in the jail in Mountain

City for one month when Victor contacted Randy and he wanted $50,000.00. $25,000.00 now and $25,000.00 later. He did not say how much later, and we did not ask any questions. Victor left Randy's house with the money that night.

Our lives and our business deals slowed down some, everyone seemed to be more careful because they were scared. I felt like I was being watched every place I went, but I was not. One of the city police that was on our pay roll was told to watch my back every place I went, and this lasted for almost two months, no one was ever seen following me, it was all in my head. Randy had the same feeling and he left town for a few weeks to settle down.

Poke and Rip was in the same cell together. Across the walkway there were two other men in a cell. Down the hall way a few feet, there was a storeroom for mops and brooms and toilet paper and such. Someone had taken a roll of toilet paper and rolled it across the floor and into the door of the storeroom that had been left open. Then the toilet paper was set on fire, and the small flame burned its way into the storeroom. The flame got bigger, and there was a lot of smoke, and that is what killed all four of the prisoners that were in the jail.

Victor was in Detroit on that Friday night, Randy was in Knoxville and I was with several friends in the bowling alley. I was off duty and we were all drinking a few beers, and since my house had not been fully repaired I was living in a motel, one block from the bowling alley. We had all walked back to the room when we got the word about the fire.

Mr. and Mrs. Ramey were heartbroken. They arranged the funeral and after the two boys were buried, they sold their farm and moved away and did not tell anyone where they were going. Jack and Emily Ramey are both in their 50's and they have a story to tell that any newspaper would pay a lot for. But they won't because they know Victor, and they know Randy.

Three months after the Ramey's had moved away Randy found out where they lived. He knocked on their door and Mr. Ramey come to the door. Randy handed Mr. Ramey $1,000.00 cash, and told him it was for whiskey that he had not been paid for, That he just wanted them to have the money, Mr. Ramey thanked Randy and Randy left. This was done so that they would know that we knew where they lived. They also know what not to talk about.

I only have a few more months in this office. No one monitors what I do, or do not do, so I am not going to work anymore. I am not going to collect any more money from payoffs, and I intend to be out of town at least four or five days every week. This office has served its purpose, I wanted this job to make money and it has done just that, I'll never have to work anymore. I told Randy my plans so that he could be prepared. Surprisingly, he accepted what I had said. He even told me that he wanted to get out also. We agreed that he took over all money deals and that during the coming holidays we would just leave. He would go his way and I would go mine. My job ended on January 1, I had not run for reelection and my deputy had run, and was elected, so he takes over.

Our group was no more. All of the politicians in the county that had been on the payroll were out. Every one of them was still in office, and I am sure they are on the take in some way with someone, but not me. The makers and haulers are on their own also. Randy and I have almost three million dollars each.

For the past five years I have lived just for money. No matter who it hurt no matter what happened to anyone else, money is all our organization wanted. But that is all in the past. Now I have a chance for a new life. Joyce and I have more money than we could ever spend. Joyce knows nothing about the buried safe, but she knows about the inside safe, however she has more money than I have ever seen before. Joyce and I think the same. We want to do the same things. We both want to travel and see the world. I met Joyce after the trouble in Tennessee.

We stayed in Europe for 90 days, then we went on a cruise to Alaska and now we are in our condo in Miami Beach. The police called me in to the station to answer questions this morning. Randy was shot and killed yesterday morning. He had been on a trip for the past four months, and on his first day back home he was murdered. The police ask me if I knew anyone that was mad at Randy, or that may want to harm him, I told them no, but that made me think about all of the rotten things that he had done in the past five years.

I could have about the same number of enemies that Randy had. We were always in business to-gather, but I tried to stay back and be quiet and let him do the talking. Anyway it will be a long time before I can go to Newport and walk the streets, without worrying that the same thing will happen to me.

Right now I am on everyone's list. The police know where I am, so everyone in Newport and Detroit knows where they can find me. The group in Newport all know that I have a lot of money someplace, any one of them would kill for half that amount. But no one knows where the money is. Victor opened that account in the Cayman Islands for me, that is where he has kept money for years.

No one in the Newport area knows Joyce; she has never been there, and has not ever met anyone from there. So I feel safe in letting her go to Newport and contacting a real estate company and trying to buy Randy's house in town. I do not know this for sure, but it is possible that the hidden room between the two closets still have Randy's money in it. If so, we may as well remove the money and then resell the house.

We rented a hotel room in down town Knoxville, and both stayed there for two days. Then Joyce drove to Newport and from the directions that I had given her she drove by the house and there it was. A big sign that said FOR SALE. Joyce found the Real estate company and asks about the house. The sales lady drove Joyce to see the property, and Joyce made a $500.00 deposit to hold the property for one week until her husband could inspect the house. The next day I was in the trunk of the car, and Joyce drove into the garage of Randy's house and closed the door. Within three minutes I had opened the hidden closet door and there was the safe with all of Randy's money, the safe door was not even locked. Joyce and I turned the safe over in the floor and dumped the money onto a bedspread and then drug it to the garage and we both loaded it into the trunk of the car. We loaded the safe also because we can use it.

After dark we went back to Knoxville and parked in the parking garage of the hotel. We left early the next morning.

Back home in North Carolina we counted the money. There was $950,000.00 in 50 dollar bills. There was $650,000.00 in hundreds. Two bundles of fives and tens and twenties that we did not count, we called it spending money. This was just an idea, but it was an idea that turned out to be okay.

During my last discussion with Victor, he had told me to go home, and he would be in touch with me. Although I was relieved to know that no one was looking for me, but is Victor telling the truth?

Three days later, Victor knocked on our door. We did not know he was coming at this time. He just said he decided to visit us and give us the good news.

My money was in the bank. My mind was already working on a plan to move more money to the Cayman Islands, but it would be later.

Our car was parked in West Palm Beach. Victor kept his plane there and drove the car the 700 miles on to Newport, the plane and the trips to the Cayman's was not known by anyone in Tennessee, it was his secret thing to do. It was his privacy, his condo on the beach, his lady friends, and his reward for the crooked, vile, and unscrupulous things that Victor had done to make the money to pay for all of this.

The plane trips back and forth from the Islands to West Palm Beach were a great advantage. We kept everything legal and followed regulations. When we left the Islands they ask what we were taking back to the states and we said nothing, and we had nothing. But Victor gave $50.00 tips anyway. When we left the States going to the Islands we had nothing but cash, but no one ask. When we carried money it was in the suitcase.

Someone had been watching us and knew our schedule here in the Islands. It had to be someone that had figured out that we bring in large amounts of cash on our regular flights to West Palm Beach. Anyway this morning as the attendant was topping off our fuel tank, a man dressed in a black suit came up to us as we were climbing into the plane and started talking. Before we knew what was happening he pulled a pistol from his belt and shot Victor in the arm. Everyone was scrambling trying to get out of the plane and the shooter fell out backwards. He shot at Victor two more times but missed, and put two holes in the plane. The attendant was still close by and saw it all happen, but said that he had never seen the man before. Within ten minutes police was all over the place. They searched the plane and our luggage and each one of us was legal. It was determined that someone had tried to rob us but got scared and muffed the job.

Victor was in the hospital for two days. While there he called West Palm and bought a new plane and had it delivered there to us. The man that delivered the plane flew the old trade in back to the States. We had to wait two weeks before we could make our trip to Florida because the Doctors would not let Victor fly the plane. Because of all of this, Victor rented a hanger in Fort Myers and was going to keep his plane there, instead of West Palm Beach. He also rented a hanger inside where there was more security while here in the Islands. Victor would have had someone to go after the shooter if he just knew who to go after. One thing he did know, that was not just a robbery, it was a hit that failed. Victor told us that we had to keep our flights secret. Not to talk about us going back and forth. When we go we will slip out of town and meet at the airport, we all agreed to do this. Then Joyce and I decided not to fly with Victor for a few weeks, but to take a commercial flight instead, it was a lot more trouble and instead of a two hour trip it turned into a five hour trip; but we wanted things to settle down some.

On Victors first trip back to the Island he was shot one time in the head. It happened in the parking garage just after the airport employee had driven Victor to his car in a golf cart. The employee just got outside the garage when he heard the shot; he immediately called the police, but there was no sign of the person that did the shooting, and there were no clues to the shooting. Victor was killed instantly. Irena was scared. She was afraid that someone was going to kill her also. If this was because of the man that robbed her, then she had a good reason to think that, but it could be because of something else that Victor had done someplace else. Who knows? Irena wants to leave and go home. She asked Joyce and I about her credit card, would it be good in Florida, and could she still use it? It is unlimited, that means that she can draw out any amount of money that the account has in it. Irena decided to keep the condo and live on the card as long as they honored it, and then she would go home. She drew out cash one time a week in the amount of eight or nine thousand dollars and kept it. Since I had an account already, I could deposit that money in my account for her, and give it to her when we got back to Florida.

Irena is slowly and quietly moving out of Victor's condo, and moving in with Joyce and

I. If any more problems arise we are moving back to the States.

Time moved on. The three of us lived in the Islands for three more months, and then we sold our condo and went back to Florida. Irena and I had been together a few times; we had not slept together at night because we never had the chance; but we had made love in the car and on the beach, and in the floor in the condo. When Joyce was not there and we were, it was our chance, and we took advantage of it. We both thought that Joyce did not know, but as soon as we got home Joyce, in a quiet, calm, voice told Irena to get her things and get out. Then she looked me straight in the eye and told me the same thing. We were not married but we had been living together for a long time. I cannot blame her for doing what she did.

The very next day, I dug up the floor in my garage. I loaded the money into two large suitcases, and after patching the hole in the floor, and loading a few of my clothes into the

Cadillac that was still in Joyce's name, I went down town and put my mobile home on the market. Then I went to a hotel that I knew Irena would be in. I ask her if she wanted to leave with me and she said yes. We did not know where we were going, but we traveled north for two days. Someplace in Georgia we turned west, and still not knowing where we were going, but we were on an interstate highway and traveled for five days.

We could not trade the car in on a different one. We both knew that we had to get rid of this car and get another one. Irena had the credit card and thirty five thousand dollars that she had withdrawn from Victors account. We bought a used ford for $9,500.00, then we loaded all of our belongings into it and I followed Irena downtown to a slum section. She parked the Cadillac on the street in a parking space and left the keys in the car, with the doors unlocked. Then we drove away in the ford and drove to a small town in Utah. Irena did not know that I had the two suitcases full of cash. She was willing to pay all of our expenses, she bought the ford and it was in her name.

We traveled for two months. We had no destination and we never stayed in one place more than one week. In Ohio is where we decided to go back to the Cayman Islands, but we was going a different way this time; we would let a travel agency arrange our trip for us, including the hotel.

I only had one problem. What would I do with the money? Irena suggested calling the bank in the Islands and ask them how to handle it, so we did. When we told the banker how much we had to deposit he gave us the name of a bank in Toledo, Ohio. We were told that he would meet us there the next day. He was there as promised; the three of us carried the two suitcases of money into a private room that had machines that counted money. I received a receipt that showed my account number and the amount of the deposit, and showed that the deposit was made in the Islands, not Toledo, Ohio. Irena and I stayed in Toledo that night, she suggested to me that Mr. Burns, the banker, probably could check on her credit card and find out what was left in the account, although her card was not from the same bank that my account was in. We decided to try that when we got to the Cayman. there we both went to the bank where Mr. Burns was, and where my account was. We ask him to check on the card and see what the balance was. We both overheard him talking on the phone and he gave no name

The travel agency took care of everything; it was a worry free trip for us. Our first day there we checked the balance on Victors card, when we asked what they wanted to identify us, the banker said "just the number on the card". The balance was $700,980.00. It was a card that could be used any place that accepts American Express. He ask if we wanted to transfer that balance to his bank and we told him no. We had 15 days to be in the Islands then we would go someplace else. Probably Mexico. It was Irena's idea to use the card money first, just in case that there was some kind of a problem, but according to Mr. Burns there could be no problem, because the money was there, and it was legally Irena's, signed over to her by Victor. We never bought anything big like cars or houses we kept it small so there would not be any phone calls to check on the account.

When our fifteen days were up we went back to Florida. On the very first day back in Florida we both made our minds up that our next trip would be to Mexico, but we wanted to stay there a couple of weeks to take care of some unfinished business.

In the grocery store the first person we saw was Joyce. She was so glad to see us that she cried, and she apologized for asking us to leave. When we told her that we were going to Mexico, she immediately ask if she could go with us, of course we said yes. The next question was 'can I move in with the two of you' and we said yes again. Our living arrangement was different. It was clean, respectable and courteous. We always had separate bedrooms. The three of us were happy with our lifestyle. We had everything that money could buy and when the sexual desire happened, it was in a quiet and secretive manner and never involved any outsiders. We had all three agreed on this in the beginning of our unusual arrangement. The three of us were tied together in a bond caused partly by having crooked and dirty money and too much money. All three of us did not want to lose that, we were all happy with it. In motels, hotels and aboard ships it required three rooms, but we could afford it.

For the first time since I got out of the army I feel like I am a free man. I own no property; the IRS does not know that I exist, I write no checks, use no credit cards and have no bills to pay. Irena pays all bills with Victors card, and Joyce is a wealthy woman. I have no bank account in the United States.

On our second month in Mexico I went out on a fishing boat with a group of people.

## stories about a Georgia moonshiner

We were 50 miles out in the ocean fishing near an old shipwreck, and had caught all the fish that we wanted, so we were just setting they're talking. The man setting next to me at the table was a minister in a Baptist church up in Tennessee. He told me this when he introduced himself to me, he and his family was here on a vacation. I had to be very careful not to let him know that I also was from Tennessee. I would have avoided the minister and not talked to him, but he had already said that he and his family was staying in the same hotel that we were in. He had asked if it was my sister or my wife's sister that was with us, he had noticed that there were always three of us together.

The minister asked me if I was saved. I did not even know what he meant so I just acted like I did not hear him. Then he asked if I had accepted the lord, again I did not understand him, so I excused myself and went inside the cabin of the boat where the food and drinks were being served. I could not ask any of these people about what the minister was

187

talking about, but I knew that I had to find out, someway.

When I was about eight or nine years old I had gone to Church with friends, but I never did hear about being saved or accepting the lord. When we get back home to Florida I'll make it a point to find out what this minister was talking about.

The crew on the boat had cleaned the fish and when I got home I had for my part, six large fish filets, and Joyce and Irena and I cooked them and we had a fish dinner. I told both of them what the minister had said and Irena knew all about it. She tried to explain it to me but I could not understand how me or anyone else, could be forgiven for as much sin as I had piled up in my lifetime, not for just the asking, not for just the confessing of the sins, and asking for forgiveness. There just had to be more to it than that. After all, I had broken all of the commandants many times and for a whole lifetime. I want to find out more about this later when I get home.

## stories about a Georgia moonshiner

While we were in Mexico my house had sold. Now all three of us were living in Joyce's home for the time being. Since the money was in an off shore bank, the pressure seemed to be off and I am not worried. We had the check for my house deposited in Joyce's name and in her bank; between the two of them they paid all the bills anyway.

How Roger got my address and phone number I did not know. On the following Wednesday, Roger called me and said that he was coming by that he had to talk to me. He was there in two hours. Roger told me that he did not know how I had got Randy's money, but he knows that I got it. Your lady friend that gave the $500.00 cash to hold Randy's house for a week had accidentally left a paper with her address on it. This is the fourth time I have been here looking for you. Then Roger told me, that before Hershel was murdered he had told him about the small room where Randy kept money. We bought the house and found the room. No money was there. We know you have it. Randy had agreed to pay us $500,000.00 for the whiskey business in Canada. He said he had to get out of Tennessee. He bought it and we quit and left. We want our money now. I told Roger that I did not get the money, I do not have any money and if I did I would give it to you. Roger said that I had ten days to pay up and then it was out of his hands. That could only mean that there would be a contract put out on me. Then Roger said, also your lady friend was there and was involved and we both know that for a fact, so you are both in danger, if we do not get the money. We were in Rogers's car, and had driven about five blocks from the house when he let me out and I walked back home.

As soon as Joyce and I got to the Islands we contacted Mr. Burns. I told him that we wanted to rent, or buy a condo in secret, if it was on the water or not would be all right but it could not be in our name. The bank owned a nice unit on the beach and we rented it for six months. Mr. Burns promised us that when the six months were up, that he would have something else for us.

We did not let Irena know where we were; she thinks that we are in Paris. We both would like for her to be able to come to us but she may be followed. This has gone too far now. Giving them the money will not stop them from killing one or both of us. I do not like it, but now I have to carry a pistol every place I go, just for self-protection.

We do a lot of Island hopping now. We spend a lot of money but we do have a good time. We have a plan that has worked well for us so far. A few selected people that we deal with, such as the private pilot and the doorman at the condo, receive large tips from us, when we get what we want. A tip is never less than $100.00. The pilot owns the plane. We can be in Miami in ninety minutes if we want to, and the cost is $1,000.00, if he has to wait more than twelve hours he leaves and if he comes back after us it is another $1,000.00. We are not checked or searched in the Islands, but we may be in Miami.

If I met Roger on the street I do not think

he would recognize me. I am fifty pounds lighter, I have a dark tan from being in the sun so much, and I keep my hair cut short. I now have a habit of watching everyone around me. When I walk down the street I am looking forty or fifty feet ahead to see who I am about to walk by, I can't help it because I am afraid of what might happen. I do not wear a bathing suit because I have to have clothes that hide my pistol. It is small, a 25 automatic with a two-inch barrel, but it will help protect us, and Joyce has one also.

Keith, the pilot, does not have a business here in the Islands. He is just a private person that owns a small plane and rents hanger space near his house from a small airport with a grass runway. Mr. Burns rents his plane sometime and he recommended me, so we are the only customers that Keith has. We help him pay his expenses and he is good to us.

I offered Keith a deal and he has accepted it. He is going to Florida alone. I gave him Irena's address and a letter and he is to hand her the letter then leave and return the next morning. Keith understands that she may come back with him and she may not. The letter explains everything. Keith has a rental car, but Irena is to leave town on the bus, Keith will pick her up at the first bus stop fifty miles away then the two of them will come to the Islands.

The letter explained that she could bring anything she wanted too, she would be safe. Irena brought all of the money she had, and everything that was valuable. She said she was not going back to live in the states.

Roger somehow and some way found out where we were. He and one of his group from Detroit got into our room in the middle of the night. Joyce and I were in bed and heard Irena screaming, and then we heard the gunshot and then just silence. I had my pistol next to the bed, but before I could get it from the drawer Victors partner was standing over us telling us to get out of the bed, I had the little 25 automatic in my hand already, but it was so small that the killer did not see it. I got out of bed as he had ordered; his pistol was aimed at us as he started ripping Joyce's clothing off of her. Roger walked into the room and yelled for his associate to stop, just then the man turned to look at Roger, during this split second I shot him in the throat. I intended to shoot him in the head but I missed. The gurgling sound coming from the man laying in the floor was sickening, he was groaning and trying to yell, but could not make any sound other than a blubbering nasty sound. Roger was surprised that I had shot the man that had shot Irena, Roger was also flustered and had forgotten why he was there in our apartment, while I had the chance, I shot Roger two times and both times I hit him in a spot that would not have killed him. If I had waited until Roger regained his composure, he would have killed both of us, he would have had to, otherwise the group in Detroit would have killed him anyway, so then I shot him in the head.

Three minutes later we were covered up

in police. Joyce and I were both arrested. I whispered to Joyce not to answer any questions, do not speak one word to anyone, except to say that we were being robbed. The man shot in the throat died. Three people in our apartment were dead.

After two hours in the police station, Joyce and I were released. The record shows that it was a robbery, and that I shot the two men in self-defense and that they had killed Irena while they were trying to rob us.

This dirty money is attracting all of the undesirables to us. We thought we had problems before, but now we really do have problems. Now we cannot live in the Islands anymore. I do not know where we will go but we have to think of a place soon.

We contacted Keith to arrange a plane ride to Fort Myers. Joyce and I packed one suitcase each. We carried what cash we had and instructed the condo manager to give our other belongings to someone, anyone that wanted it. We had prepaid for six months so we called Mr. Burns and told him we were leaving. Keith flew us to Florida, and then after one night there he was going to fly us on to Mexico. This way no one would know where we were. We had everything all planned out.

The cab brought us from the airport to Joyce's house. As we walked up the steps to enter the house five FBI agents rushed us and put handcuffs on all three of us, including Keith. Joyce and I were locked up in the Federal building in Fort Myers. Keith was taken to the airport and a search was made on his plane. They vacuumed the plane to see if any residue from dope could be found. There was none so Keith was released; he left immediately for the Islands.

In our possession we only had $6,000.00. This was not too much money for a person with a net worth like Joyce had; she could prove that her money was all legal. My wallet was in her purse, and she had my watch and ring also. I was searched and my belt and shoestrings were taken from me before being locked up. Joyce was just kept in detention overnight, she was not searched because they had no reports on her and no reason to make an arrest. She had broken no laws.

Conspiracy is what they had me for. Then the IRS made a case against me for not reporting over $2,000,000.00 in income. Money made in the United States and no taxes paid on it, not even a return was filed. I knew that I was hiding from something but this is a lot worse than I thought.

Joyce was by my side all the way. She had the information on the bank account and Mr. Burns helped her get money from the account in the Islands. Joyce spent over $500,000.00 of her money before she asks for any help. Because of the deaths that had happened in Tennessee, and Detroit, and the Islands I could not get out on bail. They could keep me in jail forever on the IRS charges, but they could not prove any killings on me in the

United States. Attorneys cost almost one million dollars. Two Judges were paid off and they still decided against me. I was in three different federal jails and it cost a lot of money just to survive in there. You have to pay for things like television, hot water, better food and protection. If the word gets out that you have some money all of the worse prisoners want a part of it, and if they do not get it they will hurt you bad. The worse person in there is the guard. If you can pay and won't, then they rough you up, or they stand by and let others do it by just turning their head. Inside cigarettes cost $1.00 each, outside they cost less than $1.00 per pack of 20.

All in all the first two years cost over $1,000,000.00 including attorneys, Judges, guards, and living expenses for Joyce. If my money had been in the United States they would have taken it all at one time. If my wallet had been in my pocket when I was arrested they would have found a way to get it anyway probably. I do not believe that any other country in the world, that is supposed to be free and honest, and run by elected officials could be any worse than this.

The Atlanta Federal Prison was better than the one here in Minnesota. If you had money you could make it all right. You could even go to school and be taught a trade, or you could finish high school. On Sundays they had church and I attended every chance I had.

Now I know the answers to the questions that was ask me by the Tennessee Preacher on the fishing boat down in the Bahamas. Yes I have been saved, and yes I have accepted the lord as my savior. I wish there was some way for me to get in touch with that preacher, and let him know about how my life has changed since I did accept Jesus as my savior. It is the first peace I have ever had. I always thought it was money that brought peace of mind, but it is not.

After the judges and attorneys finished with me, I was sentenced to ten years and that is all for the IRS. I was not even tried for anything else. They had no proof that I had ever broken any law. My time in the Army, and my time as Sheriff were in my favor, but for all the good it did, I could not tell that it helped me any.

Out of all the problems that I had I emerged with only one good thing. Joyce. She has been here regular. When she comes here she stays for a week and comes to see me every day. She still has the mobile home park and operates it by herself. She tells me every time she is here that it is all the living we need. The two of us can run the park and live well, and I am looking forward to that.

When I have a quiet moment, and I think about the past, it seems a miracle that our group in Tennessee caused so much grief to so many people for so long without me being killed also. Almost everyone connected with me then, is dead now. The line of murdered people reaches into Michigan, Tennessee and the Bahamas and it all started from a homesick soldier that just wanted to make whiskey and sell it. If I had been caught then in the beginning I would be better off. Randy, Patch, the dope peddler, Poke and Rip, the driver that delivered money to Tennessee from Detroit, the two policemen in Detroit, Hershel, Roger and his partner, Tim Oliver, my wife Lois, Dixie and my dog Tip, these were all killed on purpose, murdered. Not by me, but by my partner, so I have to take some of the blame.

According to the preacher here in the prison everyone can be forgiven of their sins, no matter what they are, I believe that, because he read it straight from the holy bible. He reads that every week, and every week it makes me glad that I am in prison, because this is the only place that I would set down and listen to God's word. When I get out I want to continue studying the Bible.

My television is small but not many have a television at all. I have a cell with a window, and I am allowed to go to the library every week. On Sunday I go to church two times and when I get out of prison, I have a job waiting, and I have Joyce. After the bad times that I have caused others, I guess that I have more than I deserve.

Every penny of the dirty money that I had is gone. I will not ever commit another crime if I am aware of it. I went from a millionaire to having no money at all. I found out that piece of mind is better than having money. I know that it will be very hard to convince anyone of that, but it is true. I had more money than I could spend in a lifetime, traveling all over the world and going first class, but I could not have peace of mind.

In here I have nothing, but it cost more to stay here and stay safe than it cost to travel to the most lavish resorts there is. I am hoping to be out in possibly six months, and if not then I have another chance in eighteen months. My record in here is good, and my money is gone, so why would they want to keep me here?

This is the end of my sad story, I lived like

a king for a few years, and then I lived like an animal in a cage for a few years. I do not know what to expect in the future.

## THE END

This story is fiction, but it is inspired by the life of a real person. The author and narrator is Larry English.

## ALL ABOUT ALVIN

This is a story about a gentle gentleman, an easy going, accommodating, and very friendly man that would do you a favor in a heartbeat. That is, if you do not do him or his family any harm in any way, then he is hell on wheels. If he is mad at you for any reason, you better leave town. He made big bad Leroy Brown look like a Sunday School teacher.

His father was born near lake Okeechobee Florida in 1891, and managed to make a living from this huge lake by selling fish, alligators and frogs. Alvin was born on a houseboat on this 28,000 square mile lake and lived there most of his young life. Naturally, he knew where every tree and bush was. He knew where every lily pad was, and every canal, island, marker and sunken boat. He seemed to know the top of the water and the bottom also, he was amazing, and he was my friend. Alvin taught me how to build fish traps, and how to cut trails thorough heavy peppergrass, and how to place the traps in the trails so that they would catch the most fish. He was not a selfish person.

One thing he did not like, and that was game wardens. The first two times that I went out on the lake with Alvin, the game warden tied to stop us, Alvin would not stop and we were chased, but not caught. It was very important for Alvin to have the fastest boat in lake Okeechobee, or any place near lake Okeechobee.

I ask Alvin one time to help me get a boat and motor just like he had, and he did. The same person built both boats for us and they were just alike, and they both had 150 horsepower Mercury motors. The day after I got my boat, Alvin traded for a 175 horsepower mercury motor for his boat.

Alvin is a legend around this lake; you can hear all sorts of stories about him. Some may not be true, but I know for certain that some of the meanest and daring ones are, as a matter of fact, true.

One night my wife and I were in one airboat and Alvin was in an airboat by himself. He wanted my wife to see how he caught alligators, Alvin had already told me about his plan. We left the house there in Lakeport just after dark, and traveled about 6 miles out to the point of a reef, there we stopped and looked all around with our headlights. Several gators were just laying out there in the moonlight and we could hear them grunting at each other. I had been instructed to stay close to his boat, but by no means to let my headlight shine in his face. I followed Alvin's instructions and when he let his boat drift up to this huge gator, even I knew that it was way too big for any one man to catch. I was not over 5 feet from Alvin's boat, with my headlight off, when he reached down into the dark, snake infested water of lake

Okeechobee and grabbed an 8 or 10-foot alligator by the lips. He managed to drag that monster into his boat, and then when he saw how big it really was he could not let it go. Alvin had both arms and both legs around that gator, but after wrestling for a few minutes it overpowered Alvin and got loose. While lying on his back in the floor of his airboat, Alvin kicked the gator back into the water. In a few minutes, after he regained his composure he just said, "I decided to let that one go".

For a couple of years right after we first met Alvin, he would occasionally come by our house and give us a half of a hog, or a quarter of a beef. He told us that some of his Indian friends had more than they needed and had given it to him. We did not believe that, but we never knew what to expect out of Alvin. Much later we found out that he would go into the woods at night and kill and dress a beef or a hog, whatever he came upon. He had a steady group of customers that bought fish every Saturday morning, and they bought beef and pork also, and of course at a discounted price.

A few times I would luck up and have a really good catch of specks [ called Crappy in some parts of the country]. When I did Alvin would come in with twice that amount. No way could he be out fished. One time I caught 1,400 pounds and knew that I had Alvin James beat. But Alvin caught 1,100 pounds in the morning and that afternoon he caught 1,300 pounds. I had to weigh mine and sell them for.55 cents per pound with a tag on each fish. Alvin sold his for $ 1.00 per pound with no tags, to his regular customers.

There are many tales around about Mr. James and some are true, but not all of them. For example, I was told by a fisherman that lived in Okeechobee, that he saw Alvin shoot the pilot of a small air plane that had landed on the dike near Sportsman Village, and take a briefcase out of the plane. At the time Alvin was supposed to be doing this, he was fishing with me and two of my relatives. This story

I know is not true. Plus, I never did hear of a plane and it's dead pilot being found, there on the dike. Because of Alvin's popularity many such stories have been rumored.

Another tall story is the one that circulated all around this area about Alvin being in a houseboat and airplanes flying over and dropping dope to him on lake Okeechobee. No way.

The one about Alvin living with his friend's wife may or may not be true. I do not know. But the part about Alvin holding his girl friend's husband prisoner, for several weeks, while he was staying with her, I do not believe. Alvin was Strong enough and mean enough to do this, but he was good enough and fair enough so that he did not have to do this. I fished with Alvin a lot and I gator hunted with him many times and I would have known about some of these things if it had happened.

One time Alvin and I were out on the lake

at night running traps on a full moon. It was light enough so that we could find the traps, dump them, separate the fish and return the traps to the water without a light. Alvin saw a 12-inch alligator there beside a grass patch and caught it; we put it into a sack to take home. In a few minutes he caught another one. Before we went home that night Alvin had caught 30 gators all about the same size. The only reason he stopped catching them was the sack got full and there was not another sack in the boat. Early the next morning Alvin went out and sold the gators for $3.00 each. He also sold the specs that he got from the traps for $1.00 per pound, that night Alvin made $390.00. His cost was 0, with the exception of a couple gallons of gasoline.

For me it was an education, the same as when we went hunting or just airboat riding. Sometimes we went hog hunting in the airboat at night. Alvin would shoot the hogs right between the eyes and within 15 minutes they were skinned, gutted with the head off and we were gone. I had never experienced these things before, I had not even thought about these things before, and if anyone told me that they had done these things, I would have thought they were lying.

One time I was with Alvin and we were running his fish traps. It was late afternoon and Alvin had about 200 pounds of large specs. As we were on the way back to the boat landing there were two black men and two black ladies fishing. Alvin pulled up beside them and asks if they were having any luck and they said no. Alvin sold them 200 pounds of fish for $100.00. Before we got to the boat landing Alvin dumped six more traps and got another 100 pounds of fish. He had traps in trails from Indian Prairie canal to Clewiston, which is about 15 or 20 miles. Like I said before, Alvin was amazing. I had a good job and a small business and Alvin made more money each week than I did.

For a few months I was there living in our mobile home so that I could run traps in the daytime. One night just after dark Alvin came and set there with me and we watched TV a while, then he asks if I wanted to ride some. I thought he meant in the airboat, I said yes. We got in his pick up and drove to Okeechobee to a bar that had a lot of black people around it. Alvin reached in the back of his truck and got a garbage bag full of something and carried it into the bar. He later told me that it was marijuana, if it was or not I do not know. But while Alvin was in that bar, I was setting there in his truck at night in the parking lot of a black bar. When he returned he asks if I was nervous at all, and I said "yes", he moved a towel that was there in the seat beside him and there was a 357 pistol under the towel. Then he told me that no one there at that place would bother him or anyone that was with him, and he could guarantee that.

One time my wife and I was in my fishing boat and Alvin was in his fishing boat. We were going down the big canal from Clewiston to near Lakeport where the canal went back into the lake. Ahead we could see a large yacht meeting us and a wake of water about 20 feet high was in front of the big boat. My wife and I were in front of Alvin. We stopped because I was afraid of the big wave. Alvin came along side of us and asks what was wrong, when I told him, he laughed at me. He said follow me. We did, and as we come to the wall of water we just rode up about 20 feet, real smooth and down the other side, that was another first for me. There was a time there that I could not see Alvin or his boat, but that was nothing to him, he had been there and done that before.

Alvin really did know people in high places. I have been with him several times when a jet plane would buzz our area that we lived in, and we may be on the lake fishing or just setting at the house, but Alvin would get in a hurry and leave fast. There was a landing strip 5 miles from our house and the small jet would land. They, whoever was in the plane, had come after Alvin. Sometime they were gone one day and sometime a week. I assume that it was the same people, or group of people, that owned the plane and owned a lot of land there in the area. Alvin was supposedly on their payroll as a lubricating engineer. I do know for sure that Alvin was the fishing guide and hunting guide for that group. When none of that group was in the area I went into the hunting camps and the water holes where they feed the deer, turkeys and wild hogs, but I never did kill anything, I was not hunting, I was just looking. I also know for sure that the person that Alvin had out fishing, on more than one occasion, had their lunch brought to them, delivered from Tampa, by jet.

One night there on Lake Okeechobee, the water was low. A lot of the shallow water area was just grass. Some places had soupy mud and at night it was just perfect for air boating. Alvin came to our house and said he knew where we might be able to kill a deer if we wanted to go. We were always ready to go when Alvin planned something like this. Alvin knew my brother in law better than he did me; I had met Alvin thorough Ralph. We went out on the grass flats and there were dozens of cows there. We had two airboats, Alvin was in one and two of my brothers in law and I was in the other one. We slid around thorough the cows looking for deer but found none. Then all of a sudden a huge bobcat jumped up and ran out thorough the grass. Alvin ran after the big cat and when he got to it he turned the airboat on the side and slid over it sideways, mashing the cat down into the mud. The cat came up ready to fight, all bowed up in the back and looking for something to attack. Alvin ran over the cat again then killed it with the boat paddle. Like I said before you never knew what to expect when you went with Alvin.

A friend of Alvin's had a small plane and the two of them would fly around over the lake and look for shell cracker beds. They decided to go up to the North Carolina Mountains and look at the mountains from above. Since I knew that area they asks me if I wanted to go, so I did. We landed in Franklin, NC. We got a car at the airport and drove into town to eat. A big bad looking cloud come rolling across the mountains and the pilot said that we better get out of here that it may storm for several days, because this time of year it does that sometime. We left as soon as the gas tanks were topped off. Instead of running out of the storm we ran into it. I recognized where we were, it was a place that I had lived in at one time. We got down to 300 feet trying to land but there was no place to set the plane down. We were in a terrible storm. Water was coming in thorough the small air vent adjusters. At times we were totally out of control, the tail of the plane was in front in the direction we were moving. The propeller of the plane was bending and the pilot said that the plane would stay together if he could keep it right side up, but upside down the plane may break up.

Lightning knocked out some of the instruments. The next time I saw the ground was when the pilot said, "there is the airport". He had seen it on the map but we could not find it. He started to land and we were not over 30 feet from the ground when he pulled up as fast as he could. This was a racetrack. He got back up to 500 feet and then saw the airport and we landed safely.

The people at the airport said they could not believe that we come in from the north, no plane could fly in the storm that they had the reports of, but we did. The mechanics replaced some fuses and Alvin and the pilot was ready to fly back to Fla. I refused to get back on the plane. I told them to go on that I would be there the next day on the bus, but they would not do that. We stayed there in that Georgia town just about 60 miles south of Franklin NC. That is one time that Alvin was not in full control.

My brother in law had a 40-foot houseboat there on his property. I had a mobile home on the other side of his property. While I was staying there to run traps, Alvin knocked on my door at 2:00 in the morning and said that Ralph had told him he could use the houseboat for a while and they would be quite. All I wanted was to go back to sleep. I never heard anything else that night, but 3 or 4 days later I was fishing from the bow of the houseboat and I saw thorough the front window 8 or 9 bags of stuff like Alvin delivered to Okeechobee.

I went over to my mobile home and closed it up and then drove to Tampa. I did not want to be there near that stuff. A few days later when I went back, and the bags were gone. I never did mention it to Ralph, or Alvin. Ralph had the boat secured with a log chain and a huge lock, welded to a large concrete foundation that had been made for this purpose. But, Alvin had the key to the cabin door. I knew that on certain occasions Alvin would use the boat to party.

One time I was going hunting with two young men that I commercial fished with. They were brothers and both of them had trail bikes. They hog hunted on the bikes. I had heard about this several times and finally

I was invited to go with them, and I gladly accepted. They ran the hogs down on the bikes and caught them. Then they carried them home and put them into a pen and would feed them corn for a few weeks, then sold them or eat them.

On this trip things worked different. I was on the bike behind the youngest of the brothers. We were a mile or so into the woods on a sand road traveling approximately 20 miles an hour. We rounded a sharp curve and there in the road was 4 or 5 pickup trucks and a game warden vehicle, a large horse trailer and 5 or 6 men, they were loading the black bags onto the horse trailer. Both brothers opened the bikes wide open; both bikes had the front wheel off of the ground. I looked over the shoulder of my driver and the speed ohmmeter read 65, which is fast on a sand road. The trucks came after us but we outran them and got away. We were out of hearing from them but they come straight to us. We out ran them again and the same thing happened. It could only be one thing. A plane was spotting us and guiding the men in the trucks to us. We turned the motors off and listened. We were right, a small plane was up there very high and after we figured this out we put the bikes under thick trees and ran on foot, staying off of the road. We went through palmettos and ditches full of water, but no one got snake bit. After we walked a few miles we heard a truck coming with the radio on real loud, we were hid but we could see the road. We knew who this was so we let them see us.

Alvin had a scanner in his truck. He listened to the plane guiding the trucks to us, then he got these young kids to drive out this road and pick us up, he knew we were out there. We knew what would happen to us if we were caught. Others had been in our situation and did not get away, but would be found later.

The black plastic bags were worth several million dollars. Everyone there in that group of men would make more money than you could earn on a job in a lifetime. These people would not hesitate to kill in order to protect that kind of money.

In this small town there were six people that controlled that part of the county. The law and the state game warden was involved. One of the largest business owners in the state, was the boss, and he and his family were already billionaires. But they were making more now than ever. They never did get caught as a group, but one or two individuals did get caught and never did tell on the others. Alvin was one of these.

An airplane, a huge D C 3, would land on a grass strip in the swamps of South Fla. Horse trailers would be waiting to get their load, and then within one hour all of the bales of dope were gone. After many loads had been hauled this way, the trafficking started including diamonds and gold, from Columbia

This is when Alvin could not resist taking more than his part. On one particular airplane that was coming in to set down there, Alvin was setting the lights to guide the plane to the center of the strip for a safe landing, because it was mud on both sides and the plane could flip and crash. The plane landed safely and it was a little early, Alvin was there alone with just the two pilots. He knew what was on the plane. His job was to light the runway and pump 100 gallons of gasoline into the planes tanks, that is all.

Alvin could not hear the trucks or see the lights from any of the trucks that were coming after their load. In the cockpit of the plane he saw a small suitcase that probably contained jewels and diamonds and gold. It was said that Alvin had to act fast, that he shot both of the pilots and grabbed the suitcase and ran.

One of the men he shot died but one lived to tell. No one knows what Alvin did with the suitcase, it was never found, that is, if he ever had it. The law was there days later, but all of the dope was gone and the plane was clean. The pilot told what Alvin did and they found a small amount of dope in Alvin's truck. Alvin got 15 years in the federal prison, but they say he still got away with murder. I did not see any of this; it is all hear say.

I did not see or talk to Alvin for the next 12 or 13 years. I talked to some of his family and I knew that he was sentenced to 15 years. His high-powered friends in high places kept telling him that he would be out soon, and that he had a lot of money deposited in his account in Switzerland. None of this turned out to be true. I was told about this Switzerland account long before Alvin was in trouble. He, Alvin, had money going into that account for at least two years for the work he was doing for Mr. Big. Alvin told me that he would be a wealthy man when they quit the business, but he could not show any money now. Alvin lived in an old house, drove an old truck, and only spent the money he made fishing. There were three of us there, with Alvin, when he talked about this. We were all good friends, and we all three believed what he told us.

One of the moneymakers that Alvin had, before the dope deal got started in a big way, was the gator skin sales. Alvin would skin the gators, roll the skins up as tight as he could get them, and tie them to keep them in a tight roll. Then place the skins into a barrel of brine. These barrels would be hauled to Louisiana and the skins sold for about $10.00 per lineal foot. Each barrel would contain as much as 400 feet. Shoes, belts, jackets, hats etc; would be made from the gator skins.

Years later, after all of these things had happened, I went to Alvin's home for a visit. We were both older and it showed, of course. Alvin had been out of prison for almost two years. He was the same stocky built, wavy haired man that I remembered back when things were so good for both of us. Alvin could not do the things that he did back then, but he got a thrill just talking about what he had done. What he told me that day was the same thing he had told me years before, so I know it was the truth.

Alvin also told me the story about how and why he was sent to prison. How he was to get out very soon and how wealthy he would be as soon as he got out. The big shot with the jet plane sure did lie to Alvin, and it cost him the last 15 or so years of his life.

That last visit with Alvin lasted about 6 or 7 hours and it seemed like he wanted me to ask more questions. He wanted to talk about things that happened back then, because then he was the cock of the walk, he had all of the big connections, with the top people, he was the best fisherman around there and everyone knew it. He was the fastest thing on the water and everyone knew that. He was the best of the best, however, gambling was not his thing. I watched Alvin lose $15,000.00 one afternoon, in a poker game that did not last over one hour. Alvin asks me to get a paper bag from under the seat of his truck. That bag had $ 5,000.00 in it and he lost that also. Then he put his truck up to stand good for a pot that five players had about $ 6,000.00 each in and he won that pot. Then he quit the game and went home. Later that night Alvin told me that, that was the last time that he would ever play poker. He admitted that he did not know how to gamble and he had tried bluffing but it did not work.

This is just some of the things that Alvin got involved in while I knew him. Alvin did not go to school very much, I do not think, but he was educated in a different way.

Alvin could make a great living from the lake, he made more money, than I have ever made, and he never had a job.

Alvin was a ladies' man, this was his problem. His 6 foot 2 inch slender frame and his curly hair attracted the females to him, he was, as I have heard him called, a swinging dick and a mean mother fucker. Alvin hung around a beer joint called the green hut, and it was a known fact that girls came from as far away as Fort Myers to try and date Alvin.

I did not know this about him for a long time.

My only interest in Alvin was fishing, he was teaching my brother-in-law and me how to trap fish, because Alvin caught fish when no one else could.

Alvin had a beautiful wife, and when Alvin was at home she would not speak to another man. But when Alvin was away on one of his trips, his wife could be found at the green hut, during the early part of the night, then she would be gone someplace until the next morning. A lot of rumors was flying around about this and everyone around there knew that sooner or later there would be a killing, just as soon as Alvin found out who she was with.

Alvin did have a girlfriend, and he did stay at her house some of the time. Alvin did call her husband out of the house and beat him with a palmetto root until he was unconscious, then taking him to a cabin in the woods and holding him prisoner for two weeks, as I heard it. The man knew that Alvin would kill him if he told anyone, so he kept quiet and shared his wife with Alvin until his death, which was only about one year. She only lived less than a year after her husband's death. They both died from fear.

In the early months of 1970, a Judge was murdered there in Glades County, and his head was cut off, his head was found on the side of the road in a plastic bag. No one talked about this, it was very quiet, the papers reported it, but in one or two days it was forgotten about. Rumors did fly. It was rumored that This judge was in the dope business himself. It was also rumored that this judge made a threat that he was going to stop the drug business in this area. All kinds of rumors were heard, but they were just rumors.

We did not see Alvin every day, not even every week, just every once in a while when he decided to come by our house for a visit. But we noticed that Alvin had not been by to visit in a while. So, I went to his house to visit him, and was told that Alvin was gone someplace, and he had not been seen in quite a while, and I was told this in such a manner that I knew to not come back here no more.

Two weeks later, in the middle of the night, Alvin knocked on our door. He ask if we were all okay, and I told him yes. Then he told me that he was having to stay hid because of money problems. He said "I owe a lot of money and I can't pay", so I have to stay out of sight for a while. Alvin ask me to do him a favor. He said "if there is an emergency in my family, will you come after me?" No way could I refuse that kind of request from a friend.

The next morning Alvin took me to the place where he was hiding. Two miles in an air boat, then on an island between Lakeport and highway 27, there was no town nearby. Alvin had a cabin there with heat, a bathroom, running water, from a well. It was all run by a generator. This cabin was on dry land, but was surrounded by water and there was another air boat tied up to his dock, but no kind of communications. Alvin stayed here for over a year, and I was never ask to deliver a message to him.

Just before Christmas in 1975, Alvin was in a very bad auto accident in Sebring, Florida. A drunk driver hit him from the rear. The drunk driver was killed, and Alvin was almost killed. He had 5 broken ribs, a fractured neck, and a broken leg, He was in the hospital for 3 months and was in a coma for two weeks.

While in a coma, Alvin said that he talked to God, Alvin says that God talked to me about every wrong and bad thing that I had ever done. I promised God that I would change, and that I would try to make things right with the people that I had offended.

As soon as Alvin got out of the hospital he went to the preacher and confessed his sins to him. The following Sunday Alvin went to the Alter and there and then he confessed to everyone about his sinful life, and he joined the Church. From that time on Alvin was in Church regularly.

Alvin lived the rest of his life as a good Christian man. He got out of prison 3 years before the auto accident.

**This is the end of my
story about Alvin.**

This story was created and narrated by Larry English. It is a work of fiction inspired by real people. **Jacob's diary** is a story about a real town in the back woods of Georgia that was bought by a large company. Then the company built a huge dam and flooded the community of Burton.

Some of the residents had agreed to move, but some did not agree. Water backed up to the houses, then the company moved the reluctant residents out and traded other property to them, for the soon to be flooded homes. The Hunt family was one of these. Lake Burton is there today in the beautiful mountains of North Georgia.

In 1857 The Hunt family lived in the second farm from the Tallulah river, on Dick's creek, in the community of Burton, Georgia. They had 40 acres there, but most of it was woods, only 15 acres was cleared for farming.

Most of the lots there in Burton was one acre, in size. Some families had more land. The

Watts, the Nichols and the Thompsons and the Lovell family all owned more property.

In 1860 there were over 100 people that lived in Burton, according to my grandmother. There were two stores and a post office. However, the population changes fast in Burton because of of the gold that was found nearby. People came from all over the country hoping to strike it rich in the gold fields, and a few did.

Indians made up the largest part of the population in this area. Most of them had lived here for years but very few had deeds or papers to prove ownership of their land and they just left, almost all of the Indians headed west.

In 1863 rumors of war were flying. And had been for a year or two. The Union Army was rumored to be burning entire villages and was coming south. A huge army of union soldiers had been on a rampage down thorough Tennessee and destroying everything they saw. This war was about slaves, but no one around here had slaves.

In the spring time of 1863, my great grandfather, Jacob Hunt, had gone to the local store, the local store was the meeting place where all of the local men gathered to gossip and brag about the big fish that they had caught. While there he overheard the men talking about the war. Seven of the local men volunteered that day for the Confederate States Army, two days later they walked to Rabun Gap, Georgia where they assembled with a group to train and prepare for a march to the north to engage the union army.

They were placed in the Rabun Gap Rifleman squad. The training they received was four days. They received no equipment or weapons, just one blanket and a bar of homemade soap for each person.

Everyone knew that they were going to fight the union army, that was over 400 miles to the north. They had no horses yet, but the plan was to join up with a group in Sweetwater, Tennessee, and then the needed supplies would be furnished.

They walked and walked, sometimes In the rain and mud they walked thorough North Carolina, Tennessee, Kentucky, Ohio and Virginia. Along the way they were involved in eight battles. Chancellorsville, Winchester, Martinsburg, Fort Royal and Manassas, was the worst ones.

Jacob was wounded and captured as his unit crossed the Susquehanna river, in March of 1865. He was a prisoner of war until the war ended in April of 1865.

He was released and set free in May of 1865, along with thousands of other down trodden, hungry, battle weary confederate soldiers. Jacobs wounds were not serious and did not prevent him from walking. He knew that his best bet was to get as far away from that area and all of the other soldiers as he could, and he knew that he had over 500 miles to walk. Jacob knew only to go South.

On the third day of his journey, he happened upon a mule where a farmer had been plowing his garden. The point of the plow was still in the ground and the gears were still hooked up to the mule, the farmer had just walked away for a few minutes, so Jacob stole his mule.

Jacob rode the mule for four days, stopping only to feed and water the newly acquired mule and himself. On the fifth day he stopped to take a nap, and while he was asleep, someone stole the mule from him.

As Jacob walked south, he would talk to the people along the way, and ask directions for the best and easiest path to travel. One old man gave him water from the well, and a few apples from the tree in his front yard. Then the old man told him about a trail that went over into Kentucky and then turned south and was the best way to travel South. He said that the trail misses the steep and rugged mountains that are south of us.

It was two days travel on that trail to the

Kentucky line, but it was easy walking. About four miles down the shortcut trail, Jacob heard children yelling and a woman's voice telling them what to do. Jacob stopped there and set down on the side of the road and listened to them. They did not know that he was there. The woman and the two kids were trying to put two large hogs into a pen and the hogs did not want to go. After a few minutes of watching them Jacob went down to them and offered his help, and they got the hogs into the pen.

Jacob started to leave and continue his journey, but the oldest child, a girl, about 12 years old, went into the house and brought out biscuits and honey for Jacob.

Jacob ask the lady if he could sleep in their barn that night and she said yes, and if you want to stay here and rest up some, and do some chores, you can stay in the barn and I will pay you $5.00 for the week. Jacob accepted.

This family had a business of raising pigs. That

lady and her two children owned 30 sows that produced hundreds of pigs each year. Each pig was sold for $2.00. The husband of the lady, and father of the two children was killed in the confederate states army over a year ago, since then the wife and kids have run the pig farm.

My job for is to feed the hogs, all of them. Besides the 30 sows, there are 15 boars and about 50 piglets running around outside of the pens. A few other small jobs needed to be done but all in all, Jacob liked this job, and when he was ask to stay on for a while and save some money for his trip home, he accepted.

Jacob cleaned out a part of the feed room, in the barn, for him to live in. He had a stove and a wash bench and a good bed, it was warm and dry in his little living quarters, and he liked it. The three years that he was in the army he never had any place half this good to live in.

The Lady's name was Lucy, her daughter's

name was Jane and the boy's name was Bobby, Bobby was 10 years old.

Jacob ate his meals inside the house with the family and when Lucy washed cloths she washed his cloths also. His arrangements there with that family was good for him and good for everyone in the family.

When Jacob left home to join the army he promised to always keep his mother and dad informed about where he was, and Jacob wrote as often as he could. His mother and dad knew where he was and they knew that he was trying to get back home. As soon as he could, he would travel the rest of the way home to Burton, Georgia and the family farm.

Jacob had missed the planting season for this year anyway, and the money that he was earning here he could save to take home with him, when he went.

After Jacob had been living there with the

family for about 3 months, it was obvious that the arrangements were very good for everyone. Jane and Bobby were very happy with Jacob being there, because he had taken a lot of the workload off of them.

On a cold and windy October night Jacob had gone to bed there in his room in the barn. Just as he was dozing off to sleep, he heard the barn door open, thinking that it was a traveler looking for a place to sleep, Jacob started to get up and chase them away when he saw that it was Lucy. The light from the lantern lit up the inside of the barn. Jacob laid very still, and pretended to be asleep. He heard Lucy set the lantern down on the floor and heard her blow out the flame, inside the lantern. Then he felt her set down on the edge of his bed and pull the covers down. She got into bed with him, there was no talking, not a word was spoken. Before daylight, Lucy was up and back in the house and breakfast was ready at the regular time.

This happened regularly for the next few

months. Then one morning as they drank coffee Lucy told Jacob that she wanted some changes made.

Lucy said that she had never gone to school, she said that she could count and write just a little bit but she wanted Jane and Bobby to learn reading, writing and arithmetic, if you are going to be here I want you and me to run this farm, and I want them to go to school. Jacob agreed and said that was a good idea, then she told Jacob that they should be married.

Jacob told her that he had to think about that for a while and he went to his room in the barn where it was quite, he lay on his bed and tried to figure all of this out, it was a lot to be put on him all at one time. After two hours of being in deep thought he concluded that he only had his parents, and Lucy only had Jane and Bobby, so there was no reason for them not to get married.

Back in Burton, Georgia, the Hunts lived alone

on a large farm. They were not able to work the farm but they did have a garden and they had plenty of food. Once in a while they sold a few acres to have money to live on.

Jacob, with his own money that he had saved up, bought a horse and surrey for Jane and Bobby to ride to school. The school house was in Cumberland, three miles down the short cut trail. Jane and Bobby went to school five hours every day, they enjoyed school. When they got home they helped with the chores, then they studied at the kitchen table until late. Lucy studied with them and she learned fast, when the test was given at school Lucy went and took the test with Jane and Bobby.

Lucy, Jane and Bobby finished school, every grade, in three years. Cumberland had a system in their schools that allowed students to go to school on their schedule, because of the farm work that had to be done. Testing was very strict, but fair. If you passed the test, you went on to the next grade. Education was what they, Lucy, Jane and Bobby wanted and all three of them worked very hard, everyday.

Jacob had gone to school in Georgia, he finished the 4th grade and was proud of the fact that he could read. Numbers was hard for him but he made out okay. Until now Jacob was the only one in that family that had any education at all.

It was now 1869. Jacob had been gone from his home 7 years, although he has been writing home regular and sending a few dollars each time in the letter, he wanted to see his Mother and Father, so he planned a trip, to Georgia. He saddled Charlie, his horse and started on the 400 mile trip. He rode hard and in North Carolina Charlie started breathing hard, he seemed to be tired and during the night Charlie died. Jacob hired someone to bury Charlie, and he bought another horse. In 27 days, from the time he left the pig farm in Virginia, Jacob was setting on his parents front porch, in Burton, Ga.

His Mother and Father were both sick. No crops had been planted in 4 years. They had sold 30 acres of the land to have money to live on. Things were not good.

Jacob had no intentions of staying there to run the farm. He knew how poor the land was and that his parents had worked the farm for years and now had nothing. He had gone to a neighbor friend to make arrangements for someone to take care of his parents, but when he returned home, he found that his father had just passed away.

Jacob then placed his Mother in the neighbors home for them to take care of her. He prepaid for his Mothers care for 6 months. He told his Mother that he had to leave and that he would be back soon.

Jacob had named his new horse Charlie, so Jacob and Charlie started back towards the pig farm in Virginia. The trip back was cut down to 24 days. Something seemed to be drawing Jacob back to Virginia, and when he got home it was late at night, and he went right to bed. He and Lucy talked for a few minutes, then, as they made love, Lucy told Jacob that she was 3 months pregnant. Then Jacob knew what it was that was drawing him back in such a hurry.

When Jacob left his home to join the army land was selling for $1.00 an acre, now it is $5.00 an acre, and people with money come mostly from Atlanta and Macon to buy a place in the mountains. It is cool in the summertime, and there is plenty of creeks and rivers to fish in. Plus, Gold has been discovered right there in that area, things were definitely picking up there in that run down little farming town.

But since The whole family had finished school in Cumberland, all doors opened up for them. Lucy was mixed up in politics and was Mayor and had been on the city council. Jane and Bobby had gone to Washington D.C. and graduated from the school of law. The family together owned and operated a hardware store and they had just recently sold the pig farm to a group from Chicago.

The family together had donated land for a Church and furnished most of the money for the material. The labor was furnished by the congregation and the preacher.

Jacob did not write his Mother any more, instead he wrote to the Phillips family that was taking care of her. He kept them paid and sent his Mother a few dollars just so she could say that she was not broke.

Time flies by. It had been two years since Jacob saw his Mother, and he had fully intended to go back to see her, but it seemed like there was no time, every minute of every day there was something that just had to be done.

Every Sunday, after Church, Jacob set down and wrote in his diary, sometimes he even wrote the letter to the Phillips family and thanked them, but he always kept the diary up to date, because he promised his Mother that he would do that.

Jacob decided that he was going to go to

Burton to see his Mother, business would just have to wait. When he told his family about his plan they told him that there was no way, that it could not happen, there was no one to run the store.

When Jacob insisted that he was going, Lucy and Bobby and his wife, Elaine, said that they would go with him, so they all made arrangements to be away, and two days later they were on the way to Bristol to catch the train. It was a four day trip so they had reservations at hotels along the way each night. They also had rooms in Toccoa, Georgia and a surrey with a driver for four days to go on to Burton.

The trip from Toccoa to Burton was beautiful but it was a long way and everyone was tired when they arrived. The boarding house was not comfortable and it was not a nice place, not worth the $6.00 a day that it cost.

The next day we all felt better, and we moved to a hotel on the river that was excellent.

From the huge front porch we could see the flow of the river and we could see a part of our farm on the other side of the river.

Jacob and Lucy walked to the Phillips house as soon as they were settled into their room. His Mother was very sick and she talked to Jacob as though he had never been away. She asked for a preacher and an attorney to come to her. Jacob had the preacher there in two hours, the preacher was in her room for a while then he left. The attorney come late that same day and Mrs. Hunt instructed him on what she wanted in her will, and she signed it that day. None of us, Jacob, Lucy, or Bobby or Elaine knew what she put into her will, other people that was there witnessed that Mrs. Hunt signed the will.

A few days later everyone went back to Virginia except Jacob. He stayed home with his Mother, 3 weeks later she passed away. After the funeral Jacob went back to his family in Virginia.

Jacob and Lucy had lived all of these years in

the log house that Lucy's grandfather built in the year of 1750, when he bought this one section of land for $360.00. He built this house himself with logs that he cut from this land. But, now we are preparing to build a new house.

On the back side of our farm there is a large lake, we own no part of the lake but our property comes to within 40 feet of the water's edge. There are no other houses within sight of the spot that Lucy wants to build on, so we are going to build our new house there. She has plans for a six bedroom house so that Jane and Bobby can bring all of their children and we can all have room to stay here. It is four miles from Cumberland.

Time moved on, we have been so busy that we did not notice that it is already, the year 1900. Entries into the diary have not been regular, because there was no purpose now that Jacob's parents are gone. He used the diary as a form of keeping records and as a habit.

In 1905 we received a letter from the family of Mr. and Mrs. Phillips. They informed us of a company in Atlanta that would buy any property in our community that was for sale. That company had bought several properties there in Burton, and wanted more.

In 1916 the Phillips family sold all of the land that they owned to the Georgia Railway and Electric Company. One by one that company bought every one of our neighbors out and told them that they could keep living there until they could find a place to relocate to.

Still there were some that refused to go. That was their home and they loved it. They believed that no one had the right to force them out, but someway the Georgia Railway and Electric Company did just that.

Everyone in Burton was told that they had to be out by June 1, 1919. Still, everyone did not go. The Company started flooding the area in December of 1919.

One family was still there when the water got close to their house. They knew that the water was rising so they turned all of the livestock loose and let everything roam free.

At the last hour or so, The company come in with mules and wagons, all of the household items and farm tools were loaded onto the wagons and hauled three miles into the next valley. That family was told that this was their new home, The Company had traded this land to them for the home place that they left in Burton.

That was in 1919.

### This is the END OF THE STORY.

# THE FORGOTTEN TRAIL©

### Fiction, Created and narrated
### by Larry English

In 1945 I was deer hunting with two of my uncles. I was only 12 years old and they would not let me carry a gun, but on that trip I made a discovery that would be on my mind every day for several years to come. The area that we were hunting in was very remote. We had to wade a wide river that was straddle deep to a six foot man, and then walk four miles across a huge mountain, but when we reached the camp area it was worth every step. It was as far away from traffic as you could get, no people, no noise, nothing but clean fresh air. We were there for one week and about the third day I went to the top of a mountain that was not in the direction that we had traveled to come here. It was new country and looked like no one had ever been there before.

I had been taught how to look for deer sign, where they had scraped the bark off of trees, and this area was full of scraps, almost all the trees had scrapes on them. I was looking at this when I found where an old road or trail had been used many years ago.

The mountainside was steep and had been dug out where the trail was. I could see the trail or road but could not imagine who was here to use it. Trees that had grown up in the old trail were over a foot in diameter. There were no houses within twenty miles of here. The road that we walked on to get here was built only about ten years ago and they did not find this trail, according to the crew that I talked with that was cutting dog wood in here. My dad told me that he had never heard of an old trail being up here.

Everyone in this part of the State knew that

Indians lived in this area before it was Rabun County. According to the history books, the army forced the Indians to go west and cross the Mississippi river to a place that is now Oklahoma. This happened in 1838 and 1839. My great grandfather was born in 1833 about 20 miles from this trail, so he was five or six years old when the Indians were run out. Did the Indians make this trail and use it?

When my uncles and I were there on the camping trip, the night after I found the trail, I went to bed and could not sleep. I had that trail on my mind, and could not wait for morning so that I could explore the trail. But about five' O clock that morning it started pouring the rain and it rained for 24 hours. Finally it stopped and we were ready to walk out of this place.

I thought about this for several years, but there was always some reason that I could not go back there. It would be foolish to go alone. It would take at least 4 or 5 days. It would almost have to be in deer season to have the excuse for being there, and I could not get a vacation from my job in November. But, 30 years later I had 3 weeks off in November. The idea of the remote area was what Ed wanted.

The river was up to my straddle and I was six foot tall. Ed was only five foot tall and the water was cold. We pulled off our clothes and boots and waded the river naked, then we had dry clothes to put on, we were only cold for a few minutes. We had our supplies in backpacks and we had to cross the river two times. Then, with good warm clothes on, we walked across the mountain to the area where my uncles and my dad had camped years ago. All three of them have passed away now, but being here in this place reminded me of them.

We got our camp fixed the way we wanted it, and got plenty of wood for the fire that first day. I recommend to Ed to go to one area to hunt and I went to where the trail was. I timed it and it took me one hour and ten minutes to go to the trail. Everything looked the same as I remembered it. I followed the old trail and it was easy because it went on a level, sometimes I could not see the trail but, then at other times, it was plain to see because they had dug it out to make easy walking in the steep places. After about one mile down the trail I found a grave beside the trail. Two rocks were stuck up in the ground to mark the head and foot; no markings were on either rock. The trail got plainer because the mountainside was very steep and there were rock cliffs that they, whoever they were, had to go around. Then there were two more graves side-by-side and marked with rocks the same way. As I set there resting and deciding if I should start back to camp now, or go a little bit further down the trail. I spotted another rock stuck up in the ground. I went to the rock and it had a name scratched out on it. Captain [something] I could not read; U S Army.

I started back to camp as fast as I could go. Tomorrow I would explore the other end of the trail and see what I could find. Next morning I went back to the trail and followed it in the opposite direction. I walked for three hours and sometimes the trail was plain and sometimes I had to search for it. It was important to watch the time of day because this was rugged mountain terrain and it was dark at 5:30, I had to be back in camp by that time for sure.

In my backpack I had a fold down shovel that I had bought at army surplus. My idea was to dig up one of the graves and see if there was anything there to tell me if it was an Indian or a soldier. There was nothing I wanted to take from the grave; I just wanted to know who had walked on this trail. Ed did not know about the trail and I would not let him know that I was going to dig up a grave just to see what was in it. No matter what, this had to be my secret.

It was 9:30 in the morning and the sun was up when I arrived at the gravesite. I raked the rocks and grass off of the area and then started digging. It was a shallow grave and the dirt was all out in half an hour. The bones were wrapped in canvas, but the canvas was rotten. There were stones of different colors there where the neck would have been, arrowheads, and buttons that were imprinted U S Army. I took nothing out of the grave. I covered it back up and tried to place the rocks and grass so that it appeared not to have been disturbed.

I was exhausted so I set there and eat my lunch and took an hour to rest. I had learned nothing. It could have been an Indian and it could have been a soldier, it was almost time to start back and I did not know any more now than I did before this trip.

That night I thought about the years that I had waited to come back here to this place. I had to do something to find an answer so I decided to not go back to the trail the next day but to rest up and go back day after tomorrow, so that is what I did.

I thought about telling Ed about my discovery

and how long I had waited to come back here and investigate this trail, but Ed was a no nonsense person, he was serious about everything and he would definitely frown on digging up any grave. Nope, I just could not let him know anything that I was doing.

On the morning that I was to go back to the trail I was up and had breakfast ready before daybreak. We both were ready to hunt, Ed for deer and me for information about the trail. I considered this to be history, and if I found anything at all it would really be worth talking about, because no one knew about the trail, as far as I could find out.

This grave was deep. The hole was over four foot deep and I was almost ready to quit digging when my shovel hit something, it was another pile of bones wrapped in some kind of cloth. This cloth had held up better than the canvas that was in the other grave but I was looking to see if there were any of the colored stones in this grave. I was cleaning the dirt out from around the spot that the neck would have been, when my shovel touched something hard, and as I kept scraping at it, I could see that it was wood. In a few more minutes as I dug deeper I found that it was a wooden box about 18 inches deep and about 2 foot x 2-foot square. The box had a lock on it that was very rusty, and on two sides of the box was written "property of confederate states army".

After taking the four bags out of the box, I put the box back into the grave and covered it back up, again fixing the top of the grave to appear as though it had not been disturbed. I wrapped one leather bag up in my coat and carried it half way to our camp then dug a shallow hole and buried it. I moved all the other bags the same way; one at a time. I was afraid that the bag would break open because they were so old, and they were too heavy to carry more than one at a time.

It was almost 4:00 0 clock now and it would be dark at 5:30, so I hurried back to camp because I wanted to be there before Ed come in from hunting. I heard a gunshot and I was almost sure that he had killed another deer. I was right, Ed had a 10-point and the one he killed day before yesterday was a six point. I helped him drag it to the camp and field dress it and hang it in the tree beside the other one. Ed told me that I was getting behind and he laughed and I laughed with him. I wanted to tell him about my find but I knew there was no way; Ed was a person that only drank once or twice a year but he was a huge liar and he loved to talk. He lied about his dogs and fishing and hunting but never a lie to hurt anyone; he had enough now to brag about on the two deer and I had told him that I had not seen anything not even any scrapings.

Next morning in camp we had a burlap bag that our groceries were in, I dumped the food out and took the bag. Just after daybreak we both left camp; Ed went to his lucky deer stand and I went to move the bags that I had found. I walked fast as I could and moved two of the bags before 10:30 then I went to the camp to rest. I had buried the bags on this side of the river, but where I could get them easy, when I come back after them. After we ate lunch and rested a while we went back hunting, as soon as Ed was out of sight I started moving the other two bags and by sundown they were all four in the same hole beside the river with a big flat rock on top of the hole. I was in the camp setting by the fire when Ed got back to camp. We had four more days to be here according to our plans, I had time to put the bags in the truck before we left but there was no place to hide them so that Ed would not see them so I decided to leave them where they are.

It is a 10-hour drive to Florida where we both live now and where we both work. This area was my home for several years but I moved to Florida to find a job.

I went back to the camp and tried to act as though everything was normal. I ate and then lay down and tried to sleep, but I could not. Now I have to figure out a way to get these bags to my home in Florida with no one knowing about it. I would expect the State of North Carolina or the United States Government to claim these bags of gold if they find out about it, and I can't let that happen.

That night in camp I ask Ed if he wanted to stay here the rest of our time, or to take these deer home before they spoil. He was 100% ready to go home, and I was too. We had been here in the woods for six days and a hot bath and good food really sounded good, not to mention the four bags that I had to figure out how to get home to Florida.

We woke up early and started packing everything up to leave. We carried all of the camping supplies first, then come back after the two deer. It was all loaded into the truck and we started down the road; we got about one mile and there was a game warden parked across the road checking for game and license. Eleven hours and thirty minutes later we were at my home in Florida. Ed's car was there at my house and in just a few minutes he was gone home.

I told my wife about the bags and not to tell anyone. We were in the car and gone in forty-five minutes; we drove half way back and stopped in South Georgia at a motel to get some sleep and the next morning we continued our trip.

We arrived in Rabun County just after 12:00 and we still had 25 miles of dirt road before we got to the river area. My wife was driving. When we got to the place where we crossed the river, we went on up the road to see if there was anyone else in that area, there was not, so we turned around and went back. I got out of the car there where I was to cross the river, and she drove back to town. She was to be back there just after dark, was the plan. I got all four bags ready to wade the river with them and at dusty dark I carried four bags of gold coins to the other side of the river

At dusty dark I was ready, I had to wait only about five minutes then here she come, she popped the trunk lid and in less than one minute the gold was in our car and we were down the road.

We obeyed all laws. We drove the speed limit and were very careful; we did not want to be stopped for any reason. That day we only went 75 miles before we got a room and then we rotated sleeping. One of us watched the car while the other one slept. We knew that there was a lot of money in those bags but we did not know how much. When we get home we will find out.

The two graves that I dug up had bones in them. In the first one I did not dig under the bones; I just wonder if there was anything under those bones? Who did this? Who buried all of these gold coins? There is no way to know but my guess is as good as anyone else's, and I believe that Indians robbed a gold shipment from the army. During the robbery some of the Indians were killed and some were wounded.

The Indians buried the gold and put the bodies on top of it, planning on returning to retrieve the gold. But something happened to them and no one came back for the gold coins. Or, some of the confederate soldiers stole the gold and hid it and later was killed before they could retrieve the bags of gold. There are many questions that could be asked about this gold and none of them will ever be answered.

My wife and I decided to try and see what we could get for the coins. Each one had thirteen stars on it, and a picture of an eagle, some had two eagles. We took five of the coins to a dealer in Miami, Florida. He offered us $200.00 each for them and we did not sell them.

One week later we flew to New York and located a gold dealer and he offered us $500.00 each and we sold all five of them. We told the dealer that we had more and he told us that he would take all that we had for cash; we had his phone number.

Each one of the bags had 600 coins and

weighed 75 pounds. The bags were leather and had imprinted on them "Confederate States Army".

We decided not to call the dealer in New York but to go back up there. This time we took 10 coins with us. As soon as he saw the coins he counted out $5,000.00. We were in a huge store like a pawnshop, but he sold everything both old and new. He told us if we had more coins to bring them to him, he would buy them. The Old Italian man must have plenty of money. There were no signatures, no receipts and no checks.

In this store they had for sale old guns made in the 1920's for $800.00, Civil war things that were very expensive. Anything that was marked "antique" cost a lot of money. I wondered what that box would be worth that held the gold for so long. How much would those buttons cost that I found in the grave; or the colored stones and what would be in those other graves? Maybe more of the leather bags.

We do not plan to sell too much at one time. Too many of this same kind of coin coming onto the market at the same time may reduce the price. We considered waiting a year to sell any more and then try to sell all of them at the same time; but not at a reduced price.

We know that this was stolen gold. But who stole it, and whom did they steal it from. Was it confederate soldiers that buried it on that trail? Or was it Indians? And was this one of the trails that the Indians used to go west back in 1838?

In 1833 my Great Grandfather was born in Burton, Georgia. At the age of 29 he moved away from Burton and that was the year of 1862. Burton is about 20 miles from the place that I found the graves. It is very possible that my Great Grandfather, Jacob Hunter, walked on that trail, who knows?

## THE END

# THE BIG O ©

### Fiction created and narrated
### by Larry English

I have spent years fishing on lake Okeechobee and I have never seen all of the lake. I have been lost in the early morning fog and rambled around for several hours looking for a canal that is only twenty feet wide to exit this big lake, finally having to just sit and wait for the fog to leave. The lake is forty miles wide and seventy miles long and all of it is surrounded by bull rush and grass, that is ten feet high in some places, and a perfect place for bass, shell crackers and crappie. It is a fishermen's paradise.

The tall grass around the edges of lake Okeechobee is like another world. Trails that

269

are just wide enough for one boat lead you from a pool of crystal clear water to another pool that is the same, and there are mile after mile like this. Fish are plentiful, but so are snakes, alligators, and mosquitoes, and birds of all kinds. I never get tired of exploring the wilds around this lake because every time I go, I find something new and different.

During my working years my family and I would spend most weekends and vacations here at our mobile home in the town of Okeechobee. We could always catch more fish than we could eat, and could sell enough fish and frog legs to pay for the expense of fishing.

Robert retired the same year that I did; he lives next door to us and is the perfect fishing buddy. He is easy going, he loves to be out on the lake and is always there to do his part of the work, that is involved with hunting and fishing. Robert and I have a few restaurants that we catch and clean fish and frog legs for, they buy all that we can supply them.

## stories about a Georgia moonshiner

In 1987 Robert and I were out on the lake at night. We were trying to find out if fish are on the beds all night the same as they are in the daytime, and we discovered that they are, and they are easier to catch at night.

On this particular night in June we were really loading the boat with shell crackers, they weighed from ¾ of a pound to a pound each, and we already had over 100 pounds in the boat. We did not use a light because we had to stay hid from the game warden, then all of a sudden there was a loud swooshing noise that scared both of us. We both thought it was the game warden in an air boat, and we both laid down in the floor of our air boat, but when we regained our composure we saw that it was a huge air plane dumping something into the water.

The moon was full and we could see for a long way up and down the lake. The misquotes were very bad and the bugs of all kind were thick, we could hardly breath for them. We both knew that we could not run the engine on the airboat so we paddled over into the grass looking for a place to hide. That big airplane made a pass about 50 yards from us then turned and come back again and we could hear the splash in the water, and see the white splash when something hit in the water, we counted 30 of these all together. Five minutes after the plane left there were four fishing boats with big motors on them out there picking up whatever that was? Each boat had two people in it. Robert and I had binoculars to watch for the game wardens and we could see surprisingly well there on the lake with the moon shinning as bright as it was. It was 12:30 when the plane made that second drop and we stayed there, hid in the bull rush, until 4:30 in the morning because we were afraid to leave. We both knew that it must be dope of some kind and if it was we had to watch out for the dopers and the law.

At 4:30 we decided to paddle out into the lake and drift as far away from there as we could get. We had heard stories about people that had seen just what we had seen, and later they would be found floating face down in the lake, so we decided to be as careful as we could be.

One thing in our favor was that we were in an airboat and we had a full tank of gasoline. This means that no outboard could catch us no matter how fast it was. We could run the tall grass or dry land or we could cross the dike that surrounds the lake and even run across the paved road on top of the dike, nothing could catch us but another airboat or an airplane.

We had dumped our fish to make the boat lighter if we had to run. We had hooked up a new tank of gasoline, and I was to stay in the operators seat and be ready to start the engine, and to keep a watch out with the binoculars while Robert paddled us out into the lake so that the slight breeze would help us to drift away from this area. We did not care where the boat drifted to, just as long as it was someplace else. The wind caught the cage on our airboat and it was like a sail on a sailboat, we were being carried toward the center of lake Okeechobee, this lake is forty miles across, it is like being out on the ocean. When it started breaking daylight, I started the engine and headed due North and forty five minutes later I turned to the west and as soon as I could see land I was relieved, then and then only did I really believe that Robert and I would make it back home alive.

Just before we reached the landing where the car and boat trailer was, Robert motioned for me to stop and I did. He said "have you thought about what happened out here tonight?" and I told him no. Then Robert said "It has to be dope they are dropping on the lake and they do it on the full moon so they do not have to use any lights, they are bound to lose some once in a while, we need to be out there more often at night, maybe we can find what they lose."

Next night we went frog gigging and at 10:30 we were there in the tall grass waiting for another plane to come in, but it did not come. We waited until 3:30, the moon come up and went down and we then knew there would be no plane that night. While waiting we both noticed that the wind blew the same direction then, as it did the night before. It was blowing into the very thick grass and if those people did lose anything, it may get hung up in the grass and still be there someplace, so we went to look around to see what we could find. Daylight came and we had found nothing, but we both believed that it was a good idea and we would look more at a different time.

Robert said that we should wait until the next full moon to go back out there, so we agreed to go two nights before the full moon and on the full moon and then one night after the full moon so that was our plan.

We fished some every day and caught frogs at night to keep our restaurant customers happy. We had a good business going and we needed the extra income for our family, but in the back of our minds we were kind of dreaming about making a lot of money.

Two days before the full moon in July Robert and I were out there hid in the bull rush, waiting for the plane to come, we stayed there all night but the plane did not show up. We both knew that it was a long shot, and may never happen again but it did happen that one time, we both were willing to set out there in the dark and swat bugs and misquotes for several hours while we dreamed of all the money that we could make.

On the third night the big plane did come. It was scary, 100 feet over the water and flying very slow, the plane dropped several packages out so close together it seemed to make one big splash. Thirty seconds and it was over. Within five minutes the fishing boats were there and again each boat had two people in it. Standing in the seat of the airboat with the binoculars I could see them plainly, they were too busy loading those packages to notice anything else around them. Three minutes and they were gone; they worked fast like fighting fire. Robert and I set completely still for two hours after all four boats were gone, and then we paddled out to the drop site. We stopped paddling and let the boat drift hoping we would drift in the same direction that a box or package would if it was floating in the water. Forty-five minutes later we drifted into a patch of thick peppergrass, it was so thick it looked as though you could walk on it, but the water beneath the grass was six feet deep, and there by the edge of the thick grass was a black plastic box. The box was so hard to see that our boat bumped into it just as we spotted it. As fast as we could we loaded the box into the boat, it was about two feet x three feet and weighed about fifty pounds. We did not know what we had but we had a good idea, and we knew that we did not want anyone to catch us with it.

To use a light now or to start the engine on the airboat would be too dangerous. We started the trolling motor and went as fast as we could toward the east side of the lake; after an hour we then started the airboat motor and in one more hour we were in sight of land. We soon found a marina and pulled in to the gas pump, the package was covered with coats and life jackets. While I filled the gas tanks Robert called our wives to come after us and they came really fast. We managed to get the package into the trunk of the car without anyone seeing it, even our wives. They all three left for home and I started back across the lake in the airboat alone.

My truck and boat trailer were at the Harney Pond boat landing. I loaded the boat and headed for home; when I got there I backed into the garage the same as I always did. I closed the doors and told Robert that we would clean the boat later in the afternoon. He knew what that meant. We had transferred the package into the boat and would open it later to see what we had.

I lay down to sleep some but there was no way I could go to sleep. Adeline was pumping, my heart was beating triple time and I was just plain anxious.

A couple of hours went by before Robert knocked on my door. He asks if I was ready to clean up and I said, "yes I guess so." We went into the garage and put the package on the workbench. There were four thick plastic covers around a heavy-duty cardboard box. Inside the box there was a sweet smelling tobacco, but we knew that it had to be dope of some sort.

There had to be someone someplace that could tell us what it was, but we were afraid to contact anyone in the town of Okeechobee. The only other person I could think of was Felix, a friend of mine that I worked with in Tampa, he drove trucks for the company part time and was part time manager of the loading docks; he knew just about everyone. I called Felix and told him that I needed to talk to him in private and it was important, that it was private. We set up a meeting in a restaurant half way between Tampa and Okeechobee.

Robert and I carried one pound of the tobacco

with us. We talked to Felix first and when we found out that he was interested, we all three went to the car and gave the stuff to Felix; it only took about one minute and he said he would give us $600.00 for the pound, and that he would give $600.00 for every pound we could get. When we told him that there were 48 more pounds right now, he almost fainted. We told Felix that if he came to Okeechobee after it, he could have it for the $600.00 per pound. I did not know what it was worth but I knew that Felix would at least double his money. We got the money for the one-pound right then and the agreement was that when he got the stuff we got the cash. Felix was to be in Okeechobee the following day with the money.

Our meeting place was McDonalds. The package was in the back of my truck with dirty clothes on top of it. Felix had $ 28,800.00 in a large tackle box and as soon as he saw that package he handed the tackle box to me and he left with the package. Robert took his half of the money and I took mine, we both agreed not to spend a lot of money for a while, and not to let our wives know about this screwy business, because if we did get caught we did not want them to be involved.

Robert and I quit the frog business but we did keep on selling fish. We put quite mufflers on the airboat and had it painted camouflage and we bought some camouflage coveralls and some bug spray. Those guys may never make another drop in Lake Okeechobee but if they do and they lose any of their packages; we want to find them.

The second time that we found anything out there it was just too good to be true. After the plane come over and the fishing boats got their load and left we waited a while then went out to the drop site to look around and there was a package in wide open water just floating around waiting to be picked up. We did pick it up and on the way back to the shoreline, we found another box, but it was only about half the size of all the others. When Felix come after it this time, he was only expecting one package so he only brought money for one, but we told him to take it on and pay us later and he did. The very next day Felix was back, he was upset, not mad, just upset. The smaller box was not the same stuff; it was cocaine. It was a lot more money, but Felix had no buyer for that yet; but he would have a buyer in one week. There was nothing to do but wait, after all Felix had been totally honest with us.

The phone call from Felix was at 7:OO AM on Saturday morning. He invited us to go fishing with him and we knew that Felix was no fisherman, so there had to be a reason for his presence in Okeechobee at this time. Robert and I met Felix at the breakfast club, a popular restaurant there in town that was always busy. In the parking lot of the fish bait stand across the street from McDonalds, Robert and I received another tackle box from Felix; this one had $180,000.00 in it. Now it was time to stop taking chances. It was time to really retire. I told Robert this and he completely agreed with me.

Later we told Felix about our plan to stop, he did not agree and begged us to try again, Felix said, "If we get another bundle like the last one, then we can all three retire and go first class". After discussing it for two or three days we decided to go one more full moon and that was the last; no way would we do this anymore, after the full moon in October.

Robert and I spent two nights hid in the tall grass there where we always hide. We had cut out a place just the size of our boat there in the bull rush and when our boat was in that hole no one could see us from any direction. The only way that we could see out was to stand up in the operator's seat of the airboat, then with binoculars we could see a large area of the lake and the place where the plane was using to drop the packages. We discovered that the mud on the bottom of the lake had a sour, rotten smell to it, and if we disturbed it in any way the smell drew more bugs and misquotes. We tried not to disturb the mud on the bottom of the lake in our hiding place.

The full moon in October was beautiful. It was very bright and we could almost read a book by the light of the moon. On the second night that we were there the plane come at 1:00 am. It made two passes on this night, and both passes were completed within one minute. Very few clouds were in the sky but just as we could hear the boats coming for the pick up a cloud drifted over us and the whole area was darkened. With our binoculars we could still see the men in the boats working; two or three minutes later we could hear the boats leaving and we could see them also. Four boats come for the packages but we could only see three boats leaving. I watched the boats closely and there were only three. Robert and I were very still; we did not move and we made no sound. We thought we could hear something, but neither of us could make out what it was. There was a breeze blowing lightly thru the bull rush and once in a while there would be a fish feeding on a bug or a frog with a splashing sound of the water, frogs were continually making their croaking sounds, but this other sound that we both heard, from time to time, was different.

Two hours later we pulled the airboat out of the hole; slowly we eased the boat out toward the drop zone. From the operators seat I kept the binoculars busy watching the open lake, thinking that the pickup boats may return for some reason.

The fact that we only saw three boats leaving the area had me worried, but it was very possible that all four boats left, and we could not see one of them. I bet if one boat were left here, that the others would have been back after it by now. The trolling motor pulled us thru the peppergrass and Lilly pads as we looked for a lost package. Just as I was about to give up looking we got the scare of a lifetime.

The forth boat that we had not been able to see leave, was right there in front of us right now. Only one man was in the boat; a Mexican with a boat paddle in his hand and he was trying to get into our boat. Robert struck him twice with our paddle. I had the 22-magnum pistol that we carried for snakes if we needed it, and the Mexican saw it as I pulled it from the holster. He dropped to his knees there in his boat, and put his hands in a praying position, he thought we were going to kill him and he was very scared. This man could speak English very well.

The tip of his gas line had broken off, and the other boats had already gone. Since all four of them went too different landings there was no way for them to know that he was in trouble. We had an extra gas tank and gas line so we gave it to him. The Mexican had 8 packages on his boat and he tried to give us one of them but we turned him down. As he left he kicked one package off of the boat into the water and said something about a restaurant. We grabbed the package and run the airboat as fast as it would go thru the airboat trails up the west shore and into Cochran pass, we went to fish eating creek and unloaded the package in the swamp by the bridge, then we went after the truck and picked up the package and went home.

As we rode down the road Robert ask what

was it that he said about a restaurant? Neither of us understood what he had said. Anyway we had agreed before we come out on this trip that this was our last time doing this. If we make it home this time you can consider us both retired.

The truck and airboat with the package still in it was parked inside of the garage. We could not wait any longer; we grabbed the package and put it on the worktable. When we cut it open we found that it was the same sweet smelling tobacco, just like all the others. Tomorrow we would call Felix but tonight I had to have some sleep.

We had been told that Felix had bought himself a fishing boat and sure enough one day after we called him, he showed up here on Okeechobee with a 14 foot john boat with a 20 horse mercury motor. A very nice fishing boat. Robert and I met him at McDonalds; he told us that he felt like a small fishing boat made him look less suspicious, because here in this area a boat is a reason to be here. This time Felix come to our house and got the last package and gave me the money, we stopped being so careful because now we were out of this business forever.

Now we can spend some of this money. Until now we had to be careful about spending because people would wonder where we got all of the extra cash, and may pay more attention to our movements, but now that we are not involved any longer we can stop worrying about that.

Robert knocked on our door and I went out to talk to him, we set on the porch and talked for a while then went to the garage and split the money for the last package. It was kind of sad knowing that this was the end of this gravy train, but what the heck, we had $ 300,000.00 of somebody else's money. As Robert was leaving he asks me if I had thought any more about what that Mexican man said about a restaurant, I told him no but it had to mean something. We both wanted to find out more about this so we agreed that when we go out to eat from now on, we will try to find a different Mexican restaurant each time to eat in, something may turn up to give us an answer.

I never did know it before but Okeechobee has 9 Mexican restaurants, we worked our way thru 3 of them with no luck on finding out anything about our little Mexican friend, but on the 4$^{th}$ one we hit the jackpot. Our table was in the rear of the dining room there were four of us eating, and the food was great and so was the service. When we were finished and started to leave,our waiter told us there was no charge. We then knew something was going on so we ask to speak to the owner. We were escorted to the office and there he was, the little Mexican that we saw out in the lake with a boatload of dope, and had left a package for us to pick up.

He told Robert and I that he felt that we had saved his life. It was not long until daylight and he would have been there in that boat with a load of dope, and could not leave because his gas line had broken. Then when he saw me with the pistol he knew that we would kill him for the dope, but instead you gave me a tank full of gasoline with a new gas line on it and that saved my life. You will never be able to pay for a meal in my restaurant, I owe you too much.

Our new friend's name was Fernando, he told us a lot about the dope operation on the lake because he wanted us to work with him. This is what he told us. "We have four boats picking up dope from the plane. Each of us is to pick up 8 bales and leave. We all go to different landings and someone is there to get our load then we go home. I am paid $1,000.00 for doing this and it takes less than one hour. We know that the police and sheriff departments and game wardens will not bother us because they have been paid off. I know that sometimes we do not get all of the bales but nothing is said.

If you will work with me I will guarantee you two bales per drop and we will split it three ways; but you will have to sell it to your customer. I am being watched all of the time to prevent me from doing this." We told Fernando that we would think about it.

It was on the Full moon of December that the next drop happened. Fernando had promised Robert and I that he would put the two bales in the hole that we cut out in the bull rush to hide in, and for us to go after it the next day; we did this and Felix was at the Kissimmee landing waiting on us when we got there with it. We got the money and split it up three ways that day, it worked perfect.

My wife and I left two days later to go on a cruise and we were gone 10 days. When we returned our double wide had burned. None of the neighbors saw anything suspicious and everyone assumed it was an electrical fire. Robert had been at home and he did not see anything wrong either, but I did not feel good about it. We left Okeechobee and went to Orlando for a few days. When we got home this time we received a letter with pictures of my airboat that was taken from the air. It was too high to see a small plane. My boat number was showing up plain on the front seat and there were two people in the boat, you could even see the rods and reels and the time was on the picture, it was 5-14-pm. You could not tell who the people were.

I got Robert outside and showed him the picture. I told him to get his wife and leave right now, do not even pack a bag and tell no one where you are going. We are doing the same thing. I already knew that the money was out of state; everything we needed we could buy, but it was time to go now.

Robert and his wife left town, but I do not know where they went. We went to a hotel in Tampa and intended to stay two weeks but on the fourth day we saw on the news where the owner of a Mexican restaurant and his family had been shot to death, in Okeechobee, Fl.

Fernando had told me that the person running

the dope ring here in Okeechobee was "John" and that he owned the boat sales there in town. I left immediately for the three hour trip back to Okeechobee, I was sure that my wife and I would never have any peace unless we got this settled now. I put her in a motel in north Okeechobee and I went to the boat yard, they were closed but a sign on the door said they were gone to the airboat races, which was only one mile away, so I went there.

I walked from the parking lot to the concession stand, which was over by the bleachers, and as I ordered a cup of coffee two large farmers come up on each side of me. They had cow manure on their boots and they smelled like a wet dog. They ordered me to go with them, and they both had me by the arm; we went to their truck and got in with me in the middle. The one on the passenger side had a knife close to my face then drug it across my arm, scratching it lightly but bringing blood. They said they knew that I had something of theirs and they wanted it back, or else. They kicked me out of their truck and I landed on my face in the mud. The races were over now and I had to wait in a long line to get out onto the road. They were already out and gone. I went to town to look for them because I intended to shoot both of them. After driving thorough town a few times I went by the boatyard and there I saw their truck setting up by the office. I turned out my lights and pulled in between their truck and the fence, and then I went inside. John was at the desk facing me; the two farmers were setting with their backs to me. As I walked in I had the 22 magnum in my hand, I hit one of them in the head as hard as I could, and blood flew all over the room, I grabbed the other one by the hair and jerked his head back as far as I could, then I shoved the barrel of the pistol down his throat and warned them that I would kill them both if they ever spoke to me or my family, or come close to us again. Then John said, "I promise we will never have any more problems, none of us will ever come near you or your family, we have all made money lets all live to spend it". They admitted to burning my mobile home and said they would pay for it. When they all agreed to do this, I still had the pistol down the big farmer's throat and the hammer was still back on it, they would have agreed to anything at that time.

The only thing that kept them away from my family was fear. They did not know what I was capable of doing, and I did not know that I was capable of doing what I did. All three of these guys swore they did not have anything to do with Fernando's death, and John swore to me that they were working for people from New Jersey.

John is the man that I had bought my airboat from and he is the one that I hired to paint the airboat. I had talked to him several times and I thought he was very nice; he financed my boat when I bought it, and he did it himself out of his own pocket and did not charge any interest, but he does this for everybody. When I had the airboat painted, I was there in the boatyard several times and John had offered me a job selling boats and motors and parts but I was doing good selling fish and I liked being out on the lake, catching the fish and selling them to the restaurants so I turned down his offer of the job.

I could not believe what I was hearing when Fernando had told me that John was the person in Okeechobee that was running this operation. I also found out that the plane come from Columbia and when the drop was made there in lake Okeechobee, that it had been in the air for 14 hours. It was 3 more hours flying time before they had a place to land and unload the rest of their load. So it is plain to see that this was a several million-dollar deal, and it happened one time each month, so anyone getting in their way or causing them a problem could be in a lot of trouble themselves.

My wife and I decided to relocate to a different place there in Okeechobee. We put the lot up for sale where the mobile home had burned and found a small house out near the Kissimmee River. It was about two minutes from the boat landing and a perfect spot to fish from and we were moved in one week. It seems that Felix's end of this deal had more problems than we did. The bales that Felix took from here was loaded onto a truckload of floor tile in Tampa and hauled non-stop to Detroit, Michigan. Some of the people involved in the Detroit operation was also involved in the New Jersey operation and they saw that the packaging and the sensamalia [dope] was the very same and it belong to them. They traced it back to Felix and Fernando. Felix knew all about Fernando and his family so he was cautious. His office window faced the parking lot there at the trucking company. Felix saw the big Cadillac pull in thru the gate; he watched them park and when one of the occupants got out with a shotgun, Felix called the police. The man with the shotgun walked up to the service window, Felix had a pistol on his desk but the gunman did not know it. As the shotgun was raised toward Felix, Felix shot first and killed the gunman. The other three men come out of the car and all three were armed, as they were halfway to the office one sheriff car and two police cars came in real fast. All three of the gunman was killed and one policeman was hit in the foot. The Tampa Tribune reported that it was a robbery that went wrong and Felix Rodrigo the loading dock manager was given credit for stopping the robbery.

Six months later Robert drove to Orlando, I drove to Orlando, and Felix drove to Orlando. We all three met in a restaurant and had lunch together. We talked about everything that had happened and we all agreed to meet there in the same place again in one year, and not to contact each other before that unless someone else come after one of us.

Robert was a good friend of mine, and the best fishing buddy anyone could have. But we saw each other often there in town and never did speak; we never recognized each other in any way, we both thought that our families would be safer this way. This was no small organization that we had been fooling with, and we knew that we were lucky to be alive.

The two dairy farmers that lived in Lakeport, Fl. were brothers. They operated a cattle farm and grew a lot of hay there near the lake on their family's farm, they were not mean people and I am not worried about them. John is a different story. He is smart, ambitious, and rich. If pressure is put on him he will tell all that he knows and he knows a lot. He will tell everything because he knows this is the tool the DEA uses. If you tell on others they go easy on you. If it is the dopers that is after you, you either tell or you disappear, this is nothing new everyone knows it.

Robert and I had a great little business going with the fish, I have been keeping that business going but now it is running into work. I do the business because I have the boat and Robert does not have one and told me a lot of times that he does not want a boat. He is welcome to have any part of the fish business that he wants at any time. Anyone can go out and catch the fish but it is the connections with the fish houses and the restaurants that make you the money, but we do not need the money now.

After all the trouble that John and I had he still come to me and told me that he had the drawing of how to build a fish trap, and he knows that it works because he uses them a lot. I went to his house to get the drawing and he had some old traps there for me to look at, he also had the tools used to build traps and he gave them to me. I bought the wire and everything I needed and now I build about one trap each day in my spare time. When I get four traps ready I take them out at night and put them out. So far I have lost almost all of them, I just cannot find them when I go back to see if I have any fish.

When I told John this he laughed at me and said tomorrow I will go with you and show you how it is done. Next day when I went after him he gave me a trail cutter. It is a pie shaped stainless steel cutter with an eyebolt on the point to drag it with. A rope goes thru the eyebolt and you drag it behind your boat to cut a 30-inch wide trail in the grass. John and I went out in the lake to a patch of peppergrass and dropped the cutter overboard into the water. We jerked the cutter along the bottom as we went real slowly and it cut the grass off and made a trail. John told me to make the trail crooked and it would be hard for others to see because game wardens look for them all the time and fisherman that has had a bad day will steal your fish. We cut a trail about 100 feet long then that night we carried ten traps out there and put in the trail. Two days later he went with me to run the traps and we had 600 pounds of crappie.

John told me that the reason we caught so many was that the moon was almost full, and that is when the crappie spawn. After the full moon you will not catch anything. You get a lot of fish for three days before the full moon and three days before the new moon other times you may catch just a few. You get a lot of fish like this but it changes from fun to work. The places we sell fish pays $ 1.00 a pound just like we catch them, or $ 2.00 a pound cleaned. It is a lot of work, but sometimes it is a good way to earn money.

One of the trails that had 15 traps in it was being robbed regularly. All other traps had fish but these were empty most of the time. John said he would show me how to stop this. We went out to the traps and John had a candle and 2 or 3 single edge razor blades. On the string of traps there would be 2 or 3, 3 inch round floats. He cut a small slit in a cork inserted a razor blade with just a little bit of the sharp sticking out and then lit the candle and waxed the blade in to hold it in place. We never had anyone else to steal our fish. I never did see anyone with a bandaged hand and I looked for them.

Our year was up, Robert, Felix and I met in Orlando again and had a steak dinner and discussed our situation. We had decided not to try our previous business anymore. We did not know if the plane was ever coming again or not. None of us needed money bad enough to take a chance like that. We had made some quick cash and got out but we did come close and five people did get gunned down because of that deal. We were the lucky ones.

Robert was going to go into the fishing business with me and we were going to hire someone to clean fish. Robert and I would catch them and deliver them to the markets. We were going to freeze the fish in one-pound packages, for something to do.

The same day that we got home John called me and ask me to come over to his boat yard and I went right on over there. John said that he needed some help and that he would pay me $40,000.00 to work for him for four days. He would give me $20,000.00 before we left home and the other $20,000.00 when we got back, it was just too much money to let get away so I accepted the job, and the first money.

John and I and three other men that I had never seen before, but John knew them so I figured they were okay. We drove to a big farm in South Georgia and soon a large plane, a D C 3 landed there. They filled the planes tanks with gasoline and then there was a gas tank inside the plane that must have held

1500 gallons, they filled it also. That extra tank was chained to the floor and the walls to keep it from sliding.

As soon as it was ready they loaded food and water and then we took off. We flew for 18 hours and while we were over the ocean, we were down to within 100 feet above the water. When we arrived wherever we were, we landed on a dirt and mud runway. About twenty people were there waiting for us with a load of packages that looked just like the ones that we got on Lake Okeechobee. The motors were shut down and the oil was checked. That tank of gasoline inside the plane had a pump on it and we refueled the plane while they loaded the packages from the truck to the plane. We then pushed the empty tank out to make room for all of the dope. All of this was complete and we took off in less than one hour. The trip back was the same thing, right down on top of the water with no lights on the plane at all. We slept on the packages. There were no seats or chairs there in the back of the plane. We had four people that could fly the plane, and John was one of them. We come back over Okeechobee and kicked out 30 packages in 8 or 10 seconds. Some place else either in Florida or Georgia we kicked out another 30 packages in a cornfield, the rest of it was on the plane when we landed. Cars and trucks were there; ready to load the rest of the dope. As soon as the motors were shut off John and I got into his car and left. We drove for an hour then stopped and got a room and a hot bath and twelve hours of sleep. When we got back to Okeechobee John gave me the other $20,000.00. That was on Thursday. On Monday night at 10:00 someone knocked on the door. It was the D E A, five of them. When they put me in the bus they were driving, John was in there also. They got everyone that was on the trip but two, and they were both D E A agents. They had pictures of each of us on the plane; they had my picture refueling the plane. All four pilots had their picture made they just had us good. Every one of us was under $1,000,000.00 bond. Every one of us pleaded guilty. Every one of us got 15 years and we all went to a different prison. I went to Minnesota Federal Prison. After three years I was transferred to Atlanta and stayed there three years, then I was sent to West Florida Federal prison and was there 4 and a half years and there I got out early.

My wife had divorced me and married again. She sold my airboat and the house and all of that dope money that we stole, was in somebody else's bank account.

Two or three times we were in good condition, and had quit that business for good and was not going to do it anymore, but we did. Before I ever knew what dope was, before I had ever seen the first drop of the stuff I had a retirement made. I had a beautiful loving wife and a home paid for. I had an airboat and could catch all the fish I wanted and was very happy. Now I am homeless and alone. I wish I were back in jail so that I could have a place to eat and sleep.

**This is the END OF THE STORY.**

# HIDDEN CREEK ©

**Fiction, created and narrated
by Larry English**

There really is a place called Hidden Creek. But until three weeks ago, as far as I know, there was no place named Hidden Creek.

I am a senior in high school and I decided to go on a camping trip alone. Across the road from my home there was a mountain named Glass Mountain. It was a useless mountain covered with rock cliffs and huge boulders. Because of the steep and rugged and rocky terrain no one wanted to go there, not even hunters, it was too hard to walk on. I looked at that mountain every day and wondered what good it was. But, I decided to go there on my camping trip. Camping supplies were simple, enough food to do for three or four days and a 22 rifle, matches, and a rainproof coat. All of this was in a flour sack for easy carrying. I left my house walking just after daylight and at sundown I was not even to the top of this mountain.

I knew that there was a community on the other side of Glass Mountain, but around the road it was over forty miles, I did not know how far it was straight thorough, the way the crow flies. Because of the very thick underbrush it was hard to travel, sometimes I had to crawl under the Ivey thickets. Just at sundown I found a small clearing and decided to camp here, I could see the top of the Mountain and knew that the next morning I would see down the other side. It was cold and Wendy there on that mountain, and the next morning I was up and walking just at daybreak. I went over the top and all I could see out there in the distance was another top, and more cliffs and more of the same terrain that I had already come through. I thought about turning back but decided to go one more day, mainly so that people would not laugh at me for coming to this place.

Four hours down the other side of Glass Mountain I found a game trail that was going North and South. I followed the trail South, because I thought it was going in the direction of the other community across the mountain. I followed the trail until almost dark and then I crossed a small stream, so this is where I camped the second night. From there the trail went back up the mountain almost to the top, then on a level it kept going south and east.

About noon on the third day I could hear the roar of a waterfall in the valley below. The underbrush was not so thick now, and I could walk easy. The rock cliffs were still a problem but the game trail went around them. The trees were bigger here, the ground was not so rocky, and this place was beautiful. I could see deer sign everywhere. I could see where Turkeys had been scratching and one place where hogs had been rooting.

The trail turned down into the valley and the lower I got the louder the waterfall got. Two hours later I came upon a creek that was crystal clear and about three feet deep in the center. I could not wait to get my clothes off and get into that cold water. The sun was shining and it was a warm day. As I bathed I could see small fish swimming near the edge of the creek. I waded downstream a few feet to look for bigger fish, but did not see any. Instead, there in the sand, I found a human footprint. A small human footprint. There was no mistake. I got out of the creek on the other side and there were a lot of footprints, and not all the same size. I scrambled back across the creek where my clothes and the 22 rifle were. I loaded the rifle first then put my clothes on. I was startled. No way could there be anyone here in this place.

From the creek there was a clean, well-worn trail going up the ridge and I followed it. I walked slow and quiet, with the rifle loaded. I saw a cave under a large rock and I saw two people run out and go further up the mountain. As I got closer a man come out of the cave with a stick, but did not make any attempt to attack me. He was as surprised as I was. We talked but he was very guarded with what he said. After about an hour the other two people came back to where we were. A woman and her daughter. This was a family of people that had been here in the mountains for a long time. They did not tell me this, I could see the food they had, the way they lived and acted, it was not hard to tell.

The young girl had long hair that covered her chest and she wore no shirt, just a pair of men's pants. The lady was fully clothed and bare foot, she did not want to talk. The young girl could not talk, but she could grunt and make a few sounds that let you know what she meant. The three of them lived there in that cave and had plenty to eat. Fish, Rabbit, honey, and pork chunks. From my flour sack we had coffee, beans and four or five biscuits that I had left over. It was a real treat for them. We had one fork and one cup and a butcher knife to eat with.

As I talked to him I found out that he had a trap to catch hogs and a rabbit trap and a way to catch fish from the stream. He had two bee trees that he got honey from and he could take honey from the trees, without destroying the bee trees

I suppose that because of my age he knew that I was no kind of law or Government official. The man confided in me as a new found friend. The only person that he had talked to in five years. He and his family have been here that long.

In 1942 he was drafted into the army, he never did report, instead he and his family came to this place to hide. He had never been out of this county and he was afraid for his life. The daughter was in the second grade in school, at that time, then she could speak a few words but she got worse as time went on. She is not mentally ill, but people thought she was. They have been here for over five years.

In the fall of the year He goes to the farms over

in my area and steals apples and peaches from the trees. If the smoke house is not locked he will get whatever he can from them. He told me that he has taken some clothes from clotheslines and that some of the dogs' sound mean but none of them are. He gives them a piece of a rabbit or squirrel and now they do not even bark at him. He told me that he can't take much and the owners will not even miss it. He travels to the edge of the woods near the houses, in daytime and to the barns and houses in the middle of the night and always on moonlit nights. He makes that trip in eight hours running on the deer trails.

None of them appear to have bad teeth, they are all skinny, and have long hair and they all three go barefoot. They bathe but with no soap, but they do not stink. They only have spring water to drink. The turkeys and rabbits and hogs that they eat are in chunks, they eat with their fingers.

The first few nights I was here I went into the woods away from them to sleep, because

I was afraid of what they could do to me, but now I see that this is the most honest, calmest, peaceful people that I know. They will only take what they must have to live. The only thing the wife brought with her when she came here was her bible; she still has it and reads to her husband and daughter every day.

Each morning he and I go to the creek, if it is warm we bathe. Later the mother and daughter go to the creek. This morning he asks if I wanted to see the start of the creek, and I said yes. About one mile upstream was the waterfall. We went to the top and three or four springs boiled up out of the ground and all become one stream then they went over this 75 foot drop and at the bottom, the force of the water had created a pool that was ten feet deep and fifty feet wide. This was not a valley. It was more like a huge hole that was two miles long and one mile wide. It was up hill every way you looked. He told me that the creek did not flow out of this place; he said tomorrow I would show you the other end of the creek.

Then he said, "I am going to show you something that is sacred". You must promise to keep this a secret as long as you live, I promised.

Half way back to their cave and high on the mountain we went to another cave. The opening was smaller but inside it was much larger than the cave they lived in. Many, many bones were there in a row. Some rocks were there in the shape of a grave. Hundreds of drawings covered the walls. Drawn with sand stone and have lasted for many years. Drawings of Indian women and children, many of them. Horses and wagons, the moon and sun and stars. Even drawings of men in uniform and on horses. Drawings of babies strapped on the backs of Indian mothers. We know this tells a story but we do not know what it is. This had to be an Indian graveyard. Also there were a few pieces of pottery and a few large pots or bowls or whatever they were.

I was told that if I mentioned this to anyone,

that someone would come here to search for this place. I promised on my life that I would never tell about his family being here or about the Indian graves. He also told me there was another cave but we would see it later. I wanted to ask all three of their names but I did not. When they want me to know they will tell me.

It was almost sundown when we got back to their cave and the fire outside had two rabbits cooking. That was it; just rabbit and we always had honey.

I was told that the trip tomorrow morning would be more interesting than today was, I did not see how that was possible, and I had a hard time going to sleep just thinking about it. Everyone went to bed at dark.

I was worried about security for a while. If someone or something came and everyone asleep we would be in a dangerous position.

When I first got here they someway knew I

was coming. I was too far away to be heard, but the two girls ran from the cave and went higher up on the mountain. Now I know how they were warned. Just after they came here one of the girls found two eggs, they hatched them out by keeping them by the fire inside the cave. That was Gray Hawks. The hawks now live in tall trees near the cave entrance, and anything different at all the hawks will warn the family. The family knows what to listen for. If no one is around both hawks will eat from any of their hands, but since I have been here, neither hawk will come down.

When I get up every morning I am hungry, but they do not eat until late in the day and only one time a day. If anything maybe they will eat honey or chew on honeycomb.

This day we are on our way to the other end of the creek. We saw the beginning yesterday, now we will see the end. There is a pool of water about thirty feet across, it is round and looks like a beaver dam but there are no beavers. This is natural. The water goes underground here and no telling where it comes back up, it may never come back up, who knows?

This is when the two of us named this place-HIDDEN CREEK. It is a hidden creek. It starts and ends in this valley.

He has trenches dug from the water inward. Fish go up the trenches and he puts a piece of wood behind the fish, and then flips it out onto the ground. We know that part of this creek is underground. We do not know how much is underground and we know that there are a lot of fish that come from someplace, there must be fish in the underground stream.

Then he wanted to show me the hog trap and rabbit traps. These two traps and the system he has devised to catch fish, feed this family. This small valley is their world and they have lived here for five years.

I told all three of them that I had to leave

and go home, because I have to go to school. They all understood. They told me their names. Jack and Louise and daughter Cindy. No last name. Then, Jack said that he was going to show me a better way to travel from my house to this valley. When I left they all three walked with me. We walked the game trails that led us a different direction. Louise and Cindy stopped on top of the first mountain and Jack went with me to within sight of the cornfields, then he turned around and started back, I told Jack that I would be back when school was out. The game trail ended on top of the ridge above the fields. It was so much better walking this way. I can see how Jack makes it in eight hours. It is an easy two-day trip for me and I will not have to crawl under the ivies.

School now was a drag. My mind was there in Hidden Creek with Jack, Louise and Cindy. I had to finish school so I had to study but it was hard for me to concentrate

In December I had some time off. I loaded all

that I could carry into a backpack, coffee and a coffee pot. Forks and cups, one fry pan a butcher knife and canned green beans. It was a long walk and I could not overload myself.

When I was about a half mile from their cave they all three met me, the hawks had warned them that someone was coming and they carried the load the rest of the way.

That night Jack told me that there was another cave that I had not seen, and tomorrow we will go to it.

The next morning it was a wet, foggy and windy day but we all four went to the other cave. It had a lot of pottery in it, a few arrowheads and several bones. It was nothing like the other cave but it had its meaning, whatever that was. We took nothing from any of the caves. It was amazing to look at this and wonder what it all meant.

There was no trail to the burial caves. As we walked through the woods going back to their cave there was a crashing, ground shaking, sickening noise. Everything around us shook. A large chestnut tree fell right on Jack. He was under that tree and he was already dead. Three days later we got him out and buried him in the cave that was nearby, by covering him with rocks the way the Indians did. Louise was behind Jack when the tree fell; she had a few scratches but was okay. Louise and Cindy cried for several days.

Now What? I can't stay here and I don't think I can leave them by their selves. Louise said they would be all right here that they knew how to get food, all but the honey. I told them that I would be back as soon as I could and I left in the middle of the day. When I got to the stream that we drank from, I stopped. I was undecided whether to leave or not, I slept there that night and next morning I went back to Louise and Cindy. They were in the creek taking a bath, in one way they both had become sort of like wild women, they thought nothing about me being there and I had no sexual thoughts about them because this was Jacks wife and daughter. I persuaded them to go home with me for a while. They did and they stayed almost two weeks, the hawks stayed in the spruce tree behind my house. On the hill out from my house we had an outdoor toilet, neither of them would use it. We had water piped to the back yard but they would not drink it because they said it taste like the pipes. They drank from the small stream near our house. They slept on the floor beside the bed I slept in. I had offered them the bed but they refused.

I had to go back with them. We left my house at mid night, and using the trails that Jack had shown me we only spent one night on the trail. We took most of the food from my pantry and it was all that we could carry, but it was enough to last them until I could take them some more. I stayed one night there and started my walk back.

I was gone from them 15 days. When I went back I carried two sleeping bags, one for each of the girls, and a few cans of food. Again, a half-mile from the cave Louise ran to meet me, she was alone. I knew that the hawks had warned them that I was coming. Louise was crying out loud, but would not tell me what was wrong.

She led me to the cave. Cindy died in her sleep two nights ago, and was still there in the cave, Louise could not move her.

That day we moved Cindy and put her beside Jack in the cave with the Indians, and covered her with rocks. We were both very sad but Louise read scriptures from her bible and told me that her and Jack were told when Cindy was born, that she may not live to be old. She had an affliction.

And that also is why she could not speak.

I could not leave Louise there alone, and she would not go home with me. I stayed there two more weeks. On our last day there we swam. It was June now but the water was cold. We both swam naked and set in the warm sunshine naked. But no sex. That night I spread one sleeping bag out for me to sleep in, and she had the other sleeping bag to sleep in. I went to bed and she lay down beside me on my sleeping bag. I zipped the bag up and there in the sleeping bag, in the cave, in Hidden Creek, we had sex for the first time. She was 34 years old and I was 19 years old. 15 years difference in age may make a difference to some people but it did not to me. It was a thing that we did every night in the sleeping bag, and sometime in the warm sunshine beside Hidden Creek.

We walked out of the woods on the game trails in the fall of the year. We both knew that we would be back but it may be next spring. We both stayed there in my house all winter and we both wanted to be in Hidden Creek, but I had to work some to have money for food.

Louise now would sleep in the bed with me, but she still would not use the toilet, she still drank from the stream and most of the time she would wear no clothes. Every other day she would take bread or corn out in the woods and the hawks would come down and eat from her hand.

Louise thought about Jack and Cindy all the time. She now wants their bodies moved out of the cave and to a grave of their own. She said that the cave was a sacred place for the Indians and the Indian Gods watched over them, Jack and Cindy are out of place, and I want them moved.

I promised her that in the spring we would go to Hidden Creek and move them to their own graves.

I went into town two or three times but she would not go. I bought her leather moccasins because I knew that was all that she would wear.

I had a job on the farm one mile from our house. It was their fields that Louise and I had to walk across to go to the trails that Jack had shown me. And there was no way that we had left any tracks for anyone to see; we had to be very careful about that.

It was springtime and the leaves were starting to grow. We were both anxious to get back to the place that we loved so much. Everything was just like we left it and on the first morning there we went to the graves of Jack and Cindy and started moving them. It took two days to do this and on the next day we swam and both lay in the warm sunshine.

Louise told me there, then, that she felt bad about those Indian graves being here in the woods the way they are. She said "I want to go to an Indian Village and ask a chief what the drawings on the walls mean". I promised her that we would do that as soon as we go back to my house.

For the next two or three weeks we both ran around there with no clothes on. Totally free, worried about nothing. We had plenty of food, a warm place to sleep and that is all that we needed.

The day after we got back to my house, we took the old ford truck that my dad had left me, and drove seventy miles to an Indian village. We ask where to find the chief of the tribe. We were directed to a huge building with several offices up stairs and stores down stairs. When we ask for the main chief we were taken to an office and left there for a few minutes, then an Indian man dressed in a nice suite came in and introduced himself. Louise started telling her story exactly as it was. She was stopped, and we were told that he did not believe the tale that Louise was telling. We were asked if we could wait two hours to repeat the story and we agreed.

Downstairs there was a restaurant; we were guided to a room in the back that had four tables. The waiter was told to give us anything we wanted to eat, at no cost to us.

In about one hour eight Indian men came

in and set down. All of them were chiefs of some tribe or village. The one that told Louise he did not believe her tale, did the talking. He introduced all of the others. Louise talked for over an hour and then answered questions for another hour. Louise asks questions too. She wanted to know about the drawings on the walls of the big cave and every one of her questions were answered. The Indian men were very gracious and polite to Louise.

There was no mention of Jack being a deserter from the army.

When Louise was finished talking all eight Indians left the room. In thirty minutes they returned and ask us if we could stay until tomorrow. We were given a very nice room to stay in and told that everything we wanted was free, just ask for it.

Again we went to the room in back of the restaurant. All eight Indians were there. We were asked if we would guide them to the caves, and Louise told them yes, on one condition. The place had to be kept secret. There could be no traffic in and out; this was a one-trip deal. They all agreed to that.

A time was decided on for them to be at my house. They were there exactly at 12:00 midnight as was planned. All eight of the men in work clothes and each one carrying a five-day supply of food in their backpack. I had some food for Louise and I and we knew we had some food there already. A driver brought them in a small bus; we all rode down to the place where we started to walk then we got out of the bus and the driver returned to their village. We walked down the rocky embankment and into the creek, we waded downstream a few feet and then thorough the woods to the trails that would lead us to Hidden Creek.

It was a hard two-day walk. We got there at sundown and everyone was tired so we eat and went to sleep. We slept there by the creek where Louise and I usually swam, we did not even go to our cave where we lived, and Tomorrow would be the time for that. The hawks followed us all the way. Louise walked away from the rest of us and called the hawks down and fed them. The Indian men could not believe what they were seeing.

We ate breakfast before daylight, when it was light enough to see we started to the burial cave. The chief went in first, ten minutes later the rest went in, Louise and I stayed outside. We could hear them crying, we could not tell exactly what they were saying but there was wailing, praying and just plain whooping.

When we went in the chief was standing there pointing to drawings on the wall. All the others were setting down watching and agreeing with what they were hearing. They allowed us to set there and listen. The story was plain even to us after it was explained, the way that it was.

The white men wanted the land that the Indians lived on because gold had been found on it. The United States ordered the Indians to go to a reservation that was many miles away. It was a hard years travel for Squaws and babies and men with no shoes. The ice and snow made this impossible, but Union soldiers forced them out anyway. Union soldiers killed some of the women and their babies and some just froze to death.

One group escaped with about 200 men, women and children. The leader was the Great Grandfather of this chief that is here now. There is no record, for all of those years, of what happened to them, they were never heard from again. This is the story that has been handed down for the last 150 years.

Now, this story that is written on the walls of this cave tells us what happened. This is the story of the 200 people that escaped the union soldiers back then.

They wandered through the mountains searching for a place to survive. They found these caves and made them their home. The drawings that were on the walls of a moon by itself means one month. The sun, moon and stars together means one year. The Squaws with empty papoose baskets means she had a baby but it died. The squaws with empty baskets and a soldier with a gun pointed at them means the soldier killed the baby. The squaws with babies in the baskets mean the baby is still alive. The deer and animal drawings mean they had food to eat and the drawings of fish mean they had fish to eat. The drawings indicate that they all lived here peacefully for four years. Then a lot of them got a sickness and had high fevers. Many died within two weeks, indicated by two quarters of the moon. After this, one half of the men left to go west and find the rest of the tribe. The others lived here the rest of their lives. This answers the questions about the bones not being in the burial cave, but scattered in the small caves. They stayed here until they all died, waiting for the others to come back.

The drawings of the soldiers with guns mean they were being forced to go. The drawings of soldiers with a knife on the end of the gun pointing to Squaws and babies mean they were killed. The drawings of all people with tears in their eyes mean they knew they were going to die, their only chance was to escape

The Indian men explained all of this to Louise and I. They were very thankful to us for bringing them the information that we did.

Each morning as the sun came up they prayed. The ritual lasted about one hour and it was held at the burial cave. The same thing was done as the sun went down. On the third day of this the chief announced that the next morning would start the work of entombment.

They found pieces of dead chestnut trees that were flat in shape. Four of the men started gathering rocks from the woods and the other four found red mud from the creek banks. They used the mud like cement to hold the rocks in place and they completely sealed the entrance to the burial cave in one day. They carried the mud on the flat pieces of wood. On the second day they did the other cave the same way.

They offered to dig graves for Jack and Cindy's bones, but Louise told them no, that they were already resting in a place that they loved.

The chief promised both Louise and I that our secret place would always be a secret with all Indian Nations. All of the chiefs of all tribes in this part of the country were here, and they all promised.

They had all worked very hard for more than two days. From sun up until sun down and it was decided that they would take one day to explore Hidden Creek and then the next morning we would all walk out of here together.

They looked at the way that Jack had caught fish, and the hog traps and the rabbit traps, they were all amazed. The animals were not afraid of us because they were used to us being here, and we never hurt them. What amazed them the most was the hawks coming down to eat from Louise's hand, and the many blooming trees and wild flowers that lined the banks of Hidden Creek.

We started walking out at 4:00 in the morning and at mid night we reached my house.

We had no phone, so I was going to take the chief to town to call for their bus to come after them. My truck would not start because the battery was dead, they all pushed it fast enough to get it started and the phone call was made. Two hours later their bus was there to get them, and then they were gone.

Two weeks later the Indian bus drove up into my yard. The driver got out and knocked on my door and when I answered he handed me a letter from the chief of the Cherokee Nation. It was an invitation for a week's vacation in the hotel where we stayed before.

Louise and I took my old truck and went up there, neither of us had ever had a vacation before. As we gave the letter to the person in the front office, we were presented with the keys to a brand new Ford truck in my name and a $ 10,000.00 check in Louise's name. The check was made out to "Louise".

We spent the week there and paid for nothing.

When we got back home all Louise wanted was to go back to Hidden Creek so we went and stayed three months. It was not the same. We swam naked in the crystal clear water, but we both felt as though someone may be watching. We had lost our sense of privacy. What we cherished most was gone.

Early one morning when I woke up Louise was gone. I found her at the graves of her husband and daughter, she had been crying and when I walked up she told me that she was ready to go back to my house for a little while.

That day, we packed everything we had their into the cave that the Indians had left open for us to live in. I, at that time, had planned on the two of us being back here to spend a lot of time; I think Louise knew what was about to happen. She was reluctant to leave. I sensed something was not right, and I just let her make all of the decisions. She made two trips to the graves, and the second time I did not go, maybe she needed some time there alone. When she came back that time she just started walking down the trail that led us away from Hidden Creek.

Louise and I were there in my house together. The hawks were in the tall spruce pine behind my house and every day she called them down to eat out of her hand. Gradually she trained them to come and eat from my hand. They were nervous about it but after a week they were taking corn from me.

Three months after we left our Hidden Creek, Louise died in her sleep, the same way that Cindy did.

I had her body cremated, and then I made that last unhappy trip back to the place where we were content and at piece.

After spreading her ashes on Jack and Cindy's grave, I left Hidden Creek for the last time. It is a beautiful place but there is nothing there for me any longer, but beautiful memories.

## END OF STORY

## BEGINNNG OF THE END ©

### FICTION
### Author/narrator Larry English

This is a narration. A story told by the author. Did you ever wonder why the United States went bad so fast? It did not just happen; it had a lot of outside help from enemies of the United States Of America.

Other country's are taking the profits from us. We, in the United States pay a triple price for gasoline, other country's take that profit. They own the service stations, motels, restaurants and they own this country of ours.

It is not the millions of Mexicans in this country, that is doing this to us but all other countries send their people in thorough Mexico. WHAT IS THERE TO STOP THEM?

My name is Frank Fernandez, I worked for a well known news magazine, for 21 years. I wrote this story while I was working undercover, spying, on a group of what I thought to be a terrorist training camp. But I found out that they are not terrorist, but just as bad. They are training to take over the Government of the United States. They can and will do it legally, with no bloodshed, it will be done according to the rules and laws of the congress of the United States of America. It will be a complicated thing for me to do, but I will try to report this story to you, just the way that I happened upon it, and how I lived there, with them, for almost two years.

Somewhere in the most desolate part of New Mexico there is a huge camp. It is not an American camp. There are no Americans there. This camp is run by Russians, North Koreans and Cubans.

Several other countries help finance this undercover movement that is gigantic in size, and expense. Turkey has a big hand in this operation and so does Iran. and Afghanistan, Mexico has more people there, than any other country.

The Mexicans that live are being duped, or exploited. First they are given everything that they want. Then slowly they start being brainwashed. The Mexicans are taught how to deceive, and fool Americans into thinking that they are dumb and uncaring. This is the furthest thing from the truth. Some of the first Mexican people that was caught up in this undercover movement was in this camp for as much as four years. Then sent to places like Georgia, Florida, Washington State, and Illinois, places where a lot of farms are. They have been taught how to mix with the locals.

75 % of the females are pregnant when they leave here. They have been schooled on how to work the system in the United

States. They have been to school on how to get food stamps, they know what to ask for and who to ask. They work for cash and pay no taxes.

At the present time there are over 9,000,000 of them that has come into the United States and are being furnished medical and other support by us, the tax payers. The money that they earn is sent back to Mexico. This strengthens Mexico and weakens the United States. Yet millions of Americans cannot get the same help that the Mexicans are receiving. [when I say Mexicans I mean all nationalities that come thru this camp] This is why the other countries work so hard to support this movement. It is a plan to cause the United States of America to fail, and fall.

Many of our politicians know exactly why this is being done, and they know who is responsible, Not all of the people here are Mexican, a lot are Haitians. A few are Russians and they are highly trained. This country can, and will be taken over if this practice is allowed to continue. Senators and representatives that make up congress have too much power. Some of them for some reason, seem to want our country to fail.

In New Mexico the camp where all of this starts is a place that is operated by scientist, engineers, and cybernetics. Although this camp is in the United States, it is near the border, and for some reason that I do not know about, the leaders of the camp want to train people here and then go back into Mexico before entering the States. I know that the camp is South of Deming, and that most of the border crossing traffic into the United States is around Sonata.

When the leaders of the camp think a person is ready to leave the camp, and enter the United States many of them are given marijuana or cocaine to carry with them when they leave. This gives them a financial start, if they are successful in their entry. If they are not successful, they are just sent back to Mexico and soon they will try again.

What can they lose? Sooner or later they will make it and join the millions of others that receive all of the free benefits. Most of the females are made pregnant one or two months before they leave the camp. They will succeed because of the way the laws are written in the United States. Or rather, the way that there are no laws written.

Huge caves have been dug out under the mountains. Miles of caves that people live in. These caves are comfortable, they stay about 72 to 78 degrees all of the time. Every convenience is there for them to enjoy.

The time that these people are in this cave they go to school 6 to 8 hours every day. A very large part of this school is programmed as a brainwash, against the United States and we all know that this works.

The main reason for all of this is to gain population. Babies born in the United States are citizens. Mothers become citizens as soon as they can. Females stay pregnant and receive the free medical attention and delivery of the babies, after they are in America. In 1991 there are 9,000,000. Of them. They will double in 18 years. In cities like Gainesville, Georgia, they can win elections any time they want to. They were born in the U.S.A., lived on welfare, and went to school on welfare. They are smart people. A lot smarter than us American tax payers.

This is what the other Countries are after. For their trained Mexicans to get the most VOTES. It may be a Mexican they vote for, or it may be a Russian that has gained citizenship.

Remember, those Mexican kids receive the same education that our kids receive. The only difference is the lunches, school supplies, some of the books, and medical insurance that we parents pay for our children, but are free to them. Spanish, Russian and English and Chinese are taught to the children in these underground caves. Money is sent to the families back in Mexico, by this organization.

My parents were born and raised in the United States, my grandparents were born and raised in Mexico, and walked across the border into the United States in 19 35, and have been here ever since. In our family there are 41 people now. There were 5 in the family in 1935. And 8 have died during all of this time. I graduated from the University of Georgia and now work for a news magazine. I have Spanish blood in my veins, and I appear to be a Mexican, but I am an American, born and raised.

I did things different. I slipped across the border and entered Mexico. After 7 months, I ask to go into the organization that I am writing about. I probably would have been shot, if I had been found out, but I felt like I had to finish all of the training and then, slip back across the border with the thousands of other immigrants. Only one out of fifty are caught, and they are just sent back to Mexico, unless they get caught with dope.

The caves are nice and big, they are comfortable they have everything that a city in the United States has. It is much nicer than the towns in Mexico, that these people lived in. The food is the best. The living quarters are top notch, and all of this is part of the brain wash, a down turn towards the United States. I lived in the caves for 17 months, and with all of the schools and speeches, it made me wonder about my own allegiance to the United States of America.

After I got my own private room, which was about 6 months, I could take a wife and keep her in my room with me. A female had to be 14 years old before this could happen. Then they were checked by the doctor every 3 months. If they were pregnant, they would be prepared for the trip across the border.

Someone was in the know about the border patrol and what sections they would be working.

And the Mexicans that were ready to enter the States, knew the best places to cross. The bus loads would go there, and smaller groups would go to the hot spots, knowing that they may be caught and returned. The border patrol had to catch some of these people so it was planned who it would be. Some had made the trip 3 or 4 times. They were trained on how to be caught. Do not fight. Speak Spanish only. Cause no trouble. Do not run. Ask for water and food only. If a Spanish speaking person questions you, tell them you have been walking for several weeks. Have a name of a town ready to tell them, when they ask. Where did you live? Many times, if a border patrolman was alone, he ask for sex, and promises to let you go if you give him sex. Do not. He will probably kill you, before he leaves.

In the caves, everyone, had to work. The life they lived here, in the camp, was the best that they had ever had, so they did not mind the work. But the big prize for them was to get into the United States Of America. The education that they received here, in the camp, made each and every one of them more eligible to get jobs away from the local people, no matter what state you went to. This was for men. Every woman's duty was to produce babies. It made no difference who the father was. Marriage meant nothing. The only important thing here, was votes.

My biggest problem was trying to hide the fact that I have the education. That I had some money and that I was an American. After I slipped across the border and was in Mexico, I went to a town that was so small that it had no name, after 2 months I walked to a larger town and lived there until I ask to be in the organization. I had taken a wife, and I had bought a donkey. My new wife had a dog, so the four of us lived in a hut on the $6.00 a week that I earned working in a bar.

The people that came to question me about the organization, ask me one question. Why do you want to be in the organization? I told them that I wanted to cross the border and live in the United States. Everyone says that you can get me there. My donkey and my wife and her dog could not go, she was too old. I gave her a few dollars and the donkey, I left that same day with those 2 men on horseback, we went to another town that was larger, and there we were joined with 20 others that were coming into the organization. We were all interviewed, and I must say that I looked and talked more Spanish than any of the others. From there we rode in an almost new ford van to the guarded gate of the organizations caves.

Every person here had a job, I had told them that I was a farmer, so I went to work in the fields. I became a regular hand on the pepper farm. We grew what we eat. Plus they grew many acres of marijuana. If anyone was caught using this marijuana they were out of the organization permanently.

There were about 100 milk cows. 25 bulls, and several hogs. One chicken house with 5,000 chickens for eggs. This was a well planned place.

Within 2 months I was in charge of the pepper farm. I did not ever know this before, but in a place like this, peppers are a necessity, they prevent people from having worms. If people get worms, they spread very fast, and soon the people start dying. Pepper is used in the food to prevent this illness. 2,000 men and woman are here most of the time. When the timing is right, and the main force of the border patrol is to the south, as many as 500 people will cross the border into the United States and make their way as far north as they can. There are several places that these trained people, can catch an organization bus, and go all the way to Georgia. From there, it is no trouble to go on to any other state.

Sometimes a few will get caught and will be returned to the Mexican border and released. They know where to get a bus to be returned back to the organization, they have already been educated and trained, so they will be on the next shipment back to the States.

When a pregnant woman goes in to the

States, within 6 months she has a baby. In 14 years that baby has a baby. During that 14 years, the pregnant woman that slipped across the border, has had 12 more babies, that is 15 babies, multiply all of that times 300 that come across with the original woman and it is easy to see how we now have 9,000,000 people in our country, and their only purpose is to multiply, and go to school, and get welfare, and medical attention, and food stamps. All of the ones born here, are as much a citizen as we are. 1/3 of the others will earn the right to be here, they can vote. How long before we can be out voted?

Because of the job that I had there in the camp, I did have a few special perks, that not many others had. A large room to live in, my private toilet and shower, and my pick of the new girls that came in, and was not living with a man. All I had to do was ask for them. I also had a truck to drive back and forth to the pepper fields. Almost everyone walked back and forth, it was less than a mile, but after 10 hours in the fields, that is a lot. I gave all of my crew a ride, and was as nice to them as I could be, because I knew that very soon, I would need some help from them. I did not know exactly how, but I had to get away from here, and back to the United States. I could not even get my stories about this camp out to my company. They probably thought that I was dead.

My first move was to pick out a friend, a 2$^{nd}$ in command, someone that I could trust to drive the truck.

I need a rainy day to carry out my plan, and since we only get about 3 rainy days each year; it may be too long to wait, I need to get out of here soon.

The pepper fields are North of us. I am in the United States now, and any place I go to, if it is North, I can get help from the border patrol or any us. law officer The pepper fields just happen to be the last thing north in the organization. It is the end of the road. No highways or roads of any kind for 35 miles. I can walk the 35 miles in 3 days, if I do not get bitten by a side winder, or run out of water. It is a dangerous 35 miles.

I had to take nick into my confidence and tell him of my plan. He thought that I was crazy. What he did not know is that he wanted to slip into the States and live there, and I had slipped into Mexico.

Nick told me that he could get burrows for the 35 mile trip, across the part mountain, and part dessert trip. Nick wanted to leave with me. He said that when we get to any kind of a road that he would leave me, and go on his own, he had been in the camp just 2 months less than I had.

Arrangements were made for a member of the pepper crew, to drive the truck to its regular parking place, and leave it there. It was always almost dark when this crew come in, but to-day it was arranged for that truck to be 30 minutes later than usual.

Nick and I had a 5 day supply of water, and a

3 day supply of food. The borrows had a load to carry, without us riding.

We crossed the small stream that bordered the pepper fields. I had a compass that I had when I came here, and now I would really need it. Yesterday I had taken my bearings, using the compass and picking out a tall mountain to start walking towards. We reached the tall mountain at the end of the second day, and we still could not see anything. I knew that we were traveling in a straight line, but Nick thought that we were going in the wrong direction. I told Nick that he could change directions if he wanted to, but that I was going to continue just as planned. We slept at least 5 hours each night and walked the rest of the time. At the beginning of the third day, we all drank a belly full of water, and a meal. So did the borrows have water. We discarded everything that was emptied or not needed any longer. Then Nick and I rode the borrows, our plan was to ride them until they dropped, and save our legs and our strength. When we needed to we could walk at least 2, maybe 3 days, and prayed that we had found the road by then.

That night we were at the foot of a mountain that we had used for a bearing. We did this so that we would not be walking in circles. We had stopped for the night, to rest. Another day was gone. We still had water for one more day, but no food.

I laid down to sleep some, but then I decided to walk up that mountain for a little ways to see what I could see. I only walked about 100 yards, then, out there, not very far, and in the straight line that we were traveling, I saw lights, car lights moving fast, and several lights on buildings.

I went back to where Nick was asleep and did not disturb him. I knew that tomorrow we would be in some town, but for now all I knew, was that it would be in New Mexico, USA.

Next morning when we got up, Nick and

I had a big drink of water, and so did the borrows.

I ask Nick that if we got out of this place alive would he go with me, and tell where we had been for the past several months. And help me tell the story about the organization. He thought that I was crazier than ever, and he said "sure, I would be honored to do that for you."

We then started on the last 5 miles of our journey. We were 2 miles from a main road, when he first heard trucks on the road, then he said "you dirty bastard, you knew the road was here, when you tricked me into helping you, but I will help you if I can.

We divided the rest of the water 4 ways, and drank the last of all of the water. It was only a mouth full each. Then we discarded all of the water bags and sleeping blankets, keeping nothing. We rode the borrows on to a truck stop there on the road, and bought a bale of hay for them. Once they were tied under a shade tree, with plenty to eat, Nick and I went inside and ate.

We had access to showers, the truck stop sold clothing. We had made it this far, but Nick was still a wetback trying to enter the United States. I had carried my money for 2 years in my pocket and it was worn thin, you could hardly tell what it was.

I called my office in Atlanta. My boss thought that it was a joke of some kind, but he was hysterical when he realized that it was really me.

I had my records all in order. That afternoon the border patrol and the sheriff department was all there at the same time. Arrangements had been made for Nick to stay with me. The border patrol treated him like a celebrity, so did the sheriff department. 5 hours later my boss was there with all of the cameras and the writers for our magazine. We went to the nearest hotel before we started talking about what all had taken place, since I saw them last.

## stories about a Georgia moonshiner

Mr. Baker, my boss, instructed me to keep quiet about all that had happened, and Nick was ordered to do the same. 3 hours later we were all on a plane and on our way to Atlanta.

I really did not know the importance of what was going on. I had plenty of time to think about it, but I just did not realize the scope of the situation.

Nick and I each had a private room in a hotel. Trouble is, there were two Federal Agents in both of our rooms. It was like we were prisoners. All four of the agents spoke Spanish, and Nick and I could not even go down stairs to eat or to get a beer.

I was in another room in the same hotel, when I was interviewed. Everything I said was taped, and at the same time, I was wearing the lie detector wires. The lie detector went crazy when I was ask what I was doing in Mexico, later Mr. Baker helped me explain my slipping into Mexico, to do an undercover story.

The federal agents checked out my history twice. They did not believe that I was American, because I spoke perfect Spanish, and had every appearance of a Mexican. They double checked my dental records, and finger prints and my records at the University of Georgia, and my 22 year record with the publishing company. Then they accepted me as an American, but they acted as though they did not want to.

Nick had no trouble, he was Mexican. Nick admitted that his only purpose was to get into the United States. Any way that he could.

I was not allowed to attend any of the meetings that were now going on. Nick and I were still being treated like outcast, but we could see military officers, and what we thought to be F.B.I. men and women. Whatever they are planning is big. I hope that this is still my story, to complete. Mr. Baker and one army general come in and talked to Nick and I. They told us that Because the compound is in the United States, there is no quarrel with

Mexico, about this. They legally own the land, they had bought a 4,000 acre ranch, But what they are doing there is a violation. Federal authorities are going to go there and take over the organization and abolish it. I will go with them, I have been told. Nick does not go.

I was also told that this is my story, I will get credit for it, but others will help with the writing because it has to come out in the next few days. Other news organizations are already after the story.

The truth about the financing of that underground camp, has been verified, the F B I has already found where the money came from, and it involved 5 foreign countries.

All of the people that are in the caves where I lived for 17 months, are already in the United States. Just two miles from the Mexican border. We know that the F B I is going to take over the camp, but we do not know when.

I had gone down stairs for an hour today, and

when I got back Nick had gone. My wallet and all of my money was gone also. I called Mr. Baker and reported it to him. He notified the sheriff and the F B I. I guess Nick saw his chance to go further North.

Eight days after Nick left, I found out that I was going back to the caves with the sheriff department, and the F B I. It was just breaking daylight when we drove up to where the front gate was, when I went there the first time. No one was there, it was empty. We drove on into the caves and found a few people standing around not knowing what to do.

The leaders had left in cars. About 1500 of the people living in the camp had started walking across the desolate place that Nick and I had crossed. All of the others had gone back into Mexico, they will cross the border soon.

The F B I went on into Mexico and searched for the car that had five people in it. They were found in just one day, and are now in jail in New Mexico.

Nick has not been heard from since he left. One time back there in the camp, Nick told me that if he ever could, he would go to Colorado and work on a ranch. I hope he did and I hope he is happy.

My story was a hit. It was true, and it happened here under our nose. That organization did not send 9,000,000 people across that border into the United States, but it did send thousands, while I was there.

20 years from now we may be out voted. We may have a president from some other country, and congress may speak different languages. This may be the BEGINNING OF THE END.

### THE END

## THE COUNTRY WAY ©

**By Larry English**

**This story is about two young boys that grew up in the hills of North Carolina. Their home was between Franklin N.C., and Dillard, Georgia. Almost the entire road going to their home was in Georgia but the dirt road curved north and crossed the state line. Part of their farm was in Georgia, and part in North Carolina, but the house was in North Carolina.**

**Some parts of this story may be true. Some parts may be raunchy, but it does show how a country boy can succeed if he has just a little bit of help.**

Tom lived almost two miles down the road from our house. He lived with his mother and father and a brother George; George had been in the Army and was kicked out for some reason. I overheard the family talking about it but never did find out why they put him out of the Army. George was six years older than Tom; Tom was one year older than I was.

The nearest neighbor in the other direction was four miles from our house, and six miles from Tom's house. The Burrell's had two girls, age fourteen and fifteen years old. The Burrell's also had a still that he made whiskey on and sold it in town every Saturday. Everyone knew this; he had been doing it for years. Saturday is when everybody went to town. Mr. Burrell had a truck and his family would come by our house and whoever wanted to go to town he would give a ride. There were only four houses on the road from the Burrell's house to town. Tom and I were on the truck just about every Saturday morning.

It cost 10 cents for a ticket to get into the

movies. Popcorn was 5 cents. Tom and I paid the Burrell girls way to the movie every time we could, because it would be dark as we went home and we were covered with blankets in the back of the truck. It was a perfect time to touch the girls and they did not seem to care; as a matter of fact, they liked it. The girls were two years older than Tom and I.

The first time we did anything, Tom and his girl was in the feed room of the barn, and my girl and I were in the loft, lying in the hay. It was her that led us on because I just did not know what to say or do.

Tom's mother had a sister that came to live with them; she was at least ten years older than both Tom and I, but she was the prettiest woman that I had ever seen. I compared her with the pictures of girls in the sears catalog, and she was prettier than any of them, but she was much too old for me; she must be at least twenty.

To make money Tom and I would help farmers

mow hay and stack it in the field. Sometime we shelled corn; we did whatever they wanted us to do and most of the time we would make at least $5.00 per day. If we had $10.00 in our pocket on Saturday, we knew that we would have a good time. We could get everything we wanted in town, and then on the ride home we really had fun. Although we knew that we had to walk back to our house, we would ride with the Burrell's on to their house, and see if the girls could stay outside for a while; and most of the time they could.

One night one of the girls asked if we had ever seen a still, and we both said no. Both girls said come on and we will show you one. It was only a ten-minute walk from their house and while we were there we got a gallon of the whiskey. We stopped for a while to talk, and while talking, we all took a sip of the whisky, then another sip, and soon we were all high.

On the way to the still we walked across a foot log over a wide creek, and when we got back to the foot log none of us could walk across it, because we were too high. We all four pulled off our clothes and waded the water, we all four were naked and on the other side, we lay in the grass for a while before going to the house. After drying off some Tom and I walked the girls back to their house and they went right in; we walked part of the way home and ran part of the way. When we got to my house, Tom just come in and slept on the couch. The next morning we were up and gone before my mother and dad got up, then we went into Toms house just as they were fixing breakfast. Toms aunt was cooking. She had a robe on and it was not buttoned in front all the way and I could see her body. I tried not to look, I couldn't help it; she knew that I saw her and that I was trying to see more.

When we started to eat breakfast, George comes to the table and he smelled like an old drunk. He was drinking last night and his breath was terrible. His dad told him to go outside and eat and he did, but he was mad about that and I thought him and his dad was going to fight, but they did not fight.

## AUNT BETTY AND ME

Tom's dad had a team of mules, and one of the things Tom had to do was feed and water the mules, so we went to the barn and he led one mule and I led the other one to the creek for water. When we got back to the barn, aunt Betty was there and she wanted to ride the mule, but she was afraid and wanted me to ride with her, and I said okay.

After the short ride we come back to the barn, and Tom had gone and left me out there with his aunt. When I went into the feed room to get corn for the mule, she was on me; she almost raped me, but it was not too hard to do.

I felt guilty as I walked into their house with Tom's Aunt but no one thought anything about it. That afternoon as Tom and I were

369

walking back to my house he asks me if I got it, and I told him no.

I was in the 10<sup>th</sup> grade in school and I was totally in love with Tom's aunt Betty. I did not care that she was a lot older than I was; she is the woman that I wanted to be with and I knew that she wanted me to. But, on Saturday morning, I got up early and went over to Tom's house and there was a car there. I had never seen that car there before. As I walked up on the porch I saw thru the window, and some man was kissing Tom's aunt Betty. The rest of the family was out in the back yard; I could hear them out there. I stopped and watched thru the window for a minute and he was touching her all over; then they come out thru the front door right by me and did not even speak. They got into the car and left. They were gone for a week, and when they returned they said they were married. In a few days she moved out of the house and moved in with that man; occasionally I would see him in town and sometimes she was with him.

Summer time was coming to an end. The leaves on the trees started turning colors and I had to study more and more for the test that was coming up. I could get out of some things that I was supposed to do, but my grades in school was not one of them, a "b" was no good on the report card. I got what I wanted at home but that "A" must be there; nothing else was acceptable. My dad had completed the 10th grade in school, and my mother quit in her senior year, and the big thing with them was my education. I just could not disappoint them. Any lesson that I had a problem with had to be studied at school during study hall, so that I could get help from a teacher, the other lessons I did at home and it would take at least two hours each day.

Saturdays I always found a job. This Saturday I was going to talk to Mr. Burrell about a regular job with him, because I know that he has a lot of work to do. When I ask Mr. Burrell for the job he looked at me and smiled. He said do you want to work, or do you want to be around my daughters? I knew he was no dummy; so I said, "I like your daughters, but I want to work and I need the money to go to school". He hired me and I went to work that day. I worked along with him; whatever he did, I helped.

Their farm was at the end of a rough dirt road. Behind their house there was thirty miles of woods, steep mountains with a lot of streams and some big creeks. On this side of the creek there was about forty acres of cornfields. There was a foot log there to cross over the creek. I had been across that foot log and I had waded that creek, but Mr. Burrell did not know that; both of his daughters were there with Tom and I when we went to the still. We worked all day until dark and he paid me before I left to go home. He was a very hard worker and he informed me that on Saturdays I would have a list of things to do there on the farm, but he had to be in town on most Saturdays; and he could tell by the amount of jobs completed from the list, if I was working or not.

My time was fully taken up. I often wondered why my life was so different than the other boys in school. They were on the ball teams and went to parties and seem to always have fun. They lived in town and had every fun thing there was and I had to work all the time and had nothing, it just did not seem right. After the third or fourth Saturday that I worked with Mr. Burrell, he ask me if I could stay later and help with a special job, and of course it will be extra money. I had an idea what it was but I never let on that I had already been to the still, because if I did, the girls would really be in trouble. Late in the afternoon we went to the barn. Behind the barn was an old building and inside the building there were several ten-gallon barrels. Mr. Burrell got a barrel and told me to get one. We walked out the trail to the foot log, crossed over the creek and then the ten-minute walk to the still. He worked there for a few minutes with me not knowing what he was doing. Then he told me to go and get all of those barrels and bring them over here, we need all of them, and there was six more barrels in the building.

When I got back to the building the youngest daughter was there, the one I was with before. We had sex, and we had to do it in a hurry because Mr. Burrell knew how long it took to make that trip. I made two more trips, and then on the third trip, the oldest daughter was there, she asks where Tom was and I told her that he was home, she just said tell him that I said hi, and then she went home. I worked four or five weeks this way. Then when I went to work on Saturday morning very early, he told me to get into his truck and we drove twenty miles into Franklin. He stopped in a car lot and went in and bought a 1937 Ford, and put it in my name. He told me that I was a good worker and he felt sorry for me having to walk home after working so hard. He said it is not a gift; you can pay me back anytime you want too. It cost $ 320.00 and it was a great little car.

I had it in my mind that I would marry that girl, and that I would live on that farm, and eventually would own at least part of the farm. Things did not turn out that way. Before the end of the school year the oldest sister run away with the druggist over in Franklin. He was older than her and had a son that was two years old. She became the cashier in the drug store, that is what his wife did before she died. All thru my senior year I worked on the Burrell farm; all day on Saturday and at least one day during the week and sometime one night, I did not always help in the still, Mrs. Burrell worked sometime and I did not have to help. I was on the farm alone on Saturdays while all of their family went to town; then I would go to town about six o clock and Ruth would wait and go to the movie with me, and I would take her home in my 1937 ford coupe.

One month before school was out in 1944, Ruth told me that she had dated a ball player from down in Ga. And they were getting married. The guy she was going out with played basketball in Atlanta for a college. I know this because I intended to give him a good butt kicking. I went to the Burrell home one night and he was there and they were setting in front of the house in the car. I was mad and really ready for a fight, so I knocked on the car door on his side of the car. He got out and he just kept unfolding; he was at least seven feet tall. I just stuck out my hand to shake hands and introduced myself to him, and said that Ruth had told me about you and I wanted to wish you good luck. He was a nice guy and a lot to big to pick a fight with. For two years almost we had been having fun, our way, and for some reason, I just thought it would be forever.

I kept working for Mr. Burrell all thru the summer after Graduation. I was valedictorian of our class, Mr. Burrell told me to forget about paying for the car that it was a present to me. He told me in a very low voice, that he had hoped that I would be his son-in-law, and "I still wish you were".

Tom and I had not been seeing much of each other for the past year because we did not have time, but he was a very close friend. Tom had broken his foot while working in a sawmill three or four years ago, and that was keeping him out of the army. He wanted to go but they would not let him. Not the case with me. If I did not get into college soon I would be drafted. I did not have the money to go to college, but my grades would get me a scholarship; but would I get it in time? Tom and I had both been so busy for the past year that we had not been any place to-gather. We had seen each other in town and talked some but that is all. But this Saturday was different. We both had time, and we both had some money in our pocket and I had a good car. We decided to go to South Carolina and buy some beer, so that is just what we did. We got a washtub and put it into the trunk of the car, then we went to Walhalla and bought two cases of Schlitz, and iced it down in the tub in the trunk of my 1937 Ford coupe.

# TOM'S BROTHER

We started drinking about dark and at daylight we only had four or five beers left. We had gone into a restaurant in S.C. and eat a big steak dinner just before we started back home; Tom started drinking then, but I did not drink until we got back to N.C. because of me doing the driving. When Tom started getting high he started talking about Ann, Ruth's sister. I never did know that he was hurt that bad, he had never mentioned it before, but he really was hurt. Not long after that, he threw up in the floorboard of my car, and we stopped by a stream and he cleaned it up. For some reason we both just wanted to drink, and we stopped at a picnic table and drank all of the beer. It was 10:30 Sunday morning when I woke up, and Tom was still asleep. He was on the picnic table and I was in the car lying across the front seat.

Then things changed and our Sunday turned bad. When we were one mile from Toms house the Sheriff come up behind us with the siren on. I pulled over because I knew that I was caught driving drunk, and I was already sick, and I sure did not need this. I set there waiting to be arrested, or whatever they were going to do to me, but the Sheriff passed us up and kept going down the road towards our house. They stopped at Tom's house. Five minutes ago Tom was close to being drunk; but now he was as sober as he could be. We went into the house and got the terrible news. Toms Father had shot and Killed Tom's brother.

George had come home drunk and started a quarrel with his dad and his Mother. George was shot in the stomach with a shotgun. They said that he died instantly. No one was arrested at that time. During that time, it was reported that George had been kicked out of the army for fighting while being drunk. The report said that he went crazy when he drank and wanted to hurt people. The investigators said it was self-defense and there would be no charges. At least I was glad of that. That was the last time that I was ever drunk. I did not realize how stupid it was not to be in control of your senses; but the night that Tom and I got plastered on beer, was enough to last me for a lifetime.

A few weeks after that Tom moved over on the coast of N.C. to work in a shipyard. I heard about him a few times thru his mother and dad; they both said that he sends money to them every month. They both also said, that he had told them about us being drunk that night, and that he has now joined the Church, and has not drank any since that Saturday night, they both said that Tom was always a good boy.

A few years ago Tom's dad, and Tom and I went on a camping and fishing trip. Deer season was open so we went to a place that had both fish and deer. It was a beautiful place but it was way back in the mountains. We had to wade across a river that was about seventy-five feet across and at one place it was three feet deep. To get all of our camping gear across, we all had to make two trips. On the second crossing Tom's dad fell into the river and all of his clothes got wet and he lost his rifle. All three of us were out in the river looking for the rifle and we finally found it. It was November and the water was ice cold. We started a fire and dried his clothing out. Next morning as we were cooking breakfast a big doe came up close to the camp and Tom shot it. We dressed it and hung it high in a tree to keep other animals from getting it. That morning I killed a buck and Tom's dad killed a buck. We had only been there one day and we had all the meat we wanted, so we just lay around the camp and eat. The next day we all three went fishing. We all had a short line wound up on a stick in our pocket, and we had brought red worms with us. We cut a sourwood pole from the riverbank to fish with and caught more fish than we could eat. We had taken salt, pepper, and flour already mixed together in a can to cook fish and to roll the deer steak in. We had a fry pan and a slab of side meat for grease; we had all we needed. Turkeys were plentiful, we could have killed as many as we wanted, but it was too much trouble to carry all of it out, besides that we had all the game we needed from the edge of the corn fields at home, we just wanted to go camping. My dad loved to hunt and fish but it seemed like bad luck followed him. The first time the two of us ever went hunting; he did not have a hunting license. The first day we were there, the game warden stopped my dad and as we were walking down the road going to the place we were going to hunt. He stopped to check my dad's license and dad did not have a license. As the warden was writing a ticket, the two of them got into an argument because the gun was not loaded, and we were not in the woods yet? My dad asked him why he was writing a ticket? The warden told him because you have the gun with you. My dad told him then why don't you get me for rape, because I have my dick with me too. They fought and my dad won. But he had to go to court and he had to pay a $50.00 fine.

## stories about a Georgia moonshiner

My dad was not a drinker usually, but the group that he hunted and fished with was. The only drinking I ever saw him do was in the woods hunting or on the riverbanks fishing. In the wintertime we would have a fire in a barrel. The water was deep there where the river ran into the lake, and several of us would set on the bank and fish and eat and talk and just have a good time. We caught fish and cooked and eat them there on the bank of the Tallulah River where it went into Burton Lake. I never drank any beer or whiskey but all the men did. I was only nine or ten years old.

We had a 1931 ford and it was a good one. It would take us right down to the river; sometime we had to put chains on and sometime we had to push a lot but it was worth it. I often thought of the rich kids not getting to do things like this, but they did things that I did not get to do, I would not take anything for my memory of those times.

Mr. Burrell bought the livestock from my dad

so he would have the money to send me to school. The $1,000.00 loan was given to my dad also. It made my dad feel better about it, he kind of saved face. No matter what Mr. Burrell did it turned out good? He is the only farmer I know of that made money farming. The sideline of his was pure profit. My streak of good luck was when he took a likening to me. If he had ever found out that his daughter and I had been together I wonder if it would have changed his mind. I doubt it, because he was an extra special kind of man. He gave the land where the church is built, to the church. Then he worked every day on the church building until it was completed. He let me know that I had help if I needed it. I still had my 1937 ford when I went to South Carolina to start college. I worked part time on campus and scrimped and did without all that I could. My dad had brainwashed me into thinking that a "B" was no good so I strived for the "A", and I got it.

Every time that I had as much as five days off I went home. I worked either on my dad's farm or Mr. Burrell's farm. Some days I would not even see the Burrell's to talk to them; I knew what was to be done so I just did it.

When I left to return to school my car would be loaded with can goods they had canned, or a ham, or a side of bacon. What made me feel good was Mr. Burrell saying "I enjoy working with you".

During my third year of college my mother passed away in may of 1948, and in my fourth year of college, my dad passed away the last week of October. I had just received a letter telling me about the hunting trip we were going on at thanksgiving time. Two days later I got an emergency phone call telling me the news. Neither of them was there to see me graduate, and it was for them that I wanted to do well, because they wanted it so much.

In the fall of 1950 I graduated with honors. I was proud, but not like I would have been if Mom and Dad had been there. Mr. Burrell was there. I wanted a master's degree but before I could apply to any school, the United States Air Force contacted me, and offered me a commission and an opportunity to further my education. I accepted their offer. In one year I had been in three schools in three different states. Then I went to California for flight training and was there for over eighteen months. During my second year I received 1st Lt. Grade, and upon graduating from flight training and getting my wings I was made Captain. At that time I was informed that I would go to Florida for combat training, and that I had forty-five days leave time coming. I got to North Carolina as fast as I could get there. My 1937 ford was in the shed behind our house and it started right up, but I had a long hill for it to roll down. My first stop was to see Mr. Burrell. I knocked on the door, and Ruth opened the door. Standing beside Ruth was a boy that was seven or eight years old. As I spoke to her Mr. Burrell walked up. He hugged me and he cried. He was frail and skinny and looked sick. He said, "I prayed that you would be home soon".

I ask Ruth where her husband was and she said that he is not here. She did not say any more about him.

We all had some cake and coffee and set there and talked for an hour or so. I was not in uniform; I had on my old jeans that I had worn in college. No mention was made of my rank or my job, or when did I have to go back; not that night. I was invited to breakfast the next morning and I was there an hour early. I went thru the barn and cornfields and down by the river just like they were mine, I felt completely at home. I wanted to talk to this family because they were the only things left, that was anything like family to me. I was also in a hurry to go find out about Tom.

As we all set at the breakfast table I brought them up to date on my past few years. I did not mean to talk so much about me, but they just kept asking questions. What I wanted to know was all about Mr. Burrell's health. He informed me that his health was fine, and he felt dam good to be seventy-six years old and still run this farm. He also told me that he had quit the still. He has made no whiskey in over two years. He said " I ran that still for thirty years and furnished all the whiskey for judges, sheriffs, attorneys and anyone else that wanted it." I quit while I was ahead.

When Mr. Burrell went to the barn to milk and feed the animals, Ruth told me all about her husband. They had only lived to-gather for six months. She was pregnant when they got married, but at that time she was not sure about it. She said that he did not touch her until after they were married. She said that she was 100 percent sure that David was my son, because until then I was the only one that she had ever been with. And since the divorce there has been no one in her life. She told me that Roy, her husband, knew that she was pregnant, and left her in Atlanta and her dad sent her money to live on. She has been living here for two years.

When Mr. Burrell came back into the house, I ask him about Tom and his mother and dad. Tom's parents were both dead and Tom moved back home about six months ago, he lives in the home place now.

Ruth's sister still worked in the drug store. I knew that I would get the right answers from her, so I left and told Ruth and her dad that I would be back later. I went straight to Franklin to the drug store. Ann was there working and she had diamond rings on the fingers of both hands; you would never think that she was the farm girl that I knew a few years ago. I just come right out and ask her about David, did she think that he was my son? Her answer was "why hell yes, everyone knows that he is." Look in the mirror then look at him, it's not hard to tell. There is no question about it. And I'll tell you something else, Ruth knows for sure. On my way back up big creek road I really paid attention to the roads. They are paved now. They are smooth, and the places where we did get stuck, now are in great shape. A lot of improvement has been made and the trip does not seem so far. I have not noticed until now, but there are a lot more houses built up here than there were before.

I stopped at Tom's house. He was in the back yard setting in the swing. I was driving my 37 Ford and when he saw me pull into the driveway, he got up and slowly walked to the front yard. He walked like he was a hundred years old, but he is really just one year older than I am. He did not recognize me until I got out of the car, then he said, "yes sir, can I help you?" Then he smiled great big and told me that he thought that I was dead. He was so proud to see me, and I found out that he really did think I was dead. We talked for four or five hours. We told each other all of our secrets and all that we had done for the past four or five years. He said that arthritis had got into his bad leg, and between the injury and the arthritis he could hardly walk. He gets a check from the sawmill company every month to live on, and he had inherited the farm and he just gets by.

He also said that "you may not know it yet"

but you have a son over at the Burrell's home. I saw him and his mother down in Clayton. I was setting in the car and they walked down the street in front of us and he is exactly like you made over. I had not seen or heard from you in five or six years, there was nothing I could do, but remember this, I was there with you and Ruth when this was happening. I left in a big hurry for I wanted to get to the Burrell home as soon as possible. Ruth and David were setting on the front porch on the steps. I ask where her Dad was and she said that he was at the barn, I almost ran to the barn because I desperately wanted to talk to him. He was shelling corn to feed the chickens and he stopped when I walked up. I ask if we could set and talk some, and he said "sure". I started by telling him how much I appreciated all of his help thru the years. Then I told him that I had always wanted to be in his family, and how I always just took it for granted that I would be, because for two years Ruth and I had been to-gather; and he stopped me right there. He said I know all of that. And I know that David is your son. And you know that I love you and David as much as I do my own two children. If you and Ruth agree on something, we will get this family mess straightened out.

We went back to the house and I ask Ruth if we could go out, and she said "yes". In an hour we left. By midnight we were back home and our plans were made. Sunday in church we would announce our wedding. It would be the following Sunday afternoon in the church. A very special invitation would be hand delivered to Tom.

I contacted the base in Florida to ask permission to be married and it was granted, as I was government property now. It was 1950 and our life was just starting, for Ruth and I, it was a restart.

The Burrell farm was 120 acres. 60 acres was on the other side of the creek and was all woods. Nice flat Land at the foot of a steep mountain, but had never been cleared of trees. The other side of the creek was all bottom land; flat rich bottom land that would grow anything.

My captain's pay in the Air Force was good. I had not spent any money in a while because I had not needed anything, but now I am going to buy Fred Burrell a new car. He had loaned me $ 1,000.00 for college, and never would accept the money back, so now Fred is going to get a new car. In Franklin a new ford was $2,225.00. I bought it and had it delivered to the Burrell home. When the salesman took it to Fred Burrell, Fred just looked at it and said, "I had rather have a tractor". So then and there Fred traded for a new ford tractor. He is on the tractor from daylight till dark every day. He has always had money and could have had that tractor any time he wanted it, but I think he was loyal to the team of mules that he farmed with. Also he was getting older and so were the mules getting older.

I have a lot of business to take care of before the wedding, and before I have to leave to go back to base in Florida.

# THE WEDDING

When my parents passed away I inherited the farm. It is a good solid house and 60 acres of land, but I want to put in an indoor bathroom and running water in the kitchen. The house is fifty years old and has never been painted. I want to fix it up for Ruth and David and me.

Everybody is all dressed up for church on this special Sunday morning. This is the first time that I have been in uniform since I have been home. Ruth and her dad both said we knew that you were a captain in the Air Force, but we did not realize it until we saw those bright shiny bars on your collar. They also did not fully understand about the wings that I wore, and what they meant and what all I had to do to earn those wings. A jet pilot is sort of a new breed, and people just do not realize what it takes to do this job. Especially country people like we are. Church went well, the announcement was made and the wedding was planned for next Sunday. Everyone was invited. Fred Burrell was the happiest person in the church. Tom was there setting right up near the front row.

On Sunday afternoon I explained to everyone in our family that when I returned to base, that I would be gone for at least a year. I have one year in Florida for training, and then three months in California for training, and then I am not sure where I will be.

Ruth told me that her dad was too old to be left there alone and her and David would help him run both farms until I got out, that is not what I wanted but for now it will have to do. I have never seen so much difference in a farm, since Fred got the new tractor. He has almost run out of anything to plow. He told me that he was going to start on my fields next week. If he plants that in corn I don't know what we will do with all of it, sell it I guess.

During the week before the wedding I drove my 37 ford to town and got the best paint job I could buy and new seat covers and tires. Everything else was good; I had rather have this ford as a brand new one. It will set in the garage until I get back home.

The wedding was as good as it could be, except it rained almost all day. Ruth and I went to Atlanta and stayed four days, and we only have two more days before I have to leave.

My base is only one day's drive from home, but I am so busy that I can't even think about going home. We start training at six thirty in the morning and at nine or ten that night we are usually still going. This week I have been in Washington State and New Mexico and that is besides all the training we have done in Florida.

When I come into the air force they promised me the chance to further my education. This week they called me into the office and told me that I could sign up for school, but that I could not start until this advanced training was completed, because it was critical to the defense of our country.

They wanted me to meet with General Thomas for a review of my records. I met with the general for forty-five minutes. He told me that it was customary to grant the request for advanced education, when a person that comes into the service that already has a degree and the desire for a masters or a doctorate. Your case is special. You are at the right place at the wrong time. We have the making of a war starting in Korea. The Jet pilot is much needed for this country.

The general went on to ask me if I would consider changing my request for school to a request for advanced training in the security field. He told me that I would still probably have to fly some in Korea, but he would issue orders to have me checked out on every heavy bomber that we have and later you will find out why. Then he said, "What we have planned for you is top secret." You are not free to discuss anything with anyone concerning this meeting or this discussion. And you will only hear from me personally about this.

I completed my combat training and then I went to Cannon AFB in New Mexico. There I flew all over the country in different heavy bombers. It was like this for eight months, and then I was ordered to Korea in an f-80 C. After twenty-five missions and six months I received orders to report to general Thomas at Andrews A F B In MD. I also had a sixty-day leave. I flew straight into Moody AFB and started my leave. Two days before I left Korea I was awarded the rank of major. I got a hop into Atlanta and Ruth was there to meet me. She was driving Fred's new ford that he had bought, she said that she could not change the gears on my 37 Ford.

We stayed in Atlanta five days before we went on to North Carolina. Everything looked the same as it did when I left. I left in May and returned in May, twenty-four months later.

After my hectic schedule for the past two years, this farm living and all of this quietness is getting to me. I started getting up at six and working five hours before breakfast. Then I worked from four o clock until dark.

Fred had really been working a lot but on the two farms there is much to do. If Ruth wants to go anyplace we will quit work and go, we can do that at any time, but she likes it at home. After five weeks at home, the sheriff knocked on our door. He told me that I had a phone call coming in at his office to-day at five o clock and he had come after me, to be sure that I was there to receive it. The sheriff ask me if I was a-w-o-l and I told him no, he said that is the only time that I get this kind of request from the military, let's go see what it is.

It was a call from general Thomas. He said that "we need to talk in private and did I

have a good place here to bird hunt"? I said, "
Yes I do have a good place." He said, "tell no
one that you are going to have company" and
I may see you soon. It was soon. The very
next day a car pulled into the driveway. The
General was alone and in old civilian clothes.
He first said we will not talk business at the
house or if anyone is nearby. I am just a friend
that you served with and I am on my way to
Florida so I stopped by to visit you.

Next day we went bird hunting. I never
had bird hunted before. Deer, Turkey, Bear,
squirrel and Rabbit but not birds. We went
across the creek behind Fred's house and the
General was impressed with the beautiful
wild countryside; he said now I see why they
call you country boy. We set on a log and
talked.

After we had talked for five minutes it was
plain to see that my life was going to change,
and it looked like it was going to change in a
fast hurry. The General told me some of the
changes that were about to take place. He

ask my permission to stay on the farm with me for three more days, and there was just no way that I could turn him down. He said his reason for wanting to stay was because we had more privacy right here than any place in the world that we could go. However I think he just wanted a place to bird hunt, and he let it be known that he wanted to fish in the creek. He said that he had not fished since he was twelve years old.

As soon as I get back to base, I would be promoted to a bird colonel, because the job required that rank. I would never be in contact with anyone but General Thomas. I would never take an order from anyone else but him. I would have top security clearance to go to any base in the world, and check out any plane that I needed, and a crew also. No one outside the White house or pentagon would have any information on me. My only contact would be General Thomas. My job was to check the security of military air bases, Army, Navy, Marines, and Air Force. It would be a full time job. I had the freedom of picking a crew and keeping the same crew all the time or changing crews when I wanted too. I decided to pick a crew and keep them all of the time for security reasons. I wanted combat veterans so I contacted the ones I had served with in Korea, all they knew was we were always on a secret mission, and we had the freedom to go where ever we wanted to go and no one ever knew where we would show up.

After discussing most of the details, the general ask if we could take one day and work on the farm and that suited me just fine. I turned the general over to Fred to work with the next day. Fred called him Thomas, and treated him like a hired hand. They both got along good to-gather, and Thomas run the tractor for ten hours. At the end of the day Thomas eat like a hired farm hand. He enjoyed being on the farm. His last day there Ruth and the General and I went to Franklin in the 37 ford, we had a nice steak dinner and went back to the farm. Next morning I got up at five thirty and the General was already gone. I wanted to tell Ruth and Fred what was going on, but I knew that I never could. They knew something special was up, but they also knew not to ask.

# WORLD WIDE SECURITY

It was 1956 already; David was thirteen years old and his only job was to get that 'A'. I gave him the same brainwash that my dad gave to me, and I know how important it is. Nothing will take the place of knowledge. It will open all doors.

Fred insisted that we all stay with him for this last week that I would be home. Ruth's sister showed up one afternoon and about an hour later Mr. Lovell, the attorney, knocked on the door. Fred said that he was dividing the farm up between the two girls. Ann immediately said she wanted no part of this farm, so Fred gave it all to Ruth, knowing that David would get his part. Ann said that her husband had more money than they could ever spend, she did not need it.

# stories about a Georgia moonshiner

I saw the General when I got back to base. It was the first day back at the base after my leave was over. He mostly talked about how beautiful it was in North Carolina, but he turned the military air base security check over to me. I was commander of a unit that sometime had only one person. And has never had over 12 personal at one time. On my first job I decided to check out an air base that was not too far away. I was not totally sure how this was going to work because after all this was a new thing even for the military. Here in Florida I checked out an f-80 c, a two-passenger jet and a co-pilot. We went to Louisiana and landed at England AFB. We were not challenged either in the air or on the ground. Upon taxiing the plane up to the hanger area I ask to see the commanding officer. He was not on the base. I did not know what to do, so I called General Thomas. When I reported to him he immediately ordered me and the co-pilot to get quarters there for the night. Next morning the General was there and they sent for me to come to his office. The Commanding Officer was a close friend of General Thomas. It was a surprise security check. The very first one. The Commanding Officer was also a Major General.

They both agreed that this was a wonderful idea and that it should have been done long ago. I was ordered to proceed with my security checks and to do it just like I did this one. General Thomas said that within thirty minutes every base commander in the world will be warned and this better never happen again. If it does you are to arrest the commanding officer and call me. This was the correct way to check security.

I filed a flight plan back to home base in Florida. When you file a flight plan they expect you, they know you are coming and when you will be there. If you do not file a flight plan, no one knows where you are. I took it upon myself to give everyone involved time to set up his or her own ground security system. No one knows but me when another check will be made. I made a request for five of the men that I was with in Korea to be transferred here. The last one will be here in four days. I also have a request in for a B-52 bomber. The reason I requested the B-52 was that it is new and two of the Men I requested and myself have been checked out on the B-52. Everyone on the ship will be a combat veteran.

Our first flight was to England AFB in Louisiana. We went in unannounced and with no Flight plan filed. We dropped down from 40,000 feet in a fast decent to try and surprise them. We landed and taxied off of the runway. When we opened the door we were looking out at three 50-caliber machine guns and a platoon of small arm weapons. We were all arrested and taken to h.q. under guard. My credentials were in order and in five minutes we were free to go, but we stayed the night in officers' quarters. After refueling we took off and headed for Travis A F B In California. We approached in the same manner only this time we were challenged in the air ten miles before reaching the base. We were surrounded from the time our ground speed got down to seventy miles per hour. This time we were held under guard until the next morning, then fed and released. As a commanding officer of a unit in the United States Air Force, no matter how small it is; it is not good to be in a situation where you do not know exactly what to do. This is how I felt at Travis AFB, when we were challenged and arrested and held overnight. I called the general and requested a meeting. He told me to go bird hunting for a few days. I knew what he meant so the crew and I left for Florida, stopping in Barksdale, La. For a security check, we were challenged so we refueled and went on to Florida. The next morning I gave the crew a ten-day leave and I left for North Carolina. General Thomas got there the day after I did. My son David and the general had become the best of friends, and they both stayed at Fred's house with him.

All four of us took cane poles and red worms and fished the creek behind Fred's house. Ruth carried us up the creek to the end of the road and dropped us off, and we fished all the way back down the creek to our house. Four miles of fishing and we all had caught a string of trout; that night we had a real fish fry. There was no talk of business on this fishing trip.

I ask the general if he had ever seen a moonshine still before and he said no. He got real excited and said can we see one? I had planned to talk to the general about business while we were at the still, but Fred invited himself to go with us so business had to wait.

I suggested that we use two F-80 C's for all over sea's checks. We can do two bases at a time with only four men. He said to use one F-80 C and just keep two men on standby and let them rotate. You go when you want too, but between the three of you it will be easy enough. Then we can bird hunt some. I was given a security card of top clearance to show any one challenging my crew or me. We got to Tom's house and we set there and drank a few beers, and it took all day for us to tell the general about the good times and the bad times that we have had. The more Tom drank the better Tom's foot got. Tom got pretty drunk, then he threw up and I told him, the last time I was out with you, you got drunk and threw up in my car. He said, "Oh hell that is right I had forgot about that", and he just laughed. We all three had the same amount to drink that night and we all three were pretty well looped, and we all three kind of went to sleep there in Tom's living room. As the sun come up over the mountain it woke me up and I got into the old ford and drove the two miles to my house. Ruth started cooking breakfast, and the smell of bacon frying almost made me sick, but I fought the feeling off and managed to eat some breakfast, then I was o.k. About mid afternoon Ruth and I drove back over to Tom's house to see how they were. We pulled the car around behind the house because the swing and chairs were there under the big oak tree where Tom usually set. They were not there and they were not inside the house and we could not find them, wherever they were they had to walk because they had no car. A few minutes later we heard Tom's dog barking up on the mountain, we knew the dog would be with Tom, so we walked toward the barking dog.

Sometime during the morning they made a deal For Jack to buy ten acres of land on the backside of Tom's property. Tom had sixty acres, and the northwestern corner was a hollow with a hickory flat just above it. The spring was on these ten acres that furnished the water for Tom's house. Jack was going to build a log house on the property, and Tom was going to oversee the building. All of this was in the talk stage right now, but they were serious. Jack was a graduate of the Air Force academy and a two star general. Tom did not finish high school. Both were honest people. In the entire world these were my two best friends. I had nothing to do with making the deal but they both ask me to help with overseeing the surveying of the land and the transferring of the deed and the building of the house, I did not mind doing it, I felt like I would be helping both of them. Tom had agreed to hire the people to get the logs and construct the house. Jack had agreed to pay all the bills and to pay Tom for his time.

I had only been home for 5 days, now this has taken place. The paper work is finished. It is time for me to leave again. My job was a very important job and I take it serious. Nothing would interfere with my work, ever.

In the quietness of my own home I made the rules for the operations officers of the United States Air Force base security systems and security checks. I gave General Jack Thomas one copy to see if he approved, and he did. I then contacted my crew and ordered them to report to the air force national security emergency preparedness office in Fort McPherson, Ga. And this from now on would be our headquarters and home base. We would have a total of four officers, all combat veteran pilots. There would always be one of us in the office. When we went overseas we would make at least five security checks before returning home. If we were met with weapons and a challenge we were to place our hands on top of our heads and say we surrender. Especially overseas. If we are contacted in the air we are to follow exactly the orders that are given to us, because for all they know we are the enemy.

On the day we are to go on a security mission, every one of us will know where we are going, but no other family or friends will know. Our first oversea flight was to be Eielson AFB, Alaska then Elmendorf AFB Alaska, Kaduna AFB Japan and Hickman AFB Hawaii then back to Barksdale AFB in La, and then home base. The other two officers would go out two days after our return, just time to check our F-80 C and refuel. The oversea trip was three days, and to check five bases in the U.S. was two days. We traveled at five hundred and eighty miles an hour and forty five thousand feet elevation. Our every move was reported to General Jack Thomas. Not by us, but by the commander of each base.

It was my plan for all four of us to be on duty twenty-one days and then all of us to be off for ten days. This plan was approved. This base is only seven hours by car from my home in N.C. Lt. Roy Evans and Lt. Moore would be on the next trip out to check five bases in the States. By way of the pilots going from base to base and the radio operators, every air force pilot in the United States Air Force knew about the security checks and this kept them on their toes. The non-commission officers running the ground security, is the ones that have to do the work now. The radar operators better not go to sleep at their post because they never know when we will show up. Now we just fly in, but soon we will be a more sneaky. Now these guys in the states are training, but the ones overseas have reason to be afraid and more serious. I believe that this job is much more important, and time consuming than I first thought it would be.

Lt. Jimmy Green, my flying partner, and I started advance training on helicopter take off and landing on our first day back and when Lt. Evans and Lt. Moore got back they started. My plan was to find a way to get into these bases and land without being detected and challenged. Not to get any one in trouble but to improve the security of every American air base in the world. With the training that we all four have had, and twenty more days here at this base, we will all be checked out on helicopters of every size.

Every member of all of our families are puzzled by our schedule and what we are doing. They want to know if we are the CIA, or the FBI or what? My orders are no one is to know what we do, and that is the way it must always be. None of us are allowed to have visitors. Everyone else on this base can have visitors except us. To make up for this we have the ten days each month off duty. While we are on duty we are on twenty-four hours a day.

# JACK'S NEW LOG HOUSE

I was gone from home a total of twenty-five days, and I can't believe what Tom has completed in that short time. The log cabin is up to the floor level, he used Fred's tractor and plowed a ditch over two feet deep and put in electric wires underground. The ditch is in a large circle going up to the cabin, when he smoothed it out, it became the road and you cannot see the cabin from Toms house or the main road. Jack wanted a cabin in the woods and that is what he has. Only thing about it, Jack planned not having electric or water in the cabin and he has both, he wanted a path to the cabin but he has a road, he may be happy and maybe not.

Jack was in some foreign country on business, I can't say where because he will be in two or three countries in one day. During this month and next he will visit every air force base there is in the entire world. Then he will be in Washington for a meeting that will last for two days. Jack is the designer of this security move. He set it up from the very start and he is working very hard to make it a success, so far it has had a lot of attention in Washington.

The location that our home is in, and the country setting is a perfect place for jack to live. He wants peace and quiet and to be away from TV cameras and reporters. He does not want to be ask questions. When he is here he wears blue jeans and a T-shirt and work shoes, and He loves to work on the farm. He will plow all day; he even hates to stop for lunch. He bought an old jeep pick-up that he drives around here, and when he goes to town it is a quick trip, just there and back. Money does not matter to him; he does not have to worry about how much anything cost. I don't think he is rich, but his salary is pretty good. His wife lives in Texas and I never did meet her, but she is Cuban or Mexican, I have seen her picture in his quarters and I know he fly's to Texas every week. Jack is not flashy, he does not want to be noticed, and he does not want folks around here to know that he is a two star general.

Ruth and I will leave in the morning on a five-day trip. David will stay with Fred and go to school. We do not even know where we are going; we are just going to drive and stop when we see a place that we want to visit.

The 1957 model cars are out now, we see them every place we go, but this 1937 ford gets more attention than the new cars do. I told Ruth that I would buy her a new car if she wanted one and she said no. I like this car; I can't drive it because I can't change the gears, but I still like it better than I do the new ones. We were in Knoxville, Tennessee and I saw a ford place with a huge sign that said deep discounts so I pulled in. I told Ruth to pick out the car that she wanted and she picked out a four-wheel drive pick-up. It was a pretty truck and it was an automatic transmission so she bought it. She followed me home driving her new truck and I could tell that she was proud of it. When we got back we stopped to see Tom and let Ruth show off her new truck, now that she has had a chance to drive it she really does like it. Tom drove it down the road and back and he said "that is a real truck". Tom told me that Jack had put him on salary. When the cabin is complete he wants me to look after things when he is away. He said that his wife would be here part of the time and she may need wood for the fire place or she may need to go to town for something, and she cannot drive so she will need some help; Tom needed the income because he does not make very much money, everything here has worked out great.

In three more days Jimmy Green and I will be flying to the Far East. This trip will probably take us longer because I am going to hit every base in the region. With Jack going to the meeting in Washington I want the records to be impressive. I want people in the white house and the pentagon to set up and take notice. Back at the base we were all there and ready for duty. I requested an F-80 C and a chopper for Sunday morning. Jimmy and I would take the plane and go into Andrews AFB, in Maryland. We would set down at 7:30 AM. If we are challenged and while we are being challenged Roy and Dan will set the chopper down near the pad that is located on the other side of the hanger from where we were. One thing is that we do not care if they like what we do or not, we do not care if they like us or not, we just do our job the best way we can.

Jimmy and I came in as quietly as we could; we touched down and taxied right up to the hanger area and got out of the plane. No one was around so we walked over to the chopper pad and Roy and Dan had just set down. All four of us walked into the hanger and found a phone; we called the officer of the day. A lone air patrol sergeant came up to us in a jeep, and we ask him to take us to the mess hall to get something to eat, and he did. We suggested that he go into the officer's mess with us. While we eat breakfast we told him who we were and what we were here for. From that point on he would not say anything. The O.D. finally showed up and we placed him under arrest. He was officer of the day and in charge of security, he was a 1st. lt. This was the first person that we had arrested and we had to use him as an example. I relieved him of his side arm, and the sergeant and I escorted him to the brig. After all of the paper work was completed, we refueled the chopper and the plane and ordered a guard to stay with each of them until we returned. At this time I explained to all three of my pilots, that this procedure would always be used in this situation. It was a lesson well learned by all of them. Since we are close to Washington and this is the first time we have a breach in security, and I have arrested an officer in the USAF, I have decided to stay here on this base for the day. I requested a car from the motor pool, and rooms in the officer's quarters for the four of us; we will leave later.

General Thomas called me. He said the report was entered into the logbook and he was happy with the situation. It was up to me if I wanted to release the Lt. from the brig or not. I did. Roy and Dan would leave the next morning for home base. Jimmy and I would go to day to Beale AFB in California and take off tomorrow morning for Turkey.

In California we landed and was met with armed guards. We were placed under guard until a call was made to General Thomas, and then released. The General told me in a joking way that if I ever made him mad, that he would tell them that he did not know me; then he laughed. The O.D. and all the security force there knew about what happened in Maryland, they were not too friendly to us, but they sure were on the ball with their security duties. Bigram airfield in Afghanistan, Ballad air base in Iraq, Incirlik air base in Turkey all three met our plane in a hostile manner. They were not sure who we were and did not seem to be happy with us being there, but they did let us eat and refuel the plane before we were rushed off. In Incirlik the highest-ranking officer there was a colonel also. I do know that he knows who we are and what we do. Our security work so far has proven that Saturday night, and Sunday morning is the time that security is lower than any other time. Fifty percent of all personnel are on liberty, and fifty percent of the ones not on liberty is drinking. Large areas like airstrips and hanger areas, are not being protected properly. General Thomas has ordered me to go with him to Washington to a meeting of base commanders. They want to question me about what they should do to improve security, since I am the one that wrote all of the guidelines on the new security checks in place now. Before this meeting, I want to pull off one more secret job. In Ellsworth AFB there are several of the new B-52 heavy bombers, this is where they train all of the crews. South Dakota is a lightly populated area, and when we were

423

there they challenged us, but only with two people in a jeep. One 2nd Lt. And a PFC. I want to go there on Sunday morning at 6:30 AM. We requested a B-52 and a crew of two. My four guys and the two new men flew to South Dakota and landed exactly at 6:30 AM. No one was there to greet us. It was Sunday morning. We had six boxes that were empty and had written on them in big letters, T N T. We placed the boxes around where they would do the most damage if they were real. We took pictures of all of the TNT boxes, and 21 bombers of all sizes. Inside the hanger was an office so we went there looking for a telephone. There we found a person on duty at the desk, but he was asleep and he had pants on, but no shirt and no shoes, we got this picture also. We found the fire alarm and set it off. People came from everywhere, but it was too late. We took names and set up a meeting for Monday morning. At ten am I called General Thomas and gave a full report. He said that he would arrange the meeting and that he would be there. At eight am on Monday morning his plane landed and I met him in the car that had been assigned to me. We went to the Officers mess hall, and he and our crew had breakfast and a preliminary meeting. We gave the pictures to him. There was no officer there in charge of security. A buck sergeant was there and that is the one that was asleep. The general conducted the meeting and I said nothing. The Lt. That was supposed to be there, and the sergeant was brought up on charges. The boxes marked with TNT was put back in our plane for the General to carry with him to Washington. The meeting was two weeks from today. We were ordered back to home base. I gave the crew seven days off and I stayed on base waiting for the General to get back.

When General Jack Thomas is on duty, he is all General and every one better act like it. When he is on the farm he is just plain ole Jack. He has a lot of responsibility and a lot of power in this USAF. I would hate for him to be mad at me; but he is a great fellow and as honest as anyone could be. He arrived late that day and told me to go on home if I wanted too. He said he would be there the next day that he wanted to see how the log house was coming along. He told me that his wife would move in as soon as it is complete. He said if we had a place to set down that we could get a chopper to go back and forth in but that would attract too much attention. I agreed with that.

I stayed on the farm for a week, and the General was there for four days. He leaves for Washington on Monday and on Wednesday I go. I will not see him or communicate with him unless it is necessary in the line of duty. We do not socialize while on duty. We both thought it would be better if we didn't.

In the meeting, US Senators ask a lot of questions of me. "What have we done" and "What do we need to do?" I told them exactly what I thought and they seemed to agree with most of it. When they ask me what was my biggest problem while out there doing the security checks, I had to say that it was confronting the officer on duty, the top man in charge. If he, or she, was equal to me or had more rank than I did, it is hard for me to reprehend them or to speak to them in the manner that is necessary to be sure that the security of our air bases and our warplanes are secure. Members of the armed services committee were there in the meeting, they ask a different kind of questions, and I am not sure they liked my answers, but I laid all of the facts on the table, now we would have authority out there or we would not. My questions were all answered, I was excused from the meeting and I went straight to the airport and left for home base.

I knew that I only had a few days off but I got into the car and drove home to N.C., I told Ruth about the meeting and she said it sounded like it went good to her. Then she said "look, you have thirteen years in the Air Force" David graduates this year, we have two farms, and you are a jet pilot, just what are you worried about? I knew that she was right, and I told her so.

# SOPHENA COMES HOME

Tom had all of the logs up and was starting the roof and the fireplace this week. He had eight people working on the job. Tom set in the truck under the shade tree, but his job was to see that the cabin was built good and the way that Jack wanted it. And he did do that. Jack come in a day later than we expected him and surprised us with his wife, she was with him. They had a motel room down in Clayton and were going to drive back and forth; she only was going to be here for a week, she wanted to see the cabin. Her name is Sophia; she is Mexican and a very pretty woman. She likes the cabin but says the neighbors live too close. Her ranch is 2800 acres and her great grandmother and great grandfather lived there, her family has had the land for over one hundred and fifty years. Her neighbors in Texas were sixteen miles away.

Sophia likes the road going to Toms farm and then on to our farm and then to Fred's farm. The main road is four miles east of Toms house. It is in Georgia and our road turns west off of the main road and is in Georgia for three miles before it crosses the North Carolina line.

Toms house is in N.C. and his barn is in Georgia. No other houses are on the road between Toms and ours and Fred's. Our place and Fred's place is in N.C. Jack and Sophia's cabin is in N.C., just about fifty feet across the line. There was an old road thru the mountains that went to a settlement called Germany. The state was going to open that road up again so they paved our road, up to the end of our property at Fred's house. Then they decided to go on the other side of the mountain with a new road and they have completed that new road. Now we still have our privacy.

For some unknown reason Jack has suggested that Ruth should go back to base with me for a couple of weeks. It has always been a strict rule that no family or friends would be allowed at our base area. I really do not care what the reason is; I want her to go if she wants to go. David can stay with Fred and go to school and he will be fine. Jack also asks if I would go back and stay in the office until he got there, what could I say? He could have ordered me back if he had wanted too. Ruth and I will leave tomorrow. She wants to drive her truck because she said that she may have to come back by herself, and she cannot change the gears in my car.

We got back to Georgia and found a motel about ten miles from the base. We stayed there until Monday morning then I went to the office and waited for Jack. Something big is up; it must be because of the meetings in Washington. Jack did not show up and he did not call, there was no word until late Tuesday afternoon then Col. Hayes, the acting C.O. comes into the office.

# MY NEW STAR

General Hayes asks that I go with him and I did. We went directly to the parade ground and there was General Thomas along with Sophia, Ruth and David, and Tom and Fred. The band was playing. General Thomas promoted me to a brigadier general, one star. I traded an eagle for a star. Along with the star was the official title of commander of the USAF base security enforcement, worldwide. I had got myself a job, that would be very hard to do and no matter what, no one could ever do it well enough. This was a complete surprise to me. Everyone was surprised and happy; but Fred cried because he knew that he had a huge part in this. It took three days for General Thomas to instruct me of all of my duties. Before now I had been in the field doing the security checks. Now, I did not know it, but the General had been spending more time on this than I had. Now I will do his job and someone else will go out and check.

Ruth and all of our crew have rooms in town at the hotel. In a few days we will all go back to North Carolina and work on the farm, then we will all be relaxed. After the promotion party General Thomas told me "I can't wait to get back on the farm". There I can relax and do not worry about all of this security all over the world. I like feeding the animals and milking the cows and I even like smelling the manure in the barn, when I am there I do not care about anything else. As soon as I can I am going to take the simple life and let this complex troubled life go. I have found out that the more you have the more you worry.

When David gets out of college, which is one more year, he said he is going to medical school. I thought he would be in the military, but he says not. His grade average is better than mine was in high school and so far in college, I know he will do anything he wants to do. He is twenty-three years old now and some of the experiences that I had when I was young, I do not believe he has had, but I am not sure about that.

Fred is eighty-four years old this month. He paid four thousand dollars on David's college. He told David and me that he wanted to do double for David's education than what he did for my education, because look what it did for me. Fred is shaky and feeble but his mind is good.

Jimmy Green is the new flight commander. He was a captain and he shipped over to accept this job and now he is a major. Roy and Dan both got out of the military and accepted a job with United Air Lines. Our new base of operations has moved to Robbins Air Force base in Warner Robins, Georgia. Still yet closer to our N.C. farm home. General Jack Thomas retires this year; he has a total of thirty-nine years in the Air Force. I ask him why he did not go for forty and he said that he had intended to, but Sophia wanted to retire on the farm in Georgia, now. I am starting my new job as a general with a thirty-day leave. It will be a new deal all the way thru. The security unit will be reconstructed from bottom to top beginning June 1st.

I had been home three days, it was April 4th and Fred and I had planned to plow the forty-five acres in the bottom by the creek, and plant it in corn. I got to the barn at Fred's house and the tractor was already gone. He was not in the house and I could see the entire cornfield from the front porch, but I could not see Fred. I got into my car and drove back to my house, but Fred was not there either. Ruth got scared and came back to Fred's with me. On the way back, Ruth saw the dog lying down by the creek. We parked the car and jumped out and ran to the creek bank. Fred had gone too close to the bank of the creek, and it had caved off with him. His leg was caught under the tractor and the dirt from the bank that caved off had dammed up the water, and it backed up over Fred and he had drowned. It was awful, we had to leave and get help to get him out. I could not let Ruth go by herself and I could not leave her there alone.

We got to tom's house and he had a neighbor friend there, the four of us went back and got Fred out of the creek. Everyone was notified except David. We drove to his college and told him in person, and we all three come home together. Fred was better to me than anyone else had ever been.

Jack Thomas saw combat in three wars, and had seen a lot of friends die. But this was worse on him than anything he has ever seen, according to Sophia. They have been married forty-two years.

Jack had been in Colorado when he received the word about Fred, he left immediately and flew into Warner Robbins. There an Air Force driver and car that picked him up and they come directly to our house. This is the first time anyone around here had seen him in uniform, now they all knew who and what he was. Jack told me later that he did not know that all those people would be at my house, but I do not care, for I am proud to be just what I am, I did not want attention.

Jack's driver stayed at Tom's house. This was a very bad week for all of us. After the funeral Jack had to leave and he told me to come back in three weeks, but if I needed more time to let him know. This place will never be the same.

The forty-five acres never got planted in corn. The tractor was pulled out of the creek and taken to Franklin and sold. No farming was done on this farm this year. David wanted to leave as soon as he could to try and get over the death of his Grand-pa. Before this, Ruth and Ann never talked very much and would only visit each other around Christmas time, but now they seem to be close. Ann's husband only cares about money; he works six twelve-hour days in the drug store and never goes anyplace. Ann has told Ruth she is going to quit work and buy a place in the country to get away from Harvey and that store. Ruth told Ann that she would give her two acres to build a house on if she wanted it. After all, Ann would have had fifty percent of the farm if she had not refused it a few years ago. Ann accepted the two acres and Ruth told her to pick it out. Jack and Sophia still have Tom on the payroll. Tom does odd jobs for them and keeps wood cut for the fireplace and the cook stove. These two people could have every convenience in the world, but they want just what they have. Jack did put in a pump at the spring to have water in the house; she did not even want that. She sold her land in Texas for a lot of money and Jack makes good, but they both want to keep it simple.

All of the land on the other side of the creek belongs to David. Sixty acres of beautiful land with lots of water. David picked it out a long time ago and has never changed his mind. When he gets out of college, our first job is to build a bridge across the creek, and then we will build David a house.

Jack has asked if he can farm the land next year. He said he did not want the farm he just wants to work it. He said he will only take what they can eat and he will buy another tractor. He informed us that as of January 1st he would be retired.

Ann picked out a flat piece of land above the road within sight of their old home place. When she had it surveyed it was just over two acres but less than two and a half acres so Ruth said O.K., you can take that. Immediately Ann hired a contractor and they started building a house, it was a big house and very nice. It took over six months to build it. Ann moved into the house as soon as she could, but Harvey did not move in with her. He stayed in Franklin and run the drug store. Now their drug store is open seven days a week.

Ann had been in her new house for two

months before Harvey come to see her and the house, and he was only there for an hour. When Harvey left, Ruth went to Ann and asks what was going on. Ann told her that she was going to live there alone; Harvey could come if he wanted to, but he does not want too. Ann told Ruth that he had only married me so that he would have free labor in the drug store. He has never loved anything but money. The next day Ann went to Franklin and bought a brand new Pontiac and paid for it with cash. She told Ruth that she had worked for twenty years, and now I am going to get paid, Harvey does not care what I spend.

I have known all the time that Ann was Toms only love, ever. But now I believe that Ann feels the same way about Tom. No one has said that, but Ruth and I both have had that same thought.

Next week I go back to work. It is my duty and my responsibility to form a squadron of flyers to check security wherever an American air base is.

Two other generals, all but my flying every other mission, approved my plans. General Thomas called me to the front porch and said, "let's talk". He told me that he had everything set for me to be home fifty percent of the time. Let the new guys go and do the work in the field, you have done your job and you have done it well, now do not try to be a hero. If you retire with twenty years service you only have eighteen more months to go, so just relax. It was more like an order than it was a suggestion, so I made up my mind right then that from now on, I intend to take the easy way out.

My 1937 ford still receives a lot of attention. It is original all but the brakes. I had hydraulic brakes put on it a long time ago. All of the officers under me have new cars and they have all offered to trade with me, but they do not know the history of that car. Fred gave me the car and I had it all thru college and everything else in my life since then, and I intend to keep it.

Back home on the farm things are becoming

normal. Fred is missed but we have to realize that death is something that is for sure for all of us.

The best thing that has happened around here is Ann moving back to the home place. Her and Ruth spend a lot of time together. They are either on Ann's front porch or our front porch, some time I set with them and we just talk. From their porch we can see the place where Ruth and I, and Tom and Ann stripped our clothes off and waded the creek. We can see the place where the still was and we can see the barn where we first made love. A lot of memories are here.

Jack and Sophia bought the farm on the other side of Tom's place. I told both of them that they could do anything on our farm that they wanted too, but she insisted on buying the place anyway. They are not going to move over there, they just bought it to keep our place private, there is only one other small farm, about eleven acres, that belong to people from Florida and they never come up here. Now Sophia wants to buy it too. Tom's, and our place, and Jack and Sophia's and Fred's place takes the entire valley. This is what jack wants, just privacy.

Ruth and Ann were on Ann's front porch talking when Harvey drove up to the house. He come on up on the porch and sit down. Ruth said that she started to leave and Ann told her please do not leave; we want you to be here. Harvey asks Ann to come in to work and Ann said no. Then Harvey asks Ann for a divorce and Ann said she did not want a divorce. Harvey said to Ann, that "he had someone else that he was in love with and wanted to marry her". Then he got up and left.

The next day, Ann went to Franklin and hired an attorney, when she told the attorney what she wanted he said that everyone in town knows about Harvey and his cashier. She has only been out of high school for two years and she had a baby while she was in school. Fred asks you for a divorce, we will give it to him.

Ann said she wanted half of the money that they have and half of the drug store and half of all that it makes in the future and all of her new house. He can have the home they lived in, and the two cars that he has. Harvey has already moved the girl into his house. I could not believe my eyes when Ruth and I went over to Ann's house last night. She bought a new john deer tractor and had it delivered to her house. She ask me if I would help her learn to operate it and Jack said she ask him too. She told Ruth that she always wanted to drive a tractor but she wanted to do it her way. She did not want to have to make a living on a farm. But she said I have my living made, so now I will do it my way. She spent a week turning the bottomland, after the third day she was running that tractor as good as anyone. She turned that forty-five acres, then she disked it up and laid it off to be planted. She has a corn planter being delivered tomorrow. Ann wants Ruth and I to tell her what we need to work with on the farm. She said she wants to get it before Harvey changes the bank account.

When jack got home he went to see the tractor, and he said that he had planned to buy one but now he will not have too. He said he would get anything else that we need, just to tell him what it is. Ruth is becoming interested now in farming, she always worked the animals, but not the crops.

Harvey took half of the money out of the bank, but he left half for Ann. He has the drug store up for sale and already a man from down in Georgia has come to talk about buying it, if it sells, Ann will get half of the money.

Jack and I set on the porch today and watched as Ruth and Ann worked down in the field, we know it will not last but it is something they want to do.

Tom has offered his land to them if they need more to work on. All three farms are there together and they say that corn is what they want to grow. Sophia will be helping them as soon as she is over the flu that she has.

## stories about a Georgia moonshiner

The Rabun County Chamber of Commerce, down in Georgia, has contacted Jack and ask him to speak at the memorial day celebration in honor of all veterans. He accepted the invitation. He is retired now, and he is the highest-ranking officer in the area. Jack is especially popular with the farmers around here, because he goes to the meetings at the co-op and talks to all of the farmers. He reads books about farming and to hear him talk, he has farmed all of his life. He even joined the 100-bushel club. That is a club that says they can grow 100 bushel of corn on one acre. Jack and Sophia have bought the small farm east of Tom's place. Now there is no more land in our little valley that is available. We cannot close off the road because the county paved the road, but we can control the road by parking vehicles in it.

One more house can be built up here and that is David's. Any of us could split up our farm and sell some of it, but we have all strived to have this valley as peaceful and quite as we could.

Tom has been coming around more and more. Especially when Ann is around. Tom has not been over to her house yet, but I think it is just a matter of time. He has always been embarrassed about talking to girls, and age has not made him any better, Ruth and I both think it will happen, but if it does it will have to be him doing it, not us.

This morning Tom and I was going fishing. We went behind the barn to dig worms for fish bait and there was Ruth, Ann and Sophia cleaning out the stalls in the barn and loading the manure on a wagon to broadcast onto the cornfield. We did not even speak to them. We dug our worms and walked up the creek over a mile before we started fishing. Below a small water fall there was a pond and the water was five or six feet deep, we set there on the bank and caught all the fish we wanted. Our stringers were full but we just kept on fishing because we were having a good time, and we were relaxed. Out of the blue, Tom asks, "What I thought about Ann". I ask what he meant; "he said do you think she would be mad if I went over to her house"? I told him if it was me that I would wait until some of us were over there, then come and ask her if you can visit. He agreed. Nothing else was said about it. We took our fish to Toms house and cleaned them, then Tom said, "what if we all have a fish fry here at my house to-night?" I told him that I would talk to everyone and let him know. Every one said yes, a good idea, Ann was the first one to say yes. And she was the first one there. When Ruth and I got there, Ann and Tom were setting in the swing out behind the house. They sat in the swing while Ruth and Sophia cooked the fish, and while we ate the fish. Jack finally carried two plates of food around there to them. They had finally got to-gather to talk.

From that night on they were close friends. Almost every day one was at the others house. They kept it respectful, but we could all tell that when the divorce was final that it would not be very long before another wedding would be. They were to-gather, then they were apart for twenty years, now we will have to wait and see.

These three girls have really worked this summer. Between two of the farms they have over sixty acres of corn, and it is really pretty. We have more tomatoes, beans, cabbage, peas, squash and okra than we know what to do with. One whole acre of potatoes and bell pepper, no way can we eat all of it. We all have a freezer and they are all full. We offered to give the rest to neighbors but they have all they want from their own gardens. I guess you could say that we live in the land of plenty.

We had to add a corncrib onto Tom's barn to hold all of the corn, I do not know how many bushels we have but I know we have more than we ever thought we would. Tom has two hogs that are ready to butcher, one weighs about three hundred pounds and the other is about three fifty. Tom said that his dad always wanted to kill hogs during Thanksgiving week, so we decided on this Saturday because the weather is right. Days are about thirty to thirty-five degrees and nights get down in the teens, it is just right.

When I got up this morning to start a fire under the wash pot to heat the water it was blowing snow. It is a perfect day, cold with snow flurries, but not too windy. Sophia has helped kill hogs before but Jack has not, neither has Ann, but the whole group is here now, even David. We shot the big one first, I bled it then we hung it up, head down and gutted it, and took off the head. Then we put burlap bags over it and poured on the hot water so the hair would release. We all scraped off the hair then washed it down good, then carried it to the cutting table in the smoke house. We did the same thing to both of them, and then we took the tender loins in the house, and cooked and eat them with hot biscuits and gravy.

We let both hogs lay there two or three days before we cut them up, the weather was cold enough so the meat would not spoil. That night it snowed five inches deep.

As we set in my living room Jack said that he felt sorry for me, when I ask him why, he said because you have to go back to work the Monday after Thanksgiving. Remember, around a holiday or on Sunday is when security is at the lowest point; you have to put a stop to that. I am not there anymore and you are the one that is responsible, so be on the ball. Jack was right, it was my job to keep everyone on their toes. I made plans to leave on Sunday after Thanksgiving. I ask Ruth if she wanted to go with me for a couple of weeks and she said yes, so I called and got us a room in a hotel. I could go to officer's quarters by myself, but they have no place for strangers on this base. I called Jimmy green and had him to contact the crew and be prepared to fly early Monday.

I scheduled two security checks for Tuesday on the east coast and two each for Wednesday and Thursday on the west coast. Then two in Japan for Saturday and one in Korea for Sunday. Then it was a long trip back to home base in Georgia. When the crew got back they briefed me about the bases they had checked. Every single one of them passed with flying colors. This looks good on the report. Ten security checks in six days, thousands of miles apart.

It is the first week in December and I am going to keep the crew here on home base for one week. Then our two weeks off will let everyone be home for Christmas, but after that I intend to use trickery to slip onto a military base.

When I got back to the hotel there was a horse trailer in the parking lot that was taking up about ten or twelve parking spaces, and I had to park on the other side of the building. Then, when I got to the room there was Jack, Sophia, Tom and Ann. Ruth had found a place in Macon, Ga. that sold quarter horses then she called Ann and Sophia. They borrowed a trailer and were coming to buy them each a horse so Jack and Tom followed them in the car. They already had the horses picked out, and will get them and saddles the next day.

$3,500.00 each for horses and $1,500.00 for bridles and saddles and such. Ruth said she would go back with them and I could keep her truck and come on, so this is what we did.

This horse talk had been going on for a while but I thought it was just talk. When they found the horses they wanted, they bought them.

Between all of us we have two hundred acres. A beautiful place to ride horses. Fred's barn is a perfect place for horses with plenty of water and grass and more corn than anyone in the county.

When I got back home it was December the 18th. It was a bright sunny day and it was cold. The first thing I saw was three ladies on horseback. They had been trimming trails out in the woods behind Fred's house, over close to where his still was a long time ago. The next house in that direction was about thirty miles, so we had plenty of room to ride in. Now it looks like Tom, Jack and I, will have to go back to Macon and buy us each a horse, or just stay at home and watch the girls ride.

# UNEXPECTED TROUBLE

We had planned on going to Franklin to do Christmas shopping the next day, but I woke up with a terrible headache. I lay there in the bed for a while and did not want to get up. Two hours later I thought that if I got up and moved around some that it may help, and it did ease off some for a while. After we started to Franklin my head started hurting a lot worse, I could not see things clearly. My arm was in pain, then my neck and jaw, and then I knew what it was. I stopped on side of the road and told Ruth to drive to the hospital as quick as she could, in ten minutes we were in the hospital. I was having a heart attack. The doctors there saved my life, but they did not operate on me. They called the hospital at Warner Robbins Air Force base and they sent a helicopter after me. I was operated on that night, they did a five bypass and I was out of the hospital in ten days. Now I feel just fine.

The only trouble is, I cannot ever pilot a jet again. I can never fly any plane for the USAF. I have spent my life in school and flying, now all of that is over. I never realized how fast a person's life can change, and I never realized how much I had to be thankful for.

The Air Force gave me ninety days to get well. Then I will be in the office of the security unit that Jack and I started. I can retire now, but if I wait nine more months my retirement is better, so I will just set around that office for nine months then move on to the farm in North Carolina.

Ruth and Ann and Sophia have joined a horseman's club down in Georgia. One time a month they go on a trip with them. They sell shelled corn to a lot of them to feed the horses; they have fun and make money too.

Some days I go to Fred's house and just set on

the porch. From there I can see the barn and the entire cornfield. I can see the creek down the hill below the house where the foot log used to be, before the flood washed it away a few years ago. In the wintertime when the leaves are off the trees I can see almost to the branch that Fred had his still on. I now wonder if Fred saw his two daughters with Tom and I, and knew a lot more than we thought he knew. Any way Fred never did say that he had seen us like that, but now here it is over twenty years later and now I have seen Ann and Tom slipping into the barn, and half an hour later they will come out and act happy and loving to each other. What is happening to them now, should have happened twenty years ago, just the same as Ruth and I.

Ann and Harvey's divorce has been final for a while and we all thought there would be a wedding by now, but not a word has been said about it. When I ask Tom about it he told me that he liked it the way it was now, he talked to Ann about getting married and she said she did not care if they ever got married or not, as long as they were together. They have both said the same thing. Some time he stays at her house and some time she stays at his house, some time they both stay at their own house. If anyone did see them it would be one of our group, because no one else ever comes on our road, except when they ride and have friends to come to ride with them. They now have over six miles of trails to ride on.

Harvey's new wife has left him already. He come home one day and caught her and a taxi driver in bed together. She left with the taxi driver.

Jack and Tom and I have horses now. We had a place to keep them and plenty of feed for them so we went to the same place in Macon and bought three more horses. Jack bought Tom one for Christmas. Jack and Tom get along like brothers and Tom is still on his payroll. I found out that tom's pay is $250.00 a week. That is great pay for a job where you do not have to work hard or regular. His main job is to cut wood for the fireplace and the cook stove. Sophia bought ten game chickens and feeds them up at their cabin. They roost in the top of the tallest tree they can find and they start crowing at 3:30 or 4:00 0 clock in the morning. She had five hens and five roosters and they are all as wild as they can be. She said that she had game chickens in Texas and she can't sleep in the mornings unless they are crowing.

I felt guilty with me being at home and getting full pay. As a one star general my base pay was $9,000.00 per month or $108,000.00 per year. When I retire I will receive 75 % of that and it is so much more than we need to live on. We already had two farms, my parent's farm and Ruth's parent's farm. Everyone in this little valley has been blessed. We need to find people that we can help. Jack had thirty years in the USAF so he retired at full pay, $126,000.00 per year, he can afford the $250.00 a week for Tom.

Harvey come to see Ann the other night and

wanted to get back to-gather. She tried to run him off and he would not leave so she called Tom. Tom was there in two minutes and there was a scuffle, Tom whipped Harvey good and as Harvey drove out of the driveway, Tom was throwing rocks at him, I doubt if he will be back.

It is time for me to go back to work. I love my home here in the mountains of North Carolina; it is beautiful all the year round. Even the winters with the cold windy ice and snowy days it is just a beautiful place. Then in the spring time when trees and shrubs start to green up and the leaves start to grow and the buds start to bud out and then blooms start to appear you know that there is a god in heaven that causes all of this to happen, it is not just an accident.

Also I feel the same about this whole country, this United States of America. For the past twenty years it has been my job to be sure that the security of the air bases of the country were safe from foreign countries, or any enemies of America. Most civilians do not know it, but America has enemies right here in our own country and I intend to do my best to protect her from them. In a few months I will be retiring, but it is because of health reasons and nothing else.

My job needs to be done by young men. The new planes and war machines advance so much each year that it is hard to keep up with. The planes that I started flying are obsolete now. I would have to go to school full time just to keep up with advances. And my reflexes are not as good as a twenty three year old pilot. I know I was one of the best twenty years ago, but now I am obsolete. Just as I have always done my best to do my duty the best that I could, it is now my duty to get out of the way and let someone take my place that can do this job better than I can. It is going to be Jimmy Greens job to keep this security going. I am going to turn it over to him, and train him the same way that Jack trained me. Jimmy has been raised to colonel already and if the job demands it he can be a general in one year, the same way that I was.

Jimmy and I have worked out another sneak attack to try and catch some base security asleep. With the use of an old B-45 A- Tornado bomber and a crew of five and one, mark 1 helicopter, with a crew of three, we are going to hop our way around the world and check every base the United States has. Jimmy wants to start in Turkey, then Afghanistan, and then Iraq. My plan is to request a bomber and a chopper in Turkey and let the project begin in Turkey. Then, when we leave Iraq go to France, Italy and Germany, staying one week in Germany and changing planes. Then in two helicopters, go to Greenland and then start in Alaska and work our way around the United States.

We will require a flight crew of nine. There will be three non commissioned officers in our office every day and I will be in my quarters, or in our office. We will be in constant contact at all times. The three non commissioned officers will rotate in the office as they see fit, but someone will be on duty twenty-four hours every day. I will be available twenty-four hours every day.

Ruth and I have a room just outside the base, only five minutes from our flight office, where all communications are made.

Jimmy and his flying police force will be gone for one month. Everyone in the crew has agreed that this is special duty. They are on duty for twenty-four hours a day and will work every day for a month and then they will be off for a month.

In Incirlik air base in turkey, we received the aircraft that we had requested. We left there and went to Afghanistan and set the chopper down first. The guards captured the crew of the chopper and arrested them, but the bomber first flew over the base and then circled back and landed, the crew had left the plane and was in the hanger before they were noticed. No one was even in the tower. When this happens the report first comes to me and then to the pentagon. An investigation was started immediately.

Within minutes of refueling, both of our craft left to go back to turkey. We arrived there at 4:30 A.M. The bomber flew over the base the same as we did in Afghanistan then circled and landed. We were stopped on the far end of the runway by two military trucks with heavy thirty caliber machine guns mounted on top. The guns were trained on us. We opened the rear hatch and major Clark unloaded to identify ourselves, the credentials were in his hand and he had both hands up as to say we surrender. An enlisted man shot and killed major Clark. while this was in progress, the chopper landed un-noticed in front of the helicopter pads near the hanger, was the report I received. Back in Georgia, I was in the office by five o clock and ordered Jimmy and the crew to take living quarters there in Incirlik air base until he received further orders from me.

I requested a jet and crew to take me to

Turkey. We filed a flight plan and left at 0800. Since my heart attack I can be no part of the crew. I have all of my other powers but I cannot fly a plane of any kind. One hour out of Warner Robbins, We were ordered to return to home base. Major General Donald Free had been ordered there to take care of the investigation because of the seriousness of the situation, and because of my health. These orders came from the president of the United States.

When I arrived back in Warner Robbins I called Jimmy and told him what had happened. I told him to have all reports ready and to be ready to answer all questions, for Turkey and Afghanistan. We, our crew, had done just exactly what we were sent to do, and it was done in a professional manner.

I called Jack and talked to him about it. He said that he had already discussed it with General Free and that everything was all right. The crew had preformed their duty as they should have, but those two base commanders and officers of the day were in a heap of shit. The enlisted man with the carbine said he made a mistake.

I returned to the room where Ruth was as soon as I had made all of the calls. One hour after I got there I was ordered to go to the hospital for a checkup for the heart and they kept me for the night, and I know that this was Jacks doings, but I do not know who he had to do it.

Ruth is the one that caused it. She called Jack and told him that I did not look so good, he called the doctor friend of his and had them to come after me and do test, and that was a good thing because they did find something. Not enough oxygen in my blood, caused from the heart not pumping correctly. I may be getting an early retirement.

First thing I saw when I woke up this morning was Jack and Tom. Tom told me that he knew, that I could not make it without him, that I never had been able to do anything without his help.

Jack said that I was eligible for retirement, full twenty-year retirement at 75 % of my base pay, and that is more than you need. I recommend that you accept it and we can go take care of our horses.

Three weeks later I was out of the Air Force and setting out on the front porch of our old house. It was shady and cool and comfortable. I could see up and down the valley. We had six horses of our own and Ruth's friends had two of their horses in the pasture. It was restful just to set and watch the horses on the green grass with the creek running thru the pasture.

My doctor said that in one month I could work on the farm and ride horses just like I did before. After three weeks the horse club had a ride here at our place. I went on the ride and it was just great, now they have miles and miles of trails and none of it is steep, they have switch backs built and the trails are mostly level. A surprise for me was that they had built a picnic area in Fred's old still house. It was nice and had so many memories.

100 feet from the barn and in the center of the old garden where Fred raised his vegetables, we cleared a spot for a pond. It was as round as we could make it and it was 200 feet in diameter and had trees on one side of it. The center was about 20 feet deep, and around the edges it was 3 feet deep. The water was piped in from 500 feet up the creek and entered the pond off of a 10 feet high rock wall, shaped like a natural waterfall.

We, Jack and Sophia, Tom and Ann, Ruth and I said that we wanted to do all of this by ourselves, but we had to hire a dragline to do the deep part of the lake, but we did all the rest. It took all winter to do it but we had a lot of fun. Now it is stocked with bass. Big bass.

Our privacy is becoming less and less. We have put up a gate with an electric eye to open and close it but we get more and more people wanting an interview and wanting to know about our duties in the Air Force. None of us have ever turned anyone away. We invite them in to talk, but some things we just do not answer. The local papers have told everyone in the world that this little valley has two retired generals living here. We have high school kids coming to find out about a career in the Air Force, we tell them all the same thing, go to college first if you can, if not go in and let the Air Force educate you. But have top grades in high school first.

A glass building beside the pond is where we entertain guest and visitors. We rarely ever have anyone in our home, our home is old, but we love it and we are not moving out of it.

Ann and Tom are getting married next week. The wedding is in the glass house and the public is invited. we expect Harvey to be there and he is welcome if he wants to come.

After the wedding is over and the guest have left all of our group will go horseback riding and meet on top of the hill for a service. Near the top of the mountain, where the branch starts the spring is big, it produces a large stream of water just bubbling up out of the ground. We figure that this is the source of our good fortune. Without this water this valley would not be so beautiful and all of our crops would not be so bountiful, so this is where we have all decided to worship god on this day and thank him for our many blessings. Not many places in the world that I know of have a water supply like this. Every bit of the water on this land comes from this spring. None of it comes from other places. And we strive to keep it clean. We have a hut built up here and a small camp and a place for the horses, but all of it is 100 feet below the spring and off to the side, so no water runs back into the branch. Today we had regular prayer time and our minister gave a sermon.

Ann and Tom have been together almost all of their life, but not completely and not only. They were each other's first love but they let that slip away. Then they got that second chance. This time it is precious to both of them.

The only two people with us here today that do not live in this valley is the preacher and the reporter from the paper. The preacher comes regular but if the reporter says too much about us, he will not be back.

The news in Turkey and Afghanistan was not good. Not good for them but excellent for us, because my men all received commendations. And it changed the security procedures for all U.S. military bases in the world, wherever they are.

Jimmy Green is now a one star general. He is not the only black general in the military but he thinks he is, he is very proud. And a good man. He has the job that I had, and he does it well.

Under orders from the pentagon there are now two sections of the security enforcement. One in the United States and one for all overseas bases and Jimmy is over all of them. The only changes made in the procedure that I started, is that any failure of security is reported to the pentagon before action is taken, and that takes about five minutes, just a phone call.

Jack and I still have flight rights and we can go anyplace we want to on Air Force planes, as a passenger. We have discussed it and found out that we neither one want to leave this valley not even for a vacation. We both have traveled the world and we both have decided that there is no other place like this. Tom has only been less than two hundred miles away from home and now he does not even want to go to town, just twenty miles. Ruth only goes if there is a horse involved. She and Ann and Sophia will load the horses and go wherever the club has a meet. She has sold almost all of the corn from the corncrib to the people with horses. She even bought an electric corn Sheller to shell the corn.

When I look into the mirror, I look the same as I always have, to me. But when I look at Ruth and Tom and all the others I see gray hair, wrinkles and receding hairlines and Jack has a potbelly. I know that we are all getting older when I see that.

David will be home in November. He writes

often but says that he can't get away from the clinic long enough to come home, but he has all of November off, and he wants to spend it here with us.

This may be the last year that the girls will be able to have a corn crop. They have insisted on doing that by their selves, the corn and the horses are their projects, their exercise, and it seems to be what they want most of all. They could be traveling the country and living high, but they are happy doing what they have done for several years now. But age is entering into the picture.

Tom's bad foot will not allow him to walk very far, I get short of breath too easy and can't do very much and Jack runs two miles every day. The oldest person in the group and the one that is in the best of health.

Harvey was killed in an automobile wreck last week. He still owned the drug store but it was leased out to a drug company and he lived on his half of the income, Ann receives the other half and now I suppose she will get all of it. Harvey died alone, after his last wife left he never got married again. He was a person that married just to get free labor in his store, he was a loner. Ann worked for him for twenty years.

A lot of times I never thought that I would still be alive in 1980, but here I am. Our group that has lived here in the valley together all of these years are still here, we are too old to work anymore but we take care of ourselves. Money is not a problem, we can pay for what we need, but money is not important anyway. I guess the most important thing that we have is memories. One or two memories are not too good but the majority of them are happy memories.

Setting here on the porch I can look down the road and see my whole life from the time that I was a child living with my mother and father, until I met Ruth and Ann and Tom's aunt Betty.

My best day was when I come home from

the Air Force and found that Ruth was home with her dad, and she had David with her, and David was mine. I knew then that my life was more complete.

We hire all of the farm work done now. Mr. Carpenter does the farming of the land and we all get what we want to eat from the land and a small percentage, but that keeps the place from running down. We have not had horses in four years and we all miss them, but we had them for a long time and that is one of the good memories.

David's wife's father owns the clinic where David is a doctor and has been since he got out of college and medical school. All of his training was done there in New York and I doubt if he will ever leave to come back home, but he has a place to come if he wants to. I know the farm life is not for him but you never can tell.

My high school class of 1944 will have a reunion next month. They have ask if General

Jack Thomas would come as a guest and that the two of us would tell something about our time in the service together. Jack has two stars and I only have one, but I am not ashamed of that. We have told them that we would be glad to speak at the class reunion. I tried on my uniform and it still fits.

My 1937 ford still runs great. I intend to polish it up and drive it to the party. I still would not trade it for a new car; we just put new tires on it because the old ones were starting to show age by cracking. This car has really been worth the $320.00 that Fred paid for it.

I have been privileged to live in this country. I have been to several other countries and I have seen how they are, and how the people live. They are not free to worship their God the way they want too, they are not free to do anything that they decide to do, they are told what to do and they risk their lives to try and get into our country because we have freedom.

In this little valley we have lived a life of plenty in a land of freedom. I consider it a privilege to have served my country and fought for our freedom that we have.

## THE END

Fiction, created and narrated by
Larry English
This story took place in the mountains
Of north Georgia, in Rabun county, Georgia

---

## THE HUNT©

---

Yep, the hunt is the thing that excites me. It always has, in years past it was a family thing that every member of my family looked forward to. About a month or so before deer season opened each one of my uncles, my dad, and some of their friends all had their list of supplies made out for the hunting trip that we knew that we were going on.

Of course that was 60 or 70 years ago. My uncles and my dad are all gone now, but the memory of those happy times, still give me pleasure.

There were two areas there in Rabun County, Georgia, that our group hunted in. One was up

Tallulah river, near Tate City, this was a hard place to hunt, and you could not get there without getting wet, crossing Tallulah river, and walking for two or three hours. When you did get to our favorite hunting ground it was worth the trip. That place was as far into the woods as you could get. The other area that we hunted on was down War women road, almost to the South Carolina State line, our camp was there. Our group bought the land and built a camp house. An old logging road, such as it was, went close to the camp. That old road was a good walking trail but if you had any kind of vehicle I guarantee you would push more than you would ride.

When we talked about our hunting trips we always called it " hunting" trips, not "killing" trips. Probably, I would be in the woods 10 or 15 trips before I would see anything at all, but that one time made it worthwhile. If I got a shot one time per season, then I was satisfied, I had done good.

Some people killed a deer every season. A

lot of them got that buck on opening day, Ken was one of these people. I hunted with Ken several years before I found out how he managed to do this. If he saw a deer high on the mountain, not knowing if it was buck or doe, he shot, and he was a good shot. With the deer down, Ken would go see what it was. If it was a doe he let it lay there. If it was a buck we drug it out to the jeep. I would only shoot if I saw antlers. Ken told me one time that those horns were no good for anything, you can't blow them and you sure can't eat them.

On one of our trips to the Coffee fields, up on the Tallulah River, Ken and I had a trip that there is no way that could ever be forgotten.

We had breakfast and was in the jeep at 3:30 in the morning. It was a cold, windy morning with the temperature at 22 degrees. We used the jeep only to cross the river, then we walked the rest of the way in. Ken had his favorite hunting spot and I had mine. I did not have a tree stand but I had a seat on top of a large rock, it was as near perfect as anyone could ask for.

Dawn was just breaking, it was now blowing snow and I was cold and miserable, my fingers were so cold I wondered if I could pull the trigger, if I needed to.

I knew where Ken's stand was, just 100 yards from mine, but a ridge and a hollow was between us so there was no danger in what direction either of us shot.

About thirty minutes after day light Ken fired his 30-30 two times, he hardly ever misses so I, in my mind, was ready to go help him drag his deer to the jeep. But, within one minute the woods come alive with deer, bucks and does, seven in all. A six pointer stopped and looked back down the direction that he had come from, I got a good shot into the shoulder with my 270 Browning, and the deer dropped right where he was, the others scattered in all different directions.

I yelled to Ken and ask if he got his deer, he answered "DOE". When I got to him he had an eight pointer almost field dressed

Because of the light dusting of snow that was on the ground it was easy to drag the deer to the jeep. At 10:30 we were home drinking coffee, and now it was snowing hard. This had been a good day, in one of the most perfect times and places that I could ever remember.

Just a couple of seasons before that, and within 100 yards of the same spot, I was walking up a hollow that had a small stream in it. Leaves covered the water and there was just a wet mushy floor of soggy leaves. I could slip up the hollow with no noise. At the head of the hollow there was a steep embankment, just a few feet, then when you looked over the top you are looking at a large flat just covered with white oak trees and so many acorns on the ground that it was hard to walk.

Almost on the top of the embankment was

a forked tree. The fork was just right right to stand by and look thru it and see the flat area on the other side. I was making my way to that tree and planned to stay there. One step from the tree I heard a twig or a stick snap behind me, when I looked back I saw a four point buck less than 50 feet from me and not a bush between us. I froze, if I moved now, that deer would be gone. I was hoping that other deer would be with that one. In seconds that buck was out of sight.

I took that other step that put me up to the forked tree, I intended to stay there for the rest of the day. Things did not happen that way.

As I leaned on that tree, not over two minutes later, it sounded like a herd of cows coming down that ridge. I counted 7 deer that I could see and I could hear others that I could not see.

Two large holly trees blocked my view. One deer was there behind that holly tree and it snorted at me 4 or 5 times, it made all kinds of noise pawing the ground and sounded like it was stomping on the ground, I got just a glimpse of the large brown side of that deer, not enough to shoot, I saw no horns, but I bet that there was some there.

Then, quick as a flash, deer ran everywhere. I then saw, I think, the same four point that I had seen earlier. I got a lucky shot just behind the shoulder and the buck stopped there. Another deer was running up the ridge, I had to shoot so fast that I was not sure what it was, but it was big. I shot 3 times and hit it twice, once in the neck and once in the hip, and it was a doe. I made a bad mistake but I shot as fast as my 270 would fire.

Life just does not get any better than it was then. I spent my vacations with my Sister and brother-in-law, Ken and I hunted every day. At that time we had the best of the best. Now, they are both gone.

Their house is still there. I can look at that

house and it brings back all of the memories of those times 50 years ago. That mountain that we hunted on 50 years ago, is still there also, but I cannot walk the distance to get there, All I can do is reminisce.

## THE END

# INTRODUCTION
# GUILTY AS CHARGED

This story is about a farm boy
that led different lives.

He had more than one family
and more than one wife.

He had more than one name
and used them to deceive.

He had lots of love, lots of land,
and lots of money for a while.

But he lost all of the respect, all of
the money, and most of the love.

Fiction created and narrated
by Larry English

This article appeared in the Knoxville Press on August 29, 1960.

Knoxville Press
Knoxville, Georgia

Bobby James, columnist for the press for more than thirty years has reported that he has located a missing person that has been missing for twenty-eight years.

Mr. James was scheduled to retire on January 15, 1960. But after receiving a phone call about a person that was assumed dead in 1918, is still alive and had taken another man's identity. The press has allowed Mr. James to pursue the story and it has taken him into four states and cost the paper thousands of dollars, but it is an amazing and unbelievable story. It will be reported to the readers of this paper in the Sunday edition beginning next week, January 4, 1961.

## Kyle smith article one

Kyle Smith was born in 1887 in Rabun Gap, Georgia. He was the only child of Fred and Linda Smith, both Georgia residents. Fred was born in Rabun Gap and Linda was born in Atlanta.

Kyle went to school in Mountain City, Ga. A four-room schoolhouse that had three classes in each room. According to the records he was an exceptionally smart boy and was never in any kind of trouble, he finished school in 1904 with the highest grades of any one in the class.

He was well known in school because of his knack for trading, he would trade for anything, a pocket knife, marbles, pencils, he would trade his lunch bag for another and not even know what was in the other bag, he just liked to trade, he had two bicycles and about a dozen good pocket knives that he had traded up to, and if he could he would get 5 cents or 10 cents to boot.

One mile south of the Smith home the Parker family lived on a farm, they were the nearest neighbors and the only neighbors that was in walking distance. Ray and Dixie Parker, and they had two daughters, June and Jane, and they were identical twins.

Kyle was one year ahead of the twins in school and when they needed help with lessons, it was always Kyle that they called on to help. Mr. and Mrs. Parker neither one had been to school, when they needed help Kyle was always there. June's room was on one end of the house upstairs, and Jane's room was on the other end of the house upstairs. The twins were allowed only one lamp up stairs at a time, because Mr. Parker was afraid of a fire starting, and a kerosene lamp is dangerous. Since the girls had different books and different lessons to be studied Kyle helped one of them at a time, and always in their own room, because they only had one lamp for light.

Kyle was still active in the trading business,

but now he was trading horses, cows and anything else that anyone wanted to deal in. He stayed very busy.

After one of his trips to the swap meet he got home just before dark, he had four horses and two mules that he had bought; they were tied to his wagon when he got home. Before he got to the barn Fred Smith come running up to the front of the house, and started yelling and cursing at the whole Smith family and throwing rocks at the house, he broke two windows. Mr. Smith went out and punched him in the face and knocked him out. When he got up he said that Kyle had made his daughter June pregnant and he was going to kill him for that. Kyle admitted that he was guilty, and he wanted to marry June, so right then they planned a wedding and in just two weeks June and Kyle were married.

One month after the wedding it was found out that Jane was also pregnant, and Kyle was the father of that baby too. It was a shock but Kyle told the Parker family that he would take care of Jane and the baby, and he did.

Kyle was a horse trader with a very successful business and he could afford the two families.

June had moved to the Smith farm and Jane stayed with her mother and father and Kyle went back and forth, he was at the Smith farm as much as he was home.

Kyle worked very hard trading; he had worked up a business that was a great success. Fred Smith had turned his farm into a hay farm to feed Kyle's animals, and had built a corral that would hold 25 or 30 horses, he also planted 40 acres of corn for feed, and the money Kyle made on trading was divided and the entire family lived on it.

On the other farm it was different. Kyle's father did not like him, and he never has. He said that Kyle was a sissy, he had wavy hair and skin like a baby's bottom, and he was too skinny and he may not be my son. Kyle's father would not help him do anything. But Kyle's mother did everything for him, she worked all the time and when Kyle was gone to buy animals, she bought and sold just like Kyle had taught her to do and she was good at it. When Kyle went to a swap meet he always brought home a wagonload of saddles, bridles, plows, and here lately he sells a lot of milk cows. A large lean too on back of the barn holds all of this and more and more people come here to buy their supplies. His business is growing fast. It keeps Linda Smith so busy that it has shamed Fred into helping her. This is the only income that they have and Fred is beginning to see that it is good for all of them.

At the last swap meet there was a rumor going around that there was a bigger and better swap meet up in Tennessee. No one had been there they just heard about it and no one knew exactly where it was or how to get there. One man said that it was in Silver Branch, Tennessee. Kyle figured that if he went up to Tennessee, which was a two-day trip that he could find out where it was. So two or three days later he left in search of the bigger swap meet. Kyle never reached Silver Branch, Tennessee. When he got to Hazelwood, N.C., he met a farmer that was selling out all of his livestock and for $100.00 he bought two horses, two milk cows and a team of young mules. Along with all of the gears and a two-horse wagon, he left to go back to Rabun Gap the same day.

June and Kyle had a son that was borne two days after he got home, mother and baby were both fine but the Doctor said that she could not have any more children because of something that happened during delivery. Kyle could not leave now to go on the trip to Hazelwood because Jane was to have her baby in about two weeks. June and Jane did visit one another and they were fine with the way things were between the three of them. They even joked about it, telling each other to go easy on Kyle because this is my night.

Jane had a son also; when he was one month

old, Kyle spent the night there before he left for Tennessee early the next morning. On this trip he stopped in N.C. at a boarding house and got a room for two days. It was not a town but just a cross road and they had good food and clean beds and it was a good place to rest up.

Bill and Rose Clark owned and operated the boarding house. It was always pleasant and they became good friends, and one or two times a week they went riding together.

In the area around the boarding house Kyle could find what he needed to sell back there in Rabun Gap. Everyone thought Kyle was in Tennessee, which was a five-day trip, but he was in N.C., which was a two-day trip; this gave him resting time from the two passionate twins.

The stay here in the boarding house was perfect. This time he had been here for almost two months, he had found a place over in the next county that he could buy anything he wanted, at a price that he could make a good profit. He bought in N.C. and sold in Ga. And no one ever knew exactly where he was.

Things were becoming very interesting at the boarding house, Bill cook had ask Kyle if he was interested in buying a 50 percent interest in the boarding house, and doing his part of the work and he would take 50 percent of the profit. Every Saturday night we will pay all the bills and then split what is left. Bill wanted $2,000.00 for the 50 percent and this made Kyle suspicious, because it was worth much more than that, bill said they had to have the help or they had to quit. It was a lame excuse but Kyle went for it; he had the money to buy horses and supplies so he used this money to buy into the boarding house business. Within two days Bill said he had to go to the North Carolina coast on a business trip. He said he would be back in about a week. Bill was ten years older than rose and rose was one year younger than Kyle. Bill went to Jacksonville, N.C. to a hospital.

He left early in the morning on his trip and

everything was normal that day; but when all the work was done, and it was bed time, Rose, in her night gown, knocked on Kyle's door and when he opened the door she just walked in and got into his bed.

Bill said he would be gone for a week but he was not; he was gone for five weeks. Kyle and Rose lived together all this time, then when bill got back home, he told Kyle that we have to talk, and at the end of the day Kyle found out the truth.

Bill had cancer and only had a few more months to live, he has had it for a year and they knew that there was no cure for him. Rose and Bill were looking for a man to take care of her. They had a way to make a good living there at the boarding house. Kyle was chosen, if they could convince him to stay. Bill also told Kyle that the money he paid for the place was up stairs, and that it was his, they were just testing him to see how interested he was, and how he could make decisions. He also told Kyle that he never lost any time getting into bed with his wife, and he said that he had his blessing for I have been sick for a long time, and I realize that her life will go on.

Jane and Kyle have three kids at the Parker farm, two boys and a girl. They are legal heirs of the 80 acres and the home place and if Ray and Dixie Parker run that place the way they were taught they would have plenty.

June and Kyle have a son that will be big enough to work soon, they have over 100 acres of land, also they have the trading barn to run, no reason they can't do well. Kyle at this time had been gone for almost six years.

It was 1921 when Kyle bought into the boarding house and business was good. The county seat was Waynesville and it was growing, but Hazelwood was at a standstill. Only four families had moved there in six years, but travelers is what they depended on. The crossroad of 23 and 107 was a busy place and it had no name. The other four families and Rose and Kyle, decided that they would name this place, so after they all discussed it they decided on Smithville, it was Kyle's family name, but none of them knew that. They knew him as Bill Clark; he took Bills name when Bill died.

They put signs up on all four roads in and out of our town and went to Waynesville and told the sheriff and the mayor about it. Rose was the Mayor of Smithville, and she was the only official.

When Bill died, Rose and Kyle took him to an old graveyard and buried him. Kyle assumed his name. Now Kyle went by the name of Bill Clark.

None of the new families lived in Smithville when the real Bill Clark passed away, Mr. Thomas had lived in Hazelwood, but that was six miles south.

There is a soft place in the road right in front

of the boarding house and when it rains it is always muddy and slick. A horse and wagon will go thru but not an automobile, they get stuck every time. Kyle noticed that in wet weather business was good, but in dry weather it was slow. Kyle got one dollar for pulling automobiles out of the mud with his mule. This gave the people time to eat and drink. Kyle found a way to slow the automobiles down in dry weather so the people would have time to buy something. At night Rose drew the water from the well and Kyle carried it out and poured it in the ruts of the road, 8 or 10 buckets on each side, by morning the water had sunk down into the ground, and it was very soft and very slick. Not one automobile got thru and the more they would spin the worse the road got. Kyle charged them one dollar to pull them out of the mud hole and that allowed them time to eat while Kyle went to get the mule from the barn. Just a small thing like that increased their business 100 %. They would water the road down just before they went to bed each night.

One afternoon a truck pulled up to the front of the building, the two men got out and come in to the dining room, Bill saw thru the serving window that it was a man he had talked to in Rabun Gap, Ga. He went out thru the back door and up to their living quarters and did not come back until the two men had left. Rose had seen him looking at them and watched as he went out the back door. She knew that something was wrong.

It had been 9 years since Kyle Smith left Rabun Gap. No one around here has ever heard of Kyle Smith, Bill and Rose Clark have always run this boarding house.

The truth is, Rose means nothing to Kyle Smith. He does not know anything about her, he is not married to her and he does not know if she was married to the real bill Clark, all he knows is that he spent $2,000.00 and he has been here for 9 years. He had plenty to eat, a warm place to sleep and a good bed partner. They got along good with each other and she is okay. But it may be time for him to move on.

In the safe there was over $6,000.00. He took the $2000.00 that he had when he got here and left her a nice note. He told her he had been mixed up with the wrong group of people, and they were looking for him and he was going to Canada. He saddled the mule and rode away. It was the only mule they had but she could not handle it anyway. She was an attractive woman with a going business so she would be all right. No one saw him leave, they did not know if he went north or south. Just that he was gone. Rose knew his real name but did not know of his families, or where he came from and she knew no one that had ever known him before.

For the past 9 years Kyle had gone by the name of Bill Clark. But now he has a clean start, he will assume his real name and live as Kyle smith.

He had found his way to Akron, Ohio. There he lived in a rooming house alone. He was 32 years old, and after a few weeks there he started working for his room rent and food. The depression was on, there were no jobs and no money and not many people had it as well as he did. Kyle was still a smart man when it came to money and he still had most of the $2000.00, but he let no one know that he had it.

Kyle stayed there for three years, mainly because he had no place to go, the owners of the rooming house were in their late 60's and had become fond of Kyle and they needed his help, sometime they gave him money for working but not always. Things were starting to pick up some; a few jobs were available so Kyle started looking around. He found a job on a construction company paving roads and he worked on this job for two years, then the company asks him to move to Pennsylvania and be a foreman and he accepted the job. Kyle did not care where he lived, and the more he moved the better he liked it. In Pennsylvania he was the boss, and he did a great job, he made money for the company. But the main part of the company was in Ohio and they had lost so much money that they went broke and out of business. The bank took all of the machinery back, even from Kyle in Pennsylvania.

Kyle had met Gloria just before going to Pennsylvania and she moved with him, now they were out of a job. In the town of Chester, Pennsylvania the city advertised for bids to pave streets in the city limits. Kyle and Gloria bid on the job and got it. They had no equipment but they had the contracts. They went to the bank that repossessed the equipment and made them a low offer because they said the machines were old and worn out, they bought the equipment on credit and for pennies on the dollar. With a few men that agreed to work three weeks before a payday, Kyle and Gloria started paving streets in the city of Chester, Penna.

In 1935 Gloria had a son and the same year Kyle was elected Mayor of Chester, he was Mayor for three consecutive years, then he did not run for it anymore.

Gloria told Kyle that she had been married

before and her husband ran around on her so she had left him and got a divorce, there were no children.

Kyle decided to tell her about his screwed up life and he told her all of it. All about the Parker twins and the four children that he had left down in Ga. And his mother and father, and about Rose and the boarding house in N.C., he cried as he told her.

Gloria told him that they both had a bad life, and because of this they had been brought together, and that they were good together and she felt like it was meant to be that way. There was a lot of love between them for the first time in both their lives.

Kyle often thought of sending money to his children, but then he thought that it would be best if everyone there thought that he was dead.

Kyle and Gloria had become very wealthy in their 12 years together and his conscience was bothering him a lot. He could not stand it any longer. He ask Gloria to go to Rabun Gap and ask around about all the people that he had left behind, and she agreed to do this so that he could rest his mind about it. If they were down and out he would see that they got help, and if they had done well he would be happy.

Armed with information on each person there, Gloria traveled to the mountains of north Georgia, there she found a very nice place to stay called the Dillon House, they had every convenience anyone could want. She hired a taxi every day to carry her around to see the area and from the instructions from Kyle she knew where to go to locate the Parker farm and the Smith farm. The Smith farm had four beautiful homes in a row, each on 10 acre lots, then there was a huge barn type building that was now a store for farm produce and canned fruits and vegetables, all kind of pies made from berries that they grew on the farm. Every bit of that farm was producing something.

Gloria went inside to look around and possibly speak with some of the family. When she asks a question of one of the clerks she had to stop, she could not say another word. Looking into the eyes of the pretty blond headed girl she could see Kyle looking back at her, Gloria composed herself and asks the girl what her name was, she said it was Cindy Smith. This was Kyle's family. If only there was a way for Gloria to find out more about his mother and father she would stay as long as long as necessary. She asks the cab driver how many taxi's they had there and he told her four. She asked who was the oldest driver they had, and he said, "it is my dad", so she requested him as her driver for tomorrow. It turned out to be a smart move. The old cab driver was in his late 70's and he knew the entire Smith family, and the Parker family, and he remembered when Kyle Smith disappeared. It was suspected that he was robbed and killed, because he always carried a lot of money with him, he was a horse trader.

Gloria found out that Fred Smith died five

years ago, but Linda Smith is alive and doing well. She owns the produce barn and lives in the same house that they lived in when Kyle was here; she never remarried after Fred died.

June never remarried and she still lives with Linda Smith, June takes care of the home and Linda and the kids run the produce barn. Jason smith is June's only child, and he is an attorney.

The family that Kyle had left behind, was running the business that Kyle started there in Rabun Gap

About 1932 a man from Rabun Gap was on his way to Knoxville, Tenn. to get a job. There were three people together and all of them from the Rabun Gap area. They stopped at a diner in Smithville, N.C. to get a sandwich. In the dining room there was a picture of three people standing in front of the same building that they were in. One of the men looked just like Kyle Smith. There were two men and one woman; the picture was old. It was almost a year later when the three men went home. One day one of the men was in the produce barn and told one of the Smith girls about what they had seen. She told her mother, and her mother called the sheriff; he went to talk with Mrs. Smith about it. The sheriff said that if you want to go I will be glad to go with you, but it has been a long time. About 15 years. They decided to go up there and the next day they were in Smithville.

They ask the lady working there about the picture and she did not know about it, but she said the owner is up stairs if you want to speak to her. The waitress went up after Rose. About an hour later Rose Clark come down and set with us and answered every one of our questions. She gave a day-by-day account of everything that had happened. She had all the respect in the world for Kyle. She loved him dearly. She told about the money in the safe and Kyle only taking what was his. She was worried that someone had harmed him, she told about him leaving in a hurry and going up stairs and staying until the three men left in their truck. The trip was successful for us, but no one knows where Kyle is, or what happened to him, but now we do know about 11 of the years, he was with Rose. We know he was alive until 1928, if Rose was telling the truth.

Back in Chester, Pa. Gloria was back home from her trip to Rabun, gap. She had told Kyle all about his family and about every one she had talked to. Kyle remembered the cab driver. That produce barn is the business that Kyle started back in 1911; they had changed from selling horses to selling farm produce, which was a smart move.

Kyle Smith was relieved to hear that his family was doing well, but he was sad to know what a beautiful family he had, and him not they're with them. What happened back then has happened, nothing can change that.

1942 was Kyle's last year of being mayor of Chester; he did not run for reelection. The last day of the year was his last day in office. Then, on February 12, 1943, Kyle was drafted into the army. After 16 weeks training he was stationed in California and sent to cooks school. Because of his age and his business experience he was told that he would not go overseas but would be stationed there for the duration of the war.

A few miles from the camp there was a horse farm that rented horses by the day or by the hour. Kyle had been going there to ride on his time off. Most of the time he rode alone but sometimes a group would be going on a ride and he would go along with them. It was on one of these rides that he met Roberta. Roberta was a Spanish girl that lived in the area and worked in a grocery store across the street from her home. After a few days of horseback riding to gather Kyle ask her out, and she said O.K., a month later they moved in together. Roberta was 35 years old and her husband was in the army in Germany. She lived alone and all of her family lived in another state. This lasted for about 6 months.

Early one morning Kyle got a phone call and it was Gloria, she was at the bus station, near the camp. Kyle hurried to go after her and they rented a motel room. For a week Kyle worked his job and when he was not working he was right there with Gloria, but she had just come to visit and only had three more days to be there. About sun down on Friday afternoon Gloria and Kyle were walking down the sidewalk near their motel. A taxi pulled up alongside them and Roberta jumped out and started screaming at them, she slapped Gloria two or three times and yelled saying that Gloria was stealing her man. Gloria ran to the motel room and called the police and they were there in about two minutes and arrested Roberta. Kyle was in uniform but he just kept quiet, but he knew that he was caught. Gloria left that night for Pennsylvania.

Back home in Chester, Pa. Gloria was broken hearted. She did not believe that Kyle would do her this way.

Gloria contacted an attorney that her and

Kyle had known for a few years; he was the city attorney and a good divorce attorney. He had the reputation of always winning. When she told Don Williams about what happened he said he could not believe it, because Kyle Smith had the world by the tail, he had everything that men work for.

Don suggested to Gloria, to be real sure about this before she goes any further, he told her that the thing to do is send someone out there to check it out and she agreed. They sent a private investigator to watch Kyle for a few days. On the first day the investigator was there when Kyle got off work at his normal time, and went straight to Roberta's house. She met him on the front porch and they hugged and kissed passionately, and it was all caught on tape. At 6 A M Kyle left her house and went to the base, which was on film also. Next day at the same time the same thing happened, except after about an hour in the house they left and went out to a restaurant and bar, they danced and drank until about 11 o clock then went back to her house. Kyle was watched for three days and that investigator had pictures of his every move. The attorney had an air tight case against Kyle, no way could he get out of this, and he did not even try.

The case was prepared and the first thing the attorney did was to call the commanding officer of the base and report his findings to him. Then Gloria filed for a divorce and Kyle had to go to Chester to try and get the judge to award him something from their marriage. He failed to do this, although Kyle had known the judge and the attorneys when he was mayor. They all frowned on his actions, they told him he was cheap, trashy, unrespectful and unfaithful and you are 'GUILTY AS CHARGED.'

Both children were given to Gloria. The entire paving company was given to Gloria. The house and two cars were given to her, and all of their property was also given to her. Kyle got one car and his clothes. He was out.

Kyle stayed right there on that base until

August of 1945 when he was discharged from the army. He did not call Gloria because he was afraid that if he asks her if he could come there, she would say no, so he just bought a bus ticket to Chester.

Kyle was 48 years old now, but on the five-day bus trip he met a woman that was about his age that lived in Arizona, they ate, drank, and rode and talked. In Texas they got a room and stayed there until they both were out of money. The last day that she was there Kyle was so drunk that he could not get up out of the bed. The woman went thru his pockets and found Gloria's phone number and called her, and told her the sad shape that Kyle was in. Gloria ask the woman if she would stay with him until we could get a car out there to pick him up, if we send money for you to live on. The woman said yes she would. So Gloria sent money to the woman, and she stayed there until Gloria and her two kids got there. The woman did not ask for anything, but Gloria gave her money to eat on and bought her a ticket to her home. Kyle and Gloria and the two kids were driving back to Chester in the same car, but they were not together.

Kyle had turned into a drunken bum. He did not care if he lived or died. He had lost all of the decency that he had ever had. He had the car that he got in the divorce and his clothes and that is what he owned.

Even Bill Cook and Rose cook were good to him. Rose Cook did everything she could to make a go of it for the two of them, and he walked away from her too, after 11 years. Kyle just did not have respect for other people's feelings. Gloria would not have anything to do with Kyle but she had to help him, because he was the father of her children, and he did start the business that she now owned. She said she was going to give him a job and that is all. He started at the bottom. That is on the tar truck using the shovel to spread gravel. He did as much work as anyone, and looked like he enjoyed working, after a few weeks he totally stopped drinking and started back to church, slowly he was becoming the man that he was before. Gloria just had to do something for Kyle. If she did not help him, he was going to die and he did not care. Would it help or hurt him to see, or talk to his family down in Georgia? Is this what was wrong with him? One thing for sure he could not get any worse, and the worst thing that Gloria could do, is to do nothing.

She discussed this with her children and the attorney that they both knew, and their minister, it was decided that there would be no harm in trying to help Kyle and maybe get him on the right track. But to do it from the family that lived in Ga. Tell them where he was and if they want to see him let them come to him, then there is no harm done to anyone, and we have not over stepped our bounds.

Gloria knew where to find the family; she had been there before and had spoken to Cindy Smith, one of the daughters.

What Gloria did not know is that Linda Smith, Kyle's Mother, knew about Rose Clark up in North Carolina, this had never made any difference in anything, but now things are different. This puzzle is slowly beginning to come together.

In the middle of the summer of 1946, Gloria went back to Rabun gap, Georgia. She had a letter written with every bit of information on, and about Kyle Smith. Exactly where to find him, and enclosed two pictures of him and gave the phone number of the office for the paving company, if they want to see Kyle, now it is possible.

Gloria stayed one week there at the Dillon house, and on the last day she had the cab driver to take her to the produce barn. The place was very busy so she looked around for a few minutes, then asks for Mrs. Smith, she was directed to a small office in the rear of the building. Gloria was almost afraid to give the letter to Linda Smith, but she did. Then she turned and walked away.

In a small town everyone knows everyone.

They saw Gloria in the cab and saw the cab waiting for her to come back out of the produce barn. Linda smith called that same cab, and told the driver that she wanted to go where he had taken the other lady that was here. Linda and Cindy went to the Dillon House and found Gloria.

Linda and Cindy knocked on Gloria's door. Gloria answered the door and Linda asks if they could talk. They were invited in. Suspicions were high, and none of them knew what to expect. Gloria asks them if it would be all right if we all went to the restaurant to talk, and that is what they did. They talked for two hours and Gloria gave all the answers for their questions about Kyle, but would give no information about her. When she was ready she got up and walked out.

Linda had Jason to trace a check, written by Gloria, to her hometown. Because they were thinking that it would be possible that this was some kind of a shake down for money, Linda contacted the press in Knoxville. The story was passed on to me. If this were a shakedown it would be a back page story. But if Kyle Smith were alive this would be a front-page story. A scoop.

When I traveled there I found out that this was a road paving company's office, I stayed around town for two days, that is all the time I needed to find out that Kyle Smith was alive and working every day. It would do no good for me to walk in and talk to them now, but I did have a plan.

This was a good story for my paper and I wanted the entire story, I want to know where he has been all of these years

I called Jason down in Ga. And set up a time to meet with him and his mother to discuss this, and I ask him to instruct the family not to talk about it, and do not let anyone outside the family know one word about it. He promised.

Two days later I was in Rabun Gap, Ga., we all

met in the produce barn after closing hours. Every member of the Smith family and the parker family was there. I gave all of the information that I had gathered to the group. There were no dry eyes in that building. Then, to my surprise, Linda Smith told everyone about going to Smithville, Tennessee and meeting with Rose Clark. She reported all that she had learned and also told everyone that 'Smithville' was named after this Smith family. She asked them to think about it and all of us decide either to go, or not to go. We wanted to go and see Kyle, but he may reject us; if he does it will be heartaches piled on top of heartaches.

I had not known about Linda's trip to Smithville and her meeting Rose Clark. This puts the topping on the cake, especially if Gloria has been with Kyle ever since they got to Chester Pa. Now we have the full story from 1918 all the way to 1946, it may change some after we talk to Kyle Smith. If he will even talk to us.

June married Kyle Smith and they had one

son, Jason. Jane Parker had three kids by Kyle smith before he left town, many think that this is why he left, but that is not the reason. Jane's three kids were named Cindy, Andy, and Phillip. They favored Kyle more than any of the rest. Cindy is a nurse, Andy will be a Doctor in two more years, and Phillip is a farmer.

June and Jane were one year younger than Kyle. June and Jane both had their first babies in 1917, one month apart.

Rose Clark was a year younger than Kyle and they had one boy named Kyle Jr., Kyle Jr. is a carpenter and builds houses for himself

Gloria and Kyle had a boy named Joe, and a girl named Jackie, Joe was born in 1931 and Jackie in 1933, Gloria and Kyle was married in 1932. Gloria and Jackie run the paving company and Joe is studying to be an engineer.

A total of six children and every one of them are fine, good looking, up standing people, well-educated business people, and professionals. The only one in the entire group that is broke, and down and out is Kyle Smith. He left a trail of young babies and broken hearts all along the way from Georgia To Pennsylvania. From 1918 until 1946, when this story became known.

I have my story now, and it is a front-page story that will take several weeks to tell, as I can only have so much space in the paper each week. But it is my desire to help Kyle Smith with his life. I know four families that need to know that they did nothing wrong in the past that caused Kyle to abandon them.

It is time for me to retire, this is my last story, and if I could make a difference in these lives I could enjoy my retirement so much more..

In 1947 I contacted every part of this group in Rabun gap, Georgia, Smithville, North Carolina, and Akron, Ohio and Chester, Pennsylvania, to ask their permission to go see Kyle, and interview him on their behalf. Every one said yes, it is all right.

## stories about a Georgia moonshiner

April 15, 1947, I found Kyle setting in a bar drinking a coca-cola. He was alone. He told me that he had lived a screwed up life, and it was too late now to change things.

I asked Kyle what it was in his life that was screwed up any more than other people's lives? Then I could not go any further, I just had to tell him who I was and what I was there for. Gloria had not told him about me or that she was in on this investigation. But she had told him how well his family was, when she went down there that first time.

My discussion with Kyle was three hours long. He cried almost all of the time. He was so ashamed of what he had done, that I was afraid that he would take his own life.

My number one question to him was 'Why did you leave home that way?' He told me that they made plenty of money. They all had everything they wanted. But he had two girls that he was having sex with, and he was in love with both of them. Both girls were over sexed and I could not keep up with them. Jane was at one farm and June at the other farm, where ever I went it was one or the other wanting sex.

When I put the question to him about "did he want to see all of the families" he said, "It is okay to tell them where I am, but I doubt if any one comes to see me".

For the full rights to this story the Knoxville press has agreed to pay for ten rooms at any hotel in Chester, Pennsylvania for three days for a reunion of this group.

The reunion was scheduled for December the 23rd, 24th, and 25th of 1947. Every member of every family was sent an invitation and a $100.00 check, compliments of the Knoxville press.

I had the room next to Kyle; it would be my duty to introduce everyone and to record it all for the paper. We had a professional photographer furnished by the paper that would be there for the three days.

First person to go to see Kyle was his Mother, Linda Smith. I went in with her and stayed about fifteen minutes, then I went out, it was privacy time for them and very touching. In about half an hour, I took Jason into his room and introduced them, everyone had mixed feelings, but they all were okay.

Someone knocked on the door, and when I opened it there was June, Jane, with Cindy, Andy, and Phillip; Kyle's and Jane's three children. From then on it was out of control. I made all of the records that I could, and we took all of the pictures that we could, it was loud, laughing, crying, praying and forgiving time.

Next to come in was Rose Clark, and she and Kyle's son, Kyle Jr. Kyle had lived with her for 11 years and they had named the town Smithville after the Smith family. There were only four families that lived there back then, it was just a crossroad.

Everyone was there except Dixie Parker. She was too sick to make the trip but Dixie wrote a letter and sent it to Kyle. After a while he went into the bathroom and read the letter, and cried the rest of the night. He never did tell anyone what the letter said.

Gloria, his last wife and their two children, Joe and Jackie, stayed downstairs in the dining room. They were as much in disbelief as Kyle was. No one in the world ever thought that this could happen

They put Kyle on the spot about where he was from 1927 until 1930. He had to think about this for a while, and then Gloria told everyone that she met Kyle in 1930 and they got married in 1932. The rest is history; everyone knows the story of the rise and fall of Kyle and Gloria.

One by one every one said their good buys and

went back to their homes, the not knowing of what happened to Kyle Smith was over. He was alive and well and after all, no one could find Kyle because he did not want to be found.

On my way back to Knoxville I will go thorough Akron, Ohio and try to locate the Beckley's. This will tie in all of the time from when Kyle left home in 1918 until after he got out of the army in 1946. Just a few minutes in the courthouse and a phone call to the county sheriff, and I had the information I needed. I had found the Beckley's rooming house. It was still in operation and it was still full with a 'no vacancy' sign out in front.

Mr. Beckley was on the porch in a wheel chair talking to his roomers. I introduced myself to him and told him why I was there. He was old and fragile, but he could hear okay. And his mind was very clear. He wanted to see Kyle and he asks me to push him inside to the phone. Mr. Beckley then called the sheriff to come to the rooming house. While we were waiting there on the sheriff to come, the old man told me that his wife had passed away seven years ago and he had no other family to come there to help him.

Then he said that he had willed the place to Kyle along with all of his other possessions, as soon as I see Kyle I will be ready to go to a nursing home. My policy has been paid up for a long time. Just then the sheriff come in and Mr. Beckley ask him if he would find out if I was who I said I was, and to please get in touch with Kyle Smith and bring him here. Apparently the sheriff and Mr. Beckley were old friends. I gave them all of the phone numbers I had to help reach Kyle. And I explained that it was a paving company's office phone and that Kyle just had a small room rented two blocks from there.

Within two hours Kyle and Mr. Beckley talked to each other. Kyle promised to get on a bus and be there the next day.

This story should have ended in Chester. But

I just have to wait and find out what is going to happen when Kyle gets here.

Sheriff Darby met the bus in town and picked up Kyle. They went directly to the rooming house and Mr. Beckley and Kyle and the sheriff had a long talk. Then they all three went to the county judge in the courthouse and Kyle was given the deeds for the rooming house and the farm on the edge of town. Along with the property were everything in the houses, and all farm equipment, and a 1941 Ford pickup truck. Mr. Beckley had $1,500.00 in the bank. He gave Kyle $500.00 and the sheriff $500.00 and the cook in their kitchen $500.00. Then he said, "Now I am ready to go, I have exactly the same thing that I started with". "Nothing."

Now this story is ended. No one knows what will happen to Kyle now, but I hope it is all good.

## THE END OF THE STORY